WEST OF REHOBOTH

ALEXS D. PATE

West of
Rehoboth

A NOVEL

WILLIAM MORROW • 75 YEARS OF PUBLISHING
An Imprint of HarperCollins*Publishers*

HarperCollins books may be purchased for educational, business,
or sales promotional use.
For information please write: Special Markets Department,
HarperCollins Publishers Inc., 10 East 53rd Street, New York, NY 10022.

FIRST EDITION

Designed by Kate Nichols

Printed on acid-free paper

Library of Congress Cataloging-in-Publication Data has been applied for.

ISBN 0-380-97679-X

01   02   03   04   05   QW   10   9   8   7   6   5   4   3   2   1

For sons,

and especially mine

When I was young and in my prime,

I could get my barbecue any old time.

TONI MORRISON, *BELOVED*

Acknowledgments

Life is story and so many voices, both past and present, live there. To my mother and father, my sister, Wanda, my brother Billy and all those many more Williams, Pates, Wrights, Browns, Sawyers, Cheeks, and Childs who make up my family, my deepest gratitude. And thanks especially to my aunt Minnie and her son Adolph, who provided good reason to be in Rehoboth Beach when I was young; my aunt Ruth and uncle Colwell and their sons (Colwell, Jr., Terrance, and Stephen), who were often summer companions; my aunt Margaret and uncle Bill and their children (Ricky, Jean, and Anita); and my aunt Louvenia and her sons, Lonnie, Bryant, and Dennis.

I want to thank Gyanni for her early reading of this book and for being a wonderful daughter. To Alexs, my son, I want to say that this life has so much more meaning now that you amplify it with your presence and your love.

And, for continued support and love, I must thank Me-K Ahn,

Ralph Remington, Katherine Link, Damu McCoy, Marcela Lorca, David Mura, Susan Sencer, Dine Watson, Walter Allan Bennett, Janine Balfour, John and Serena Wright, Katie Leo, Judy Kessel, Natalie Moore, Taiyon Coleman, Rose Brewer, Rohan Preston, Angela Shannon, Mary Rockcastle, Dominic Saucedo, E. Ethelbert Miller, Paul Boyer, Duchess Harris, Archie Givens Jr., Carol Meshbesher, Julie Metanich, Tom Nelson, Richard Adams, Bill Banfield, Dwight Hobbes, Alan and Diane Page, and my colleagues in the African American and African Studies Department at the University of Minnesota.

Thanks also to my editors at Morrow, Meaghan Dowling and Kelli Martin, for their sensitive and careful nurturing of this story, it has grown under their touch. And to my agent, Faith Hampton Childs, whose guidance and belief in me has been the one constant throughout my writing career.

And, finally, for the fuel and the light, the amazing Soo Jin. Thanks.

WEST OF REHOBOTH

1

The soft summer held them all. They gently sat upon the shimmering flecks of sun hidden in the cut grass. They came together like this every Fourth of July. It was a time when Lemon Hill Park was at its height of sweetness. They came together to grill hot dogs and hamburgers, to play catch, to escape the raging heat of North Philly. They sat among the trees and flowers, and for a short time the adults could throw their heads back and sigh. Inhale fresh life.

It was 1962. It was what white people called a holiday and the folks from the neighborhood were at the park. Doing what they wanted to do. Laughing. Telling stories. There were five blankets spread over the ground—a blanket for each family. The young folks were all over the place. The girls were playing dodgeball, some of the boys were playing catch. The mothers were huddled together playing bid whist. The fathers weren't there. A baseball game on television held most of them at home, although Edward was pretty certain his father was firing up the grill. This was no place for fathers anyway, he thought. None of the fathers he knew could so completely relax and just "be" like his mother and her friends could. A day in the park almost never included the men.

Edward Massey was the only boy not playing. There were times when he just couldn't be like everyone else. Even though if he could control everything, he really wanted to be doing whatever the other boys were doing. Playing whatever silly game they were playing. Or talking about girls or sports or even sneaking a puff on a cigarette. But there were moments, like this moment, when sitting still, in thought, burrowed deep into his own mind, was all he wanted to do.

"Paradox," he said in the barest of whispers. It was a word he'd only recently learned.

The boys were now choosing sides for a baseball game. They had discovered another group having a picnic and realized there were enough kids to maybe play seven to a side. Edward knew that any minute somebody was going to run over and try to get him to play. After all, he was the best catcher out there. He was the thickest of them all, chubby even. The perfect size to sit behind the plate and throw runners out. But he would have to confess that he just plain did not want to play. Beside him sat a book which he intended to read a little of and the rest of the time he just wanted to think. The peace of the park was rare. The air, laced with the happiness of so many of his friends at one time, rarer still.

Sure enough, his best friend, Sonny Goodman, was jogging in his direction. "C'mon, Eddie, man. We're gettin' up a game. We need you."

"I don't feel like it today, Sonny," Edward said quietly, hoping his mother who sat behind him wouldn't interfere. He knew she sometimes worried that he didn't play enough. Luckily she was so caught up in her card game she didn't even turn in his direction.

"We need a catcher."

"I'm reading," Edward said as he picked up his book.

"You can read later, man. Let's play some ball."

Edward could see Sonny's body already turning back toward the other boys. "I don't feel like it."

"Don't be lame, man. We just need one more player."

"Sorry, man. I don't want to right now." Was all that Edward had to say to finally send Sonny on his way. He opened his book.

Fifteen minutes later Edward sat, his back against his mother's back, reading *Poirot Investigates*. Hercule Poirot was his favorite detective. No one could compete with the brilliant deductive powers of the Belgian sleuth except perhaps Sherlock Holmes. There was something seductive about Monsieur Poirot that pulled Edward into the stories. Edward loved Poirot's arrogance, his profound self-confidence, and especially the fat Belgian's use of his "little gray cells."

Edward was nearly always reading. His mother paid him a dollar for every book he read in addition to the one he was assigned in school. That meant that *every* book during the summer was worth a dollar. It didn't matter which book, but if he finished it, after a brief quiz, he was given an additional dollar over his allowance. He was up to two dollars a week. His goal was to read three books a week over the remainder of his vacation.

As he sat reading, he felt the pressure of his mother's body against him. When her time came to play a card, she would lean forward. He would try to anticipate her and hold his back stiff, awaiting her return. And even as he tunneled into the mysterious world of Paris high society, the banter of the women penetrated. It was rapid-fire, free-ranging, bouncing from neighborhood news to card-game boasts and taunts.

Edward looked up from his book. His own gray cells stimulated, he focused on the other boys. They were always playing.

They never hardly talked about books. Even Sonny, one of the smartest, never seemed to be serious about anything. And Rooster, well, to Edward, Rooster was one step away from being a member of one of the many gangs that surrounded them. They were both the same age as Edward—twelve.

He often had to suffer the teasing and ridicule for being so much of a "bookworm." But what else was he supposed to do with his time? Aside from the fact that he actually did love to read and his mother literally fed him books like snacks, he had nothing else to occupy himself. Yes, he could play baseball in the summer and football in the winter, which he did a little of, but he would always get bored. There were no girls lining up to kiss him after school like there were for Sonny. He never got invited to the secret "sets" where the cool kids were doing more than kissing.

Instead, he would think of problems, unanswered questions, mysteries, and attempt to solve them. He would create elaborate stories to fuel him on these intellectual jaunts.

His eyes found his sister, Sarah, sitting under a tree with her friends. She was ten, and he guessed they were huddled together talking about boys. He pushed back his Phillies baseball cap and wiped the sweat from his brow.

He wanted to solve crimes one day. He wanted to dress in sophisticated clothes and have an assistant, Sonny perhaps, and be asked to consult with the police. He prided himself on occasionally anticipating Poirot's hunches and conclusions. He knew he was smart enough. If he got the chance he could be just like Hercule Poirot. He could sit in an overstuffed chair and solve crimes by just thinking about them.

"Girl, you know that man's gonna kill her." He felt his mother's words, their lilting clarity pass through him.

Gwen Goodman, Sonny's mother, wiped the tip of her nose with a tissue. "I don't know. I wouldn't be surprised if he don't ever come back. He's been gone now over a year. I heard from Sadie that he's staying in South Philly with some loose trash."

Angela Massey let out a light chuckle. "Gwen, you don't have to worry about that. He's definitely coming back home. You know that man ain't gonna leave Doris in that house forever. I know for certain that he's done paying on it. The house is his free and clear. Besides, if you ask me, he still loves her."

"All I know is he better hurry back. There's something strange going on in that house, if you know what I mean."

There was a brief silence and then the voice of Beaulah Freeman, Gail's mother, who had bid a six in hearts and had obviously underestimated her hand, got everybody's attention. "Mm-hmm. That's right, ladies. You got to come by me. I got the board. Come on now, Angela," she said, pointing to Edward's mother. "Come on now, ain't no use in studying. I got this." Edward could feel his mother tense. She was beaten.

"That's right, Angela, you study long, you study wrong." That was Esther Roberts, Rooster's mother.

Edward felt his mother relent and toss her card.

They all screamed. Beaulah had taken every book. She had "rubbed head"; that was the term for having an unbeatable, take-every-book kind of whist hand. There were screams and hollers. Laughing women. A new hand was dealt and the conversation shifted back to Mrs. Robinson. Edward's ears perked up again.

"I just think she had better be a little cool with it, though. You can't be acting like that around here. They'll run her out of this neighborhood."

"She's got one foot out already, if you ask me. It ain't right. It ain't God's way."

Edward looked up at the sky. His little gray cells popped. Yes, he knew by the way they talked in code, by the way they never actually said what they were talking about, that it had something to do with sex. And he knew that Mrs. Robinson's husband had disappeared nearly a year ago. And he knew that a woman friend had become a very frequent visitor to the Robinson house. And this was the first year neither the mother nor the children, Emily and Frank, had joined them for the Fourth of July picnic.

"*Oui, mon ami,*" Edward couldn't help but say it. "It eez so eeezee."

"What are you saying, Edward?" His mother leaned her head back, startling him.

"Oh, ah . . . I was just thinking." His mother was already back to the game. What he knew was that there was something very odd about the way these women responded to the Robinson situation and her new friend. *Voilà!* It was obvious that Mrs. Robinson had taken a woman lover. Their attempts to hide the subject of their speculations were futile against his razor-sharp mind. Unless something further aroused his interest, there was nothing more to this mystery.

And then his mind slipped ahead two days. In just two days he would be away on vacation until Labor Day. This was really his last day in the neighborhood before his mother, his sister, and he would relocate to Rehoboth Beach for the remainder of the summer, which they did every year after the Fourth.

But he was especially looking forward to their trip this year. He had particular business in Rehoboth. This summer he was determined to solve one of the biggest questions of his young life: exactly who was the man who lurked around the edge of his aunt's property that everyone called Rufus. Whom Edward was told to call "Uncle" Rufus, even though he had no idea how they were related.

Last year when he was in Rehoboth he'd only seen Rufus two or three times, mostly as the old man disappeared into the woods. Whenever he asked about Rufus everybody changed the subject.

But it became a real mystery when Edward discovered that Rufus had eaten Mr. Peabody. That topped it. Who would do such a thing?

Edward's thoughts were interrupted by a flurry of activity near the entrance to the park. Suddenly there were at least fifteen boys clustered together. Edward could see, even from the distance, that it was the 2–8 Oxford gang. His stomach trembled. He knew many of the members from hanging around the Athletic Center. The Athletic Center was one of the prime meeting places for the 2–8, so if you were a healthy young neighborhood boy with even a slight interest in playing sports, you had to negotiate your way through. If not, you could end up stomped into the ground. Or sliced up by the whistling sting of a broken car antenna being wielded as a sword.

But even though he knew most of the gang, he was always scared when he was around them. You never knew when somebody would just start picking at you, goading you just to see if you'd get mad. If you did, then you had to fight. And if you weren't in a gang and you ended up in a fight with a member of one, you were dead meat. You weren't fighting one boy, but all of them. Edward had seen it happen over and over.

The card game ended abruptly. Without speaking, the women were instantly up, extinguishing the stationary brick grills, gathering their children, rewrapping food, and plotting an alternate route out of the winding narrow road that turned off of Girard Avenue and up into the part of Fairmount Park that was named Lemon Hill. Edward's mother had him by the collar. He saw Mrs. Goodman swoop up Rainy and Sonny and push them along.

No words were necessary. The gang wars were raging throughout the neighborhood. Had been for more than three years. Philadelphia was the gang-related-death capital of the country. There was a gang at nearly every corner. In Edward's neighborhood alone there were more than five "corners," as the gangs were called, to deal with. But the war between 2–8 and its rival the 2–4 Ws from Whither Street was fought up and down Seybert Street, the street on which Edward lived.

That was the primary reason he and his sister were shuttled out of the city every summer. His parents knew the threat that walked the North Philadelphia streets. They knew that the summer heat provided the perfect backdrop for violence and death.

Still, without any spoken strategy, the women herded the children directly into the crowd of gang members. Somehow they had decided, collectively, to push through them instead of going the long way home.

Edward was sweating blood as they passed amid the boys. All of his interest in crime and detection was gone. He only wanted to get by them without trouble. Under the wing of his mother he was reasonably sure they wouldn't do anything. All of the women, especially Sonny's mother, were very active in the neighborhood and knew most of the boys. Indeed, as they walked into the shadow of slick hair, baggy tan khaki pants, and Stacy Adams soft leather shoes, Edward actually heard a series of mumbled "Hi, Mrs. Goodman; Hi, Mrs. Roberts; How are you, Mrs. Massey?"

The mothers knew how to handle the situation. They could have stopped and said, "Now, Scott, you know you should be at home with your family instead of running around out here in the park like some kind of lunatic." They didn't because they knew it would provoke and they were too far from home.

Besides, something was about to happen. Edward could feel it. So could everyone else. And once things began happening on the streets of North Philadelphia, it was too late to start trying to get people to go home.

Like goslings in tow, they shuffled through and were quickly out of harm's way. They had barely made it to the street when it became clear what was happening around them. Edward looked up Girard Avenue and could see an encroaching crush of people moving toward them. They were still more than a block away, but Edward knew it was 2–4. He could tell by the way they wore their pants, rolled up high over their shoes. The 2–4 Ws, 2–8's arch rival, were in the midst of an ambush, and unless their group made a detour, Edward and the caravan he was traveling with were right in the middle.

It was then his mother spoke up. "Gwen, Esther, I think we better cut over to Whither Street. I don't like the way this is looking. We've got too many kids here to get caught up in this foolishness." They had barely crossed Girard on their way to Whither when the 2–4 Ws began running toward the park. Edward looked back, his throat holding a sizable lump. He was sweating now. The shade of the park trees, the breeze slicing through the leaves were gone. They were on hot concrete, stepping over hot tar and steaming bricks. They were on their way home. Behind them the gangs were banging.

As they turned down Whither, Edward listened as Sonny and Rooster talked about the gang war.

"I don't know why 2–4 even wants to jump bad with 2–8. They always lose." Sonny was tossing a baseball up and down as he talked and walked.

"No kidding. Man, I would never be from 2–4." Rooster's high-pitched voice went perfectly with his long-legged gait.

Out of nowhere a hand reached out and smacked Rooster hard against the head. "You better not be from *anywhere*." Rooster's mother, visibly upset, held her hand up, poised for another attack.

"I'm not, Mom. I swear, why you had to hit me?"

"Because if I see you acting like those fools back there I'm gonna skin you alive, that's why. And after I skin you alive they're probably gonna put me in jail. So I'd rather beat your sorry butt now. Maybe I can smack some sense in your head."

The other kids laughed quietly. They all knew that Rooster was already spending time with 2–8, already drinking wine with the corner boys on Friday nights. He was the one who came back with stories of gang wars, parties with drinking and smoking, and girls.

As they neared home, the group broke up. Some to Whither Street, some to Twenty-sixth Street, Edward and his family to Seybert. But even as they turned into their narrow street of tight-packed red-brick row houses, Edward could see the retreating 2–4 Ws, racing back to their turf. He assumed it had been another futile attempt to inflict injury on their enemies.

Just as they reached their front door, 2–8 materialized at the corner. There were seven of them. Edward quickened his step. His mother held the door open. "Get in here right now, Eddie. Sarah, don't go near the window," she said.

But before Edward could get inside, the boys came running down the street. And as the screaming started, Edward realized that members of 2–4 had been hiding in alleys and behind cars. They materialized. There was a series of popping sounds as car antennas were torn off cars. And in the middle of the block, in the middle of the street, almost directly in front of him, the two groups clashed. Edward was frozen, one foot on the top step. He heard the cursing and felt the anger. The antennas sang through the air. One boy slipped and immediately three boys were on him, stomping and punching until someone came to his rescue.

Edward's mother snatched him inside and shut the door. The fight was still going on when they heard the sirens of the police approaching.

Once in the house, they all stood fixed like chess pieces.

Edward, his mother, and his sister. And then, slowly, each trembled, and in a flash the reality of how close they'd been to the
heat of battle melted into just another moment. One of many. A
part of the world they lived in. The natural consequence of the
way things were. A story that Edward would one day tell his white
friends to enhance their appreciation for his survival.

Eventually the gangs scattered, although two boys were cap-
tured by the police. Edward, Sarah, and their mother watched
from the window after the police arrived. Within the hour it was
quiet again.

When there was nothing else to see in front of them, they,
almost in unison, turned to the interior. The house was thick with
afternoon shadows. It was about four-thirty. There was still
enough time to celebrate the Fourth. Edward knew his father was
in the backyard. He could smell the seared, basted sweetness of
his father's barbecue sauce and the slab of ribs it enfolded, cooking. The thick smoke wafted through the kitchen window and
traveled, ever thinning, throughout the house like a spirit. Like a
sugar spirit in search of salivating mouths.

His mother put her thick-wristed, light brown arm around
both him and his sister. "Everybody okay?" she said with a
matter-of-factness that soothed them. They both nodded.

"Good. You were both very good. Actually everybody behaved
themselves pretty well. All things considered."

Sarah looked up at her mother. "Were you scared, Mommy?"

"Scared? No, girl. I wasn't . . . I'm not scared of those little
boys. I have to take care of you. And I ain't letting nobody hurt
you." Edward watched his mother give Sarah an extra hug. His
body still trembling a little from the adrenaline of fear and movement. But he'd been through this before.

"I'm going to see what Dad's doing," he said, hoping to head
off any unnecessary sentimentality. There were gang wars every

weekend, usually at night, when the little kids and the non–gang members were inside. The only difference this time was that they'd almost gotten caught up in it.

Sarah broke from their mother's clutch and headed upstairs to play in her room. Their mother, who still had not released Edward, now held him at arm's length and just stared into his eyes.

"What?" he wondered. "What's wrong?" But he knew. She was looking at him like he was made of glass. Like someone had just thrown a rock in his direction.

"Nothing. Nothing's wrong. Everything okay with you?"

"Yeah." He waited for her to let him go. He was careful enough. He didn't need her to worry over him all the time. He would be a man soon. Besides, he was the one who had to walk to school or home in the evening after playing with his friends. He already knew what it was to be stealth-like. Spiritlike. He could duck into alleys and hide behind cars when things around him starting falling apart. He was already skilled in inner-city survival.

"You're sure now?"

"Yes, Mom. I'm fine."

She let him go. "All right, then. If you say so." As she released him, she eased herself onto the couch.

When Edward walked out into their small fenced-in yard, he saw that sure enough, his father was there tending a slab of ribs like it was a religious ritual.

"Hey, Dad."

"Hey. How was the park?" His father, Earl Massey, didn't talk much. He was a tall, thin, dark-skinned man, who stood in contrast to his wife, Angela, whose soft smooth roux complexion accounted for the milk-chocolate skin of their children. Earl was a concrete pourer at construction sites. Nobody ever believed him when he said he worked construction. People would take a step back and eye him up and down. "Naw," they'd say. "Naw, you lyin', man, you too skinny, you ain't hardly strong enough to work at no construction job." But Earl would always answer, "You don't want to find out how strong I am."

"It was okay." Calm now, Edward tried to reflect that in his voice.

"Well, how come y'all back so soon?" Edward watched the flames caress the long slab of meat sizzling in front of his father.

"Gang war."

"So that's what was going on out there. I kind of figured that. I didn't know y'all was back; otherwise I would have come out there." His father stepped back from the grill, turned, and looked him in the eye. "Eddie, those guys ever try to recruit you?"

Edward took a breath. There were always so many questions. Everybody was constantly trying to calculate his movement into the pit of despair that the neighborhood could be or his ascension to a life of education and success. Toward safety or danger? Which way are you leaning, little black man? His mother. His friends. His father. He was measured every day.

He thought about the question. He was almost embarrassed to say that no gang had ever approached him. "No, sir."

"That's good. Those kids aren't playing out there."

"I know." Edward understood what his father was saying. Even he had noticed how knives and zip guns had given way to shotguns and pistols. People were dying.

"Listen, Eddie, you can't let nobody make you fight a ghost. You can't beat a ghost."

Edward listened to his father but didn't understand what he was talking about. "What ghosts?"

"Those kids out there. They're fighting ghosts."

"No, they're not, Dad. They're fighting each other. One gang just don't like the other one, so they fight."

"That's what it looks like, Eddie. But it only looks like that. The truth is they're fighting air, emptiness." Earl put his hand on his son's shoulder. "If they win the fight, what do they get?"

Edward had never thought about that. What did they get? "Well, they get respect. They make other people scared of them. People get out of their way."

"But what do they *get*, Eddie? Really. What you call respect is useless when everything is chaos. People wasn't meant to duck and dodge like you have to do out there. When people respect you they smile at you. They think good things about you. You got to learn the difference between respect and fear. When people fear you, they will eventually figure out a way to take you out. You can count on that. You understand?"

"Yeah. I guess."

"Well, we'll be eating soon. Go tell your mother to get out here and say hello to me."

.   .   .

Later, after they had eaten, the entire Massey family sat in the darkened living room watching *Peyton Place* on television. Edward was once again thinking about Rehoboth Beach and Rufus. Last year the kids he had played with had told him count- less stories about Rufus. There were any number of theories about why he didn't live in the house with Edna. Why he lived in a broken-down shack on the fringes of her property, almost near the woods. Why he never came into her house. This was the year Edward would put his investigative powers to work. He would unravel the story about Rufus once and for all.

Edward watched the luscious image of Constance Mackenzie on the flickering small screen. His mind slipped into the box of projected images. He wondered about the world those characters lived in. The small towns outside the ghetto wall. What was out there? It had been a mistake for his mother to make him read so much. He'd experienced so much. He knew about nineteenth-century England from Dickens, Harlem from Langston Hughes, read about urban Chicago from Sinclair, and tested his soul in the wilderness of Jack London. How was he to be comfortable with North Philadelphia? The world was truly wide. There was life out there. Mysteries. Lies. Beauty. Crime-filled and crimeless streets and places without streets at all.

It was strange. He lived a life of contradictions. In a pinch he'd admit that his family was closer to the images of family he saw on television than the pictures of black families he saw in *Life* magazine. Not exactly *Leave It to Beaver* or *Father Knows Best*, but not that far from it. Within the walls of his house he always felt safe. But outside the front door, it was clear from the houses packed tightly on the block and the narrowness of the street and the frustrations of the people around him that danger and threat existed there.

It was a world of shadows and alleys. A world of denseness. Black sweet shadowy denseness. On a Saturday morning the sun could fill his street with the most wondrous light. Could carve beautiful images into the bricks and cement that surrounded him. But when night came or on the dark days when clouds hovered, his world trembled with sorrow. Sorrow that darted between the music that floated from windows, carrying Little Anthony or the Drifters or Gloria Lynn through the air.

And then, of course, there were the created worlds of the books he read. But, at night, when he lay in bed reading, no matter where the story took him, he was still serenaded by the sorrow around him.

Edward watched the television as yet another infidelity was revealed. You could count on *Peyton Place* to show the troubles of rich white people. It was here that he discovered that sorrow also visited tree-lined, manicured-lawned streets and could be dressed in formal wear. White men and women struggled without mussing their hair or substantially changing the appearance of their lives. Nobody lay destitute on street grates in Peyton Place.

And then, in the midst of his reverie, there was a muffled explosion just outside the house. Sarah screamed, pulling herself out of her mother's lap, her pigtails matted to her head. Earl was up and moving to the window; Edward looked at his mother. She sighed. Through the part in the drapes his father created, they all could see that the storefront at the corner was ablaze.

"Damn, the Stoykos' place is on fire," Earl said with surprising force. But he didn't move, seemed almost frozen at the window.

"Maybe you better get away from the window, Earl."

And, as if Angela's voice had shaken him from a light dream or a nod, he said distantly, "Yeah, maybe I better. Something very strange is going on out there."

Edward watched his father turn away from the window. His mother was already on the telephone to the fire department. Sarah walked over to Edward. "The fire engines are coming. I can hear them."

"I don't hear anything."

"I do. There's three of them coming." Edward looked into his sister's eyes and saw absolute certainty. But before he could protest again, he heard them, too. She was right. Three engines were on the way.

His father was now heading to the front door. Edward jumped up to follow, Sarah tagging behind him. But just as the three of them reached the front door there was a shatter of glass and a curtain of flames shot up in front of them. Earl immediately turned and swept Sarah into his arms.

"Get out of here," he screamed to Edward and Angela as he

pushed them all toward the back of the house. Edward was terrified. Someone had tried to set their house on fire.

"Earl, what's going on? What happened?" Angela's body was moving toward the kitchen, but her face was turned in Earl's direction.

"I don't know. Just as I was about to open the door, I heard glass shattering and our front steps burst into flames. Scared the daylights out of me. I don't understand it." Now they were all in the kitchen looking at each other in total bewilderment. The back door was open just in case they needed to exit.

"Was it just the steps, Earl, or what was on fire?"

"Baby, I really don't know. The fire engines are out there now. I'm gonna go out through the back and see what's what. You keep these kids in here till I get back. Don't y'all move a muscle."

His wife nodded and then, just as he disappeared through the back door, she said, "Now, you be careful."

After about three minutes of silence, Edward tugged at his mother's dress. "Mom, can't I go out and find Dad? I'll be all right."

"You heard your father. You'll stay right here with me and your sister."

After a few more minutes, Edward's father walked back in, his hands buried in his pants pocket, his jawbone jutted out in anger. "It's those goddamned thugs. Somebody threw bombs. One went in the Stoykos' and one almost came through our front door." Angela reached for him and he took her in. "How do you know?"

"The cops told me. They figure one of those idiots thought either the Stoykos or us must have called the cops on them this afternoon. So they were trying to bomb us out. Leastways, that's what the cops are saying. But that's not the worst. Old lady

Stoyko got taken to the hospital. They think it was a heart attack."

"Is she gonna be okay?"

"I don't know. They said she was in pretty bad shape. It's a shame. One of the last white people in the neighborhood. I tell you, Angela, it's a crying shame."

"I don't believe it. I never heard of such foolishness. They tried to set our house on fire, too? You must be joking. I can't believe that. Who would do that? We know all those boys. They wouldn't do that."

Edward listened intently. He could tell that Sarah was becoming increasingly frightened. He felt her trembling body standing next to him. Somebody had tried to bomb their house. But they had missed. He thought about the front of their house. It was just like the one on either side of them. Five stone steps that led up to the door. No porch, no railing. The only thing separating the houses was a strip of bricks one foot wide. They had been saved by the only thing that separated one house from the other.

"Can I go to the front door and see?" There was too much going on to be content huddled deep in the house. He wanted to survey the damage.

His father looked at him, the anger lifting. "Yeah, I guess it's okay now. The cops are out there. But, Eddie, don't go outside. You hear?"

Edward nodded and made a quick dash toward the front door. Sarah looked up at her father. "Can I go, too, Daddy?"

"Just be careful, Sarah."

Edward felt his sister pull up just behind him. He stood on his tiptoes and looked out the front-door window, but he couldn't see very well. So he stepped back and opened the door. Now, just on the other side of the screen door, he saw the splattered glass. He could see the charred dark green tint of the Thunderbird wine bottle now reduced to shards. The front steps were all black with the mud made from soot and water. There were still a lot of police and lights and firefighters around. There were also a lot of bystanders gawking at the burned-out storefront that had been the Stoykos' home. Edward's sensitive nose twinged from the acrid sting of the smoke. When personal things burned, they carried a unique odor. You could always tell when someone's house had burned because the neighborhood would be heavy with the smell of singed and charred memories.

Edward carefully made a mental note of everyone who was standing around. He knew almost everyone. But among the crowd was one figure that caught his attention. His little gray cells began to vibrate. MommaButch was standing there among the crowd. What was MommaButch doing here, almost in 2–4 territory, when he was a warlord for the 2–8? But there he was. Standing next to Mr. Bell and Mr. Wells as if he, too, was a homeowner and a concerned neighbor.

He knew MommaButch fairly well. They had played touch football together on Ingersoll Street. There was only one explanation for MommaButch's presence. He must have had something to do with the firebombing, Edward thought. Why didn't anyone else see that? It would be just like a hard-core gang leader like MommaButch, a boy with incredible arrogance, to stand there daring anyone to implicate him. Standing there, actually, to make sure no one would.

He thought about saying something to his father but didn't. The whole affair made him uneasy. No one had ever done anything like that to his family. Instead he just stood at the door watching the movement of the people as they gradually went back to their houses. And after about five minutes, Edward watched MommaButch disappear into the night.

Slowly, as the night wove its darkness deeper, Edward grew

tired of the sharp air, the abstract kaleidoscope of color, and the sounds of men speculating and tending to their jobs. Sarah had already gone upstairs to bed. His father and mother were back to the couch and the television. He closed the door, and after retrieving his Agatha Christie book from the dining-room table, climbed the steps himself. He read four more Poirot stories before he went to sleep.

.   .   .

The next day, after he had packed his clothes for the trip to Rehoboth, Edward left his house looking for Sonny and Rooster. He found them sitting on Rooster's front steps on Ingersoll Street.

"What's happening?" he said as he joined them on the hot steps.

"Nothing, man. We just been playing some b-ball. I cleaned this sucker's clock." Rooster stood up and bounced the ball on the steps in such a way that it hit the edge of the step and careened into Edward's chest. Edward was caught completely by surprise. The ball hit him and knocked him backward.

"You ain't shit, Eddie." Rooster cut a sly smile and retrieved the ball. Edward had never liked Rooster. He hung out with him only because he was Sonny's friend.

"Leave him alone, Rooster. He ain't done nothing to you."

"He's a punk."

Edward turned into Rooster's face. "Your mother's a punk." He held his breath a second and sat down next to Sonny. The truth was that Edward was afraid of Rooster, but then, in a way, Edward was afraid of most of the boys who moved around him. But he also knew when he had to pump his heart up and show them he wasn't a complete pushover. Every fight he had had began with him feeling pushed into a corner. A corner from which the only way out was to act as crazy and as bad as the boy

who put him there. This was one of those moments. At least
Rooster wasn't a cornerboy. There was no army of violent wild
teenagers to back him up.

Sonny broke into laughter. "That's right, Ed, man. Tell that
chicken-bone, no-basketball-playing, funky-breath sissy where
to get off."

Sonny knew how to handle Rooster. He knew that Rooster
would not escalate his conflict with Edward if he perceived that
Sonny was on Edward's side.

Rooster looked at Sonny for a second and chuckled to himself.
"I heard there was a fire on your block last night."

"Yeah. Somebody bombed the Stoykos'. They almost got our
house, too." Edward was glad to be talking about something different.

"For real?" Sonny hadn't heard about it. "What happened?"

But before Edward could answer, they all looked up to see
MommaButch cross the street, coming toward them.

"I swear," Sonny said under his breath. "Here comes one of
those goons."

"He's cool, man. MommaButch is all right." Rooster spoke
through sly teeth.

"Yeah, all right if you like hardheads."

Edward tensed. He remembered the scene the night before
with MommaButch's tall figure outlined by the spinning red
lights of the fire engines.

"What's going on, youngboys?" MommaButch's voice was
pitched and full of menacing energy. He talked and moved like a
power, a force. And he was. This was a guy you couldn't cross.

"Nothing, man. We're just laying." Rooster could sound just
like a gang member when he wanted. Now *his* voice was edged.

"Yeah, well, I'm looking for some punks from 2–4. I'm gonna
get me one today." Edward wanted to get up and leave, but he

couldn't. He could feel even Sonny's anxiety rising. But Rooster seemed to be calm, even glowing from this personal attention.

Rooster was still bouncing the ball. "I heard y'all kicked much butt last night."

"Yeah, buddy. You can believe that shit. But one of my boys got locked up 'cause of some bullshit snitches, so I had to deliver some payback, in my own kind of Fourth-of-July-barbecue style. If you understand what I mean?"

"You did that?" Rooster was sporting a wide grin and looking directly into Edward's stunned face.

"You heard it here first." MommaButch let the words slither through his teeth and then grabbed the ball out of Rooster's hands.

Edward was trembling inside. It *was* him. It *was* Momma-Butch who had almost destroyed his house. What was he supposed to do? Rooster was still grinning at him. Sonny instinctively put his arm around him, as if he were trying to tell Edward not to speak. Not to erupt. Not to say anything that would provoke MommaButch. Edward took a deep breath. He felt tears gathering just behind his eyes. This wasn't a mystery anymore. His first instincts had been right.

"Well, if you see any of those punks sneaking around here, I'll be down at Barnett's getting me a hoagie. Come and get me."

Rooster nodded as MommaButch tossed him the basketball and headed down the street. Sonny turned to Edward and said, "You did good, man. That crazy fool would have dusted you right here. I'm sure he didn't know that was your house. He thought they were white people."

"It don't matter who they were, Sonny. He ain't got no right to go around trying to set people's houses on fire. Old lady Stoyko is in the hospital, man. She's a nice lady. You know that. She'd do anything for us. I mean, no matter what somebody's selling—

candy, cookies, magazines, whatever—if you stop at the Stoykos'
you know you gonna make at least one sale for sure. It ain't
right, man."

"I know."

Rooster sat down on the step below them. "Aw, man, what are
you whining about? It didn't burn your house. It wasn't no big
thing. Anyway, them white people don't belong down here no
way. This is our neighborhood."

Edward had heard enough. "You know, man," he said, looking
down at Rooster, "I ain't gonna miss *you* at all. I can't wait to get
out of here. Because I can't listen to your stupid talk anymore.
Hurting people, no matter who they are, ain't right. Anyway"—
he was now standing—"I got to get home and finish packing." He
paused again. "You want to walk me home, Sonny?"

"Yeah, man, I'll walk you."

"Oh, so that's the way it is. You want Sonny to walk you."
Edward almost felt sorry he'd said what he'd said and was about
to apologize when Rooster let him off the hook. "It don't mean a
thing to me, you understand. I got to be going anyway, you dig?"
And with that, he turned and strolled toward Twenty-sixth Street.

Sonny and Edward went the other way, with the July sky high
above them. Edward was quiet as they put distance between
Rooster and them. He was thinking about what he'd said to
Rooster about not missing him. He wouldn't. And he really
wouldn't miss all the conflict that whirled around them. "You
know"—he turned to Sonny—"I wish you could come with me. I
like going away and all, but . . ."

"I know," Sonny said quietly. "Maybe one of these years I
could go with you, or maybe your parents will let you stay home
for the summer."

"Yeah, if I stayed here for the summer we'd probably have a
cool time, huh?"

"Jay-straight we would. But it's hip that you get to go away, too. The gangs are already acting crazy. You're lucky you don't have to stay here. Safer, too."

"Yeah, I guess." Edward then said good-bye to his friend and went into the house. There was still a sharp smell of gasoline and charred cement in the air around the front door. His mother and Sarah were in the kitchen. He hollered at them and headed up the stairs to his bedroom. Even though it was only late afternoon, he felt tired. He sat down on his bed and picked up his book. But he didn't feel like reading; his mind was fairly racing. He first thought about MommaButch and how it was that a boy like him could get away with so much mischief. He could beat up people, rob people, even burn other people's houses down without anybody making him stop. It made no sense at all to him.

Then, inevitably, his mind turned to Rufus. Rufus, the man who, like a deranged thief . . . no . . . who *was* a deranged thief, had ruined his vacation last summer when he'd inexplicably snatched Mr. Peabody. Edward had been completely unhinged by the loss of Mr. Peabody. Distraught actually. Late one afternoon, after sitting on the dock by the Rehoboth Canal crabbing, he had returned to Edna's only to find everyone—his mother, Edna, three women he didn't know, Bud the Iceman, and his uncle Sam who lived down the road—sitting in Edna's private social parlor, each with a bowl in their hands. Everyone smiling and licking their lips. When they saw him, all eyes averted. Edward knew instantly that something was wrong. Such a silly ruse. They must have known that even at eleven he could detect such immature behavior. He could smell the air of guilt swirling. They were all guilty of something. Some crime had been committed. But what was it?

The bowls. Yes. It had something to do with the bowls. They all had one. And they had all become 4:00 A.M. quiet. His first instinct had been to sit down next to his mother and wait until everyone started talking again. He knew they couldn't remain silent forever. And when they did speak he knew one of them would make a mistake. One of them would *think* what they were saying was safe, but Edward only needed the slightest slip and he would know whatever it was they were trying to hide.

But he didn't sit down. He employed quite a different approach. He eyed each person carefully, and then he quickly left for his room. The staircase that led to his room opened into the parlor, so when he reached the top he stopped, leaned over and turned the knob to his door, pushed it a little, and let it close. It made just enough noise to satisfy him.

He then slowly crept back down the stairs. Trying to anticipate each creak. Trying to make himself lighter. He tried to make himself think of himself as weightless as he descended. The creaks seemed to dissipate. This was his strength. The ability to fit his slightly round adolescence into spaces he wasn't supposed to be in. Each step brought the sound of their conversation clearer to his ears.

"Somebody should tell him," Edna had said.

"I'm his mother; I'll tell him. I know Edward. He probably already knows. But if he doesn't, I'll be the one."

Edward then heard Sam's voice. "City kids don't understand about all this stuff. Rufus didn't know that damned turtle was somebody's pet. He just saw the main ingredients of a hot pot of snapper soup. And a damn fine soup it is. That Mr. Peabody sure do gots some taste."

They all laughed. "Well, I got my bowl full just like y'all, but I'm not looking forward to telling Edward."

Edward knew then what Rufus had done. The mystery had quickly lost all of its complexity. Rufus had stolen Mr. Peabody, skinned him, and cooked him up into a soup. Edward's very own pet turtle. The snapping turtle he had found his first week in Rehoboth that summer. The turtle he had fed and played with and planned to take home to Philly with him as a present to Mrs. Butters, who was to be his eighth-grade teacher, as a class pet. What a heinous crime. What a horrible person Rufus was.

Edward swallowed hard and began a silent return up the steps. This time he quietly slipped into his room and collapsed on the bed. Horrible. Horrible. He'd intended to read one of the Archie comics he'd brought. But instead he couldn't stop himself from bolting out of the room and rumbling loudly down the stairs. When he reached the bottom, he took another deep breath and blazed by them out into the cooling Delaware early-evening air.

He thought he'd heard his mother say his name weakly as he emerged from Edna's, but he took off running, heading around to the back, where Mr. Peabody's cage was. He crumpled to his knees hugging the empty box like a lover. He cried. It startled him. He was crying over a turtle.

He remembered his mother picking him up and enveloping him in her arms. Kissing him. He could smell the pungent floral aroma of turtle soup on her breath. He forgave her. He forgave them. But Rufus? Rufus . . . This summer. His intense interest in Rufus was of course mostly driven by a desire to know the man who had killed and eaten Mr. Peabody. To know why. But another curiosity nagged him. He'd never been able to clear his mind of the images of black men lying akimbo on the steps of vacant buildings. Dirty muttering men. Men with hands that were nearly white with dryness and with palms as dark and dull as their faces. And when his mother or father took him downtown, they silently led him by even more desperate-looking men sprawled in front of restaurants, begging. Who were these men? he wondered. Where did they come from?

When he asked his parents about it, they never answered in a way that brought clarity. Yes, they couldn't find a job. Yes, they were hooked on drugs. Yes, they were mentally unstable. Yes, they were sick. He understood that. But there had to be more to it than that. To his young mind, his parents' responses did not explain the emptiness. The absence of anything resembling a shame about what they were. Why weren't they ashamed? Embarrassed?

From the moment he'd seen Rufus, Edward recognized that same emptiness in his eyes. He knew from the very first that Rufus was the type of man whom people whispered about. Pointed at. Avoided. Feared. He was just like the men his friends called "bums," no-accounts. What was their story? What was Rufus's story?

2

Going south from the city into rural Delaware was revelatory. After Dover they would pass field after field of corn, slowly turning lush with its sweet fruit. And then later, in Milford, they would pass the orchards of apples and peaches. And in between, the pigs, horses, and cows stood as grazing witnesses to the ignorance of all those who passed.

They had been driving since just before dawn, as was his father's custom when they traveled long distances. And, for the Massey family, a four-hour drive was considered long-distance. At this time in the morning, the scenery that moved by them revealed itself slowly. Showing itself through the disappearing shroud of night in glimpses of increasing brilliance.

Edward was crammed in the back of his father's 1960 Cadillac, between bags of fried chicken, his sister, and a cooler of ice and sodas. They had traveled under a fog of sleep and dreams.

Every time Edward awoke, he'd lean forward, toward his mother, and ask, "Are we almost there yet?"

Invariably his mother would turn to him with a look that said, "Go back to sleep, read a book, look out the window, do whatever you want, but don't ask me that stupid question again, please."

When awake, Edward had counted the overpasses and the bridges. He knew from previous trips that when they passed the Mispillion River they were getting close. Indeed, the bridge that spanned the narrow river had a big sign with the river's name painted in black and white. Every time he had driven over the Mispillion, he thought about the girls on his block and how when they were playing double Dutch they'd often chant the letters of the other river—M-I-S-S-I-S-S-I-P-P-I—putting an exaggerated emphasis on the "Pee-Pee" part. Maybe it was the Mark Twain novels he had read that year that made him so enamored with the great river. There were mysteries there he was sure, floating down the Mississippi.

And on they rode—past the chicken coops and hog pens, the lonely farmhouses; past the roadside shanty stores which offered bargains in fresh produce and fireworks.

They rode past them all. Edward's father was a man unafraid of the accelerator. Once he set his sights on a target, got in the car, and started moving, only gasoline and absolute necessity would stop him. Those absolute necessities were limited to bathroom stops for the children.

Even when he was forced to stop for Edward or Sarah to go to the bathroom, he usually pulled over to the side of the road. They were expected to go into the bushes.

Edward's father never parked in front of a Howard Johnson's or a Stuckey's or a Bob's Big Boy for anything. This infuriated Edward. He couldn't figure it out. No matter how hungry for a hamburger or desperate to go to a real bathroom Edward was, his father would not take his cement foot from the gas pedal. Once Earl Massey started driving long-distance, he would fight all attempts to get him to stop for anything until they reached their destination. But Edward didn't know that his father had grown up in the segregated South. Had never felt welcomed on the highway.

Even though it was the early sixties and civil rights was the coming thing, there was still the chance of seeing one of those "Coloreds Served in the Back" signs or the "Whites Only" tags over the bathroom doors. Edward's father kept his stopping to a minimum. He knew anything could happen if he wandered into the wrong joint at the wrong time. Entire black families had been broken up or destroyed by such heroic acts as pulling over for a soda pop or a cone of ice cream in the old South. And Delaware, for all practical purposes, was as "Southern" as a city boy could get without *going* to Mississippi.

.   .   .

Rehoboth Beach was a place of summer resort. It was the type of seaside town that survived on the availability of wealthy summer tourists. Edward's family was not in such a fortunate category. The Masseys came to Rehoboth for different reasons. The main one was an attempt to relieve Sarah and Edward from the stress of North Philly summers. But there was another reason. Angela went to Rehoboth to work. She would wait tables all season. It was her way of taking some of the pressure off of Earl. When she and the children returned to Philadelphia in September, the day after Labor Day, she would bring five or six hundred dollars home with her.

"Rehoboth" is a word with biblical connections. As Job searched for his new turf, he led his flock of followers to a place where they would be safe, where everyone could live, where there would be "room enough." That is what Rehoboth means: "room enough."

In the beginning, before there was a city, a group of Methodists came to the area from various locales in Delaware and Maryland. They came in religious unity hoping to establish a resort, free from the moral decay that they saw creeping throughout the country. Jim Crow joined them there, perhaps to help hold time still.

State Highway 1—the only road into Rehoboth, split into a two tined fork as it approached the city. The right road led over a bridge which spanned the canal, tributary of the Chesapeake, which snaked through the heart of the bustling resort town and took the eager tourists to the open arms of the Atlantic Ocean.

But before reaching the water, at the very edge, a dried-out, weather-beaten boardwalk sat, propped up by wooden posts which were driven into the sand. On this boardwalk were a bevy of stores filled with seasonal scalpers who sold caramel popcorn, saltwater taffy, and cotton candy to the tourists who oozed into the sun-washed city.

The tourists braved everything. Lying body by body on the hot harsh sand. Noses white, smelling of cocoa butter, against the background of the breaking ocean and the sound of nasal sprays wheezing, the privileged enjoyed their summer days by the sea. They collected in formless hulks, basking in the sun of Rehoboth's segregated beaches—Jim Crow's basement tanning salon. There they would stay until the sun waned with the wake of autumn.

But down the left fork of Highway 1, the direction Earl Massey headed, led you to West Rehoboth.

The black people who lived there never called it "West" anything. It was just Rehoboth Beach to them. But to the officials at City Hall, it was an important distinction. The citizens of unincorporated, annexed entities do not vote, were not counted, and had virtually no social services offered to them.

The folks of West Rehoboth were crab catchers, clam shuckers, dishwashers, waitresses, maids, and lawn mowers. They provided the human arms which kept the bustling Rockwellian town bristling clean. They were the tillers of the field. And when they were done with their chores in Rehoboth Beach, they were remanded to the western province. Their own little *bantustan*. No black person had ever lived on the other side of the canal. They sat in the balcony at the theater. They were prevented from eating in the restaurants. They could not drink at the bars. They could not stay in the hotels. But the greatest restraint laid upon them, the greatest indignity, was the Crow's Nest.

The Crow's Nest was a small area of sand about the length of a city block at the mouth of the Atlantic, on which black people were allowed to sun and bathe. Everyone called it the Crow's Nest. You had to be black to be there. If you were black you had no choice.

But in spite of all of Jim Crow's creations, the barriers and preventions laid on these people, they fashioned West Rehoboth into home. They laughed and cried there. They smoked and drank there. They played with their children and picnicked there. It was there that they had a safe place to sleep and somewhere comfortable to eat dinner.

The people of West Rehoboth went barefoot when they could. But it was difficult. For years the roads and driveways of West Rehoboth were paved with clamshells, leavings from the clam-and-oyster-processing factories in the adjacent town of Lewes. They were spread about in painful reminder to the barefoot traveler that a new pair of flip-flops might be useful.

Flip-flops were just becoming the big thing in beachwear. It was a newfangled idea, like canned potato chips. Essentially

made from two pieces of rubber, flip-flops made people feel holy
as they walked no matter what they walked on: clamshells or the
hot sand at the beach. But when it was time to get dressed up, on
a Friday or Saturday for example, these usually barefoot people
wanted, just like their brothers and sisters in the city, to step out
in fine patent leather, Cuban-heeled, mock-celebrity boots in an
effort to escape the jagged ends of the crushed clamshells.

Jim Crow was an enigmatic, unseen, but important resident of
Rehoboth. He could formulate any disguise, feel comfortable in
any surrounding. He could be the manager of the bowling alley,
the desk clerk at the Henlopen Hotel. He could even be the usher
at the only movie house. He could be making less than minimum
wage. He could be a woman. And she could have muscles in her
lips which made them as stiff as a half-opened drawbridge when
she slammed the cash register closed in the face of a black person.

That was the thing. A perfectly nice person could turn sour,
become a blotched red-faced swelling when merely presented
with the necessity of being civil to someone black. Jim Crow
could usurp the foreground of a life, a person's individuality, and
render it background. Obliterate the details of a God-loving soul.

Jim could sneak into a white person's heart and whisper
enough fear that suddenly black people were not good enough to
eat inside their restaurants. A wavering soul would need only a
kiss to the fading lips by a seductive Jim Crow.

. . .

Edward stretched as he rolled his chubby body out of the car. His
sister was still curled into the corner of the backseat of the car.
His father was already at the trunk and his mother was making
her way into Edna's house. They were finally there. Rehoboth
Beach, Delaware. This was where he'd spend the remainder of
his summer.

Edward stood in the yard of his aunt Edna's large house. Actually, Edna's was much more than a house. The enclosed porch was the candy store, replete with a Coca-Cola refrigerator that sat like an upright red coffin. You could find Lance sandwich cookies, Sugar Babies, and bubble gum clipped like laundry to the walls. You could get a pickled pig's foot and Polish sausages, fished from a big jar on the rickety counter which divided the room, for fifteen cents each.

Inside, there was a large dining area with ten small tables which doubled as a restaurant and later, at night, as a dance floor. Edna had extended the back room to accommodate three full-size pool tables. Nearly everybody in West Rehoboth came to Edna's for something. A Log Cabin candy bar, a barbecue sandwich, a game of pool, a night out dancing. If they wanted to have fun in a safe place, Edna had a corner on the market. The only other option for black folks was the Do Drop Inn—and there was considerable risk in simply walking through the Do Drop's doors.

Edward looked up, his nose full of honeysuckle and his ears with the buzz of insects—june bugs, flies, and mosquitoes—and saw his mother emerge from the porch with Edna's arms draped over her. Edna smiled when she saw Edward. Sarah was now running to her. As Edna leaned over to embrace Sarah, she grimaced. Her arthritis had intensified over the years and this summer she could definitely feel more pain than at any other time in her life. Edward wondered if it was her joint pain which made Edna's smiles seem weirdly frightening or whether she just wasn't used to smiling and didn't really know how to do it. He wanted to like Edna. To love her. But even when she was trying to be nice, she managed to irritate him. When she smiled it was never purely joyous. There was a sort of cynical twitch in the corner of her mouth which made him uncomfortable. And when she complained or criticized someone, it degenerated into a harangue that could last the length of a full day.

Edna Hull, a potato-skinned woman, sixty-two, and a resident of West Rehoboth for more than forty years, was a genuine small-town king-, or perhaps queen-pin. She was the resident loan shark, numbers runner, landlord, and barbecue expert—the only one from which to get an ice-cold Nehi grape soda. There, at Edna's, one could also acquire the peculiar taste for Royal Crown Cola with Planters salted peanuts dumped into the bottle. The peanuts, all pushing to the top, the salt mixing with the sweetness of the soda yielded an experience worthy of a summer vacation.

In West Rehoboth, there were two places a person could go to have a good time: the Do Drop Inn and Edna's.

The Do Drop was wild and rangy. Untamed. It smelled of wine-soaked wooden floors and the sweat of hardworking black men. There, after a hard day of serving food and cleaning the summer homes of white people, the most daring sought passion and excitement. Behind the Do Drop, a perpetual crowd huddled over the rolling dice of craps.

At Edna's, no one played craps. The only gambling done was small time on the pool tables. Ten-dollar, eight-ball wagers raised an eyebrow at Edna's. No cards. No heavy alcohol drinking. Edna didn't want the troubles of the Do Drop in her place, so she kept a tight hand. Anybody who even looked like he or she might cause trouble was asked to leave. Besides, Edna sold no alcohol. She'd turn her head if she saw customers drinking beer, but if she saw a whiskey bottle, she kicked them out. Of course, people would just come there already drunk or sneak sips from the brief flash of a partially hidden flask.

Edna's had the Seeburg jukebox and a small dance floor.

Edna's had the food, and most especially on a warm July evening, Edna's had the women and the music for dancing.

Nearly everyone, black and white, owed Edna for some kind of favor or loan or job that she had arranged for them. She was at least as effective as any phantom government employment office. If there was an available job within driving distance, she knew about it first. If you had a problem with the law or needed medical help and couldn't pay for it, Edna could probably help—if she liked you.

But make no mistake. Edna was not selfless. She understood the troubles that plagued and would try to help when she could, but she was not to be taken advantage of. Indeed, Edna expected to be repaid for every loan, every favor she issued. She was known as tough and fair. She could evict tenants without a tear if they had promised but not delivered their rent. But she could *forget* to ask for the rent from a person who had been sick and unable to work.

As a ten-year-old girl—living with her family on a small peanut farm her father sharecropped—Edna had a face full of sunflower brightness. She was as thin as a fence post and as fast on her feet as the flapping wings of a hummingbird. Even in that world, one step removed from slavery, young Edna was worry-free, happy, and mostly a blur. She would run everywhere. To the barn in the morning to milk the cows. Through the subsistence cornfield. Back to the house to get the garbage, then to the barn to get the feed and then to the pigsty, where she donned her rubber boots and climbed into the mud with the pigs.

Her mother was fond of looking out the kitchen window and calling out, "I never seen a soul what liked sloppin' hogs more than you, girl." And then, in a voice meant more as a mark of bewilderment to herself than for Edna, she'd say, "It's the only time you ain't wearin' out yo' shoes, rippin' and runnin' 'round here like you do."

But there was one other place Edna slowed to a stop: church. She'd been baptized at eight and had fully embraced Jesus from that moment on. Her innocent faith was like a shield that extended the boundaries of safety that her family already provided.

When Edna left her mother's house in Goldsboro, North Carolina, bound for Philadelphia, she was young, energetic, and naive. But the city almost immediately began to change her. From the beginning she was hurt by the way she was treated. In the city it was often other black people who acted like they were better than her. She could feel them looking down on her as if she was little better than a hillbilly. They openly laughed at her Southern accent. No matter that most of them had only recently come from the South just like she had. In fact, that was the first big lesson. You had to at least try to talk like you'd never been farther south than South Philly.

And then there were the men, slick city men whose flirtations and lies had left their mark. Had challenged her faith. It was her stay in the city which drew the lines for her life. It didn't take long for her to realize that her survival would depend on her ability to use what she could to keep others from using her.

She had been accustomed to a different world. In the South, the fiery monster of hatred was visible, tangible. A mix of contradictions and paradoxes. She knew it as a place where a white man would just as soon spit in her face as give her the key to the only bathroom in a gasoline station. That same man might also send her a get-well card if she was ill.

At home in North Carolina, black folks were different, too. They knew how to suffer together. The family extended into history and they held hands against the onslaught. There was intense strength, warmth that was spread as thick as fresh raw honey throughout the community. This was what she had left.

Over the middle and later years of her life Edna had consolidated her power and her influence on the lives of the people of West Rehoboth. And because of that, folks tended to patronize her place, slobber on her apron, and smile as much as they could when they came face-to-face with her. She'd had to build a large thick wall around her heart, but it was still there. Beating.

3

Edward's father stayed in Rehoboth exactly twenty hours. Just enough time to sleep, eat, pack up more food that Edna had prepared, make one trip to the beach, gas the car, and head home. Edward watched his father turn the Cadillac onto the clamshell-paved road and kick dust and shells back at Rehoboth. His mother had already gotten a job and was scheduled to work the next day, and Sarah was just as quickly another dust urchin with the other kids who played in Edna's yard.

Later that afternoon, Edward was sitting on the front step, two cinderblocks lying side by side, wondering how long it would be before he saw Rufus, when Edna opened the porch door and asked if he wanted to accompany her to the dairy.

Riding with Edna to Milford for apples and peaches at the orchards there, or to Seaford to the chicken factory for fresh chickens in quantity, or to Milton for hair pomade was one of the benefits of being there. So he was happy to formally begin his vacation with one of those unpredictable rides with Edna.

As Edward slid into her car she turned to him. "You sure are growing up fast, Eddie. I wish Christine was here to see you, but she's with her mother this summer." Christine was the daughter of one of Edna's relatives who lived with Edna. She was about the same age as Edward. "Seems like it was just yesterday when you was nothing but a little softshell."

It was getting late, into the early evening, when they left the yard, drove down Hebron Road, and then turned left onto Highway 1 and proceeded into the heart of Rehoboth Beach, Delaware, proper.

Edward didn't know what to say. He wanted to be around her for investigative purposes. But she made him very uncomfortable. He couldn't quite figure it out. Perhaps it was age. He had seen her teeth in the bathroom, sitting in a glass. Just sitting there. Maybe that was what was wrong with her smile.

"My dad thinks I should be taller." Was all he could manage to say.

"Your daddy can't make you grow. You're tall enough. What does he want, a giant?"

Edward fidgeted. "A basketball player probably." This was already too much. His father wouldn't like them talking this way. Besides, he didn't feel like it was a desire or anything his father had. He just thought Edward was a little short for his weight.

"Well, are you glad to be down here for a while?"

"Yes." He really didn't feel like talking. Not about himself anyway. He wanted to know about Rufus. He had been watching Rufus's shack almost since the moment they arrived and had seen nothing going in or coming out. "Aunt Edna?"

"Yes, sugar." Edna was busy maneuvering her car into the dairy's parking lot.

"Um, ah . . . where is Uncle Rufus? I haven't seen him since we been here."

The door slammed shut and Edward watched Edna's back as she wobbled into the store. He got out of the car and caught up with her. There would be no answer. When adults didn't want to talk about something, he knew from his detective mentors, there was definitely a story worth discovering.

They bought five gallons of regular milk and a half gallon each of chocolate and buttermilk. While Edna paid the bill, he loaded the backseat of the car. Edna was still silent as they made their way back. Not exactly silent. Edward could hear a slight humming coming from her body. She was cruising along in her '57 Oldsmobile, a dusty black car with a smirking grille and razor-sharp fins. It chortled erratically. Edward was lost in thought. Where was Rufus?

It wasn't like he really *knew* Rufus. He'd maybe only talked to him once in the five summers he had been coming to Rehoboth. But he'd seen him in the yard occasionally. Or staggering down the road. Or sitting on his steps staring into the Delaware sky.

He made a mental note to start asking some of the other kids, especially Anthony, a boy he had befriended on other visits. He hoped Rufus was still in Rehoboth. His shack certainly was. It sat there like an unused outhouse. He remembered that last summer he had heard two women talking in Edna's restaurant. Something about how Rufus was known to appear and reappear like magic. No one ever knew where he disappeared to or when he'd come back. But when Edna delivered their barbecue-rib sandwiches all talk of Rufus had ended.

"Oh Lord." Edward heard Edna's voice, which brought him back to his place in the car. He looked at her. The night shade rising around them.

"What's wrong?"

Edna squirmed in the leather seat. "These fools out here tonight. I shoulda guessed it."

Edward could see the flashing lights of two police cars just ahead. "What's going on?"

But Edna said nothing. The car came to a stop and within seconds a state trooper walked up.

"Nice evenin', Miz Edna." Edna nodded at him. She could hear the creak of his leather motorcycle boots. The chin strap of his hat cut across his square jaw, making a mark on his flushed tanned face. When he talked the chin strap inched its way toward his mouth until he had to pause long enough to let it slip back into place.

Edward heard Edna sigh before she spoke. "It *is* a nice evening, Horace. It's quite nice. How come it's always you, Horace? Every time the law got something to say to me, it's always you who's the one saying it?"

Horace looked down at Edna. He wanted to get this over with. He had had no idea that the last car in this night of routine inspections would be Edna's. He tried to maintain distance. There was a history between them and it would have been much better if she hadn't been driving the car.

"Y'all got a driver's license and owner's card?"

"You know I do, Horace."

"Mind if'n I take a look at it?" He paused, hitched up his pants, and looked at his partner, who had already started walking around to the back of the car. "You see, this here's a road check to inspect the fitness of these here cars that come ridin through here."

"I don't mind, Horace. How's your mama?" Edward was now turned toward Edna, watching her expressionless face.

Horace peered at her from under the brim of his trooper's hat. The ridges in his jowls tightened as he clenched his teeth. Begrudgingly he spat out, "Fine. She's just fine, Edna."

Edna continued: "Horace, how come you on this road? All the tourists come down the other road, the one goin' into town."

"I know that, Edna; now I got to do what the chief says. You know that. Now turn yo' windshield wipers on."

Nothing happened.

"Blow your horn, Edna."

The barest of sounds startled the crickets as they chirped in the bushes alongside the road.

"The brakes, Edna, would you put yo' foot on the brake pedal, please?"

Edna, sitting behind the steering wheel of her car, a little woman, a bit drawn and slow, but alert and mentally quick, looked up at him. She turned to Edward and mumbled, "Guess he thinks we stopped this thing by draggin' our feet on the ground."

Edward's hand immediately covered his mouth as he stifled a laugh.

"Edna, do you know that one of your brake lights is on the blink?"

"No, Horace, I didn't know that."

"And did you know your muffler is hanging by a thread and—" He stopped, straightened himself. "Edna, do you realize that this here whole entire automobile is fallin' apart? When's the last time you got it inspected? I don't know how you keep it runnin'."

Edna looked straight ahead. "With gasoline, Horace."

"Now, don't y'all go gettin' indignant with me, Miz Edna. I'm only doin' my duty. We'se gon' hafta take a trip back on into town to see the magistrate."

"Magistrate? You must be kidding?" For the first time Edward felt fear in the car.

"Naw, Edna, this ain't no joke. I got my orders."

Edna was silent. Horace shifted his weight. It was a dangerous game to play with Edna Hull. Even at headquarters, the guys talked about her in hushed tones. She was one of two or three Negroes he had been warned to steer clear of. Over the years, he had seen her often, but one particular time they had faced each other with fear and apprehension. Rufus had brought that on. But that eventually faded into lore. Now they spoke when they passed each other. Edna had somehow discovered that Horace's mother owned a candy store in Milton. Whenever she went there she would stop by to have a soda and talk. His mother had mentioned it to him once. "That's a nice colored woman, that Edna Hull."

Horace's heart had slowed when she said it. Not Edna Hull. Not in my own house, he thought.

Edna had a special way with white people, especially the older ones. On the surface, they all trusted her and sought her counsel. In fact, Edna's presence as the center of black life in Rehoboth over the past thirty years had taught her all kinds of tricks and ploys to go along with the knowledge of the details of private white life.

Horace felt as if he was pressing his face to a shattering mirror. He knew it wasn't safe. The headlights of an approaching car flashed in her eyes.

"Listen, Horace, I was thinking about getting me one of them new cars just today. I know this thing ain't running right. I'd make me drive into town, too, if I was you. But this thing"—she hit the steering wheel with the heel of her hand—"this thing ain't really worth it. That magistrate probably got a lot more important things to do than dicker with me on this stupid piece of car. Besides, I don't think I got enough gas to even get to town and back."

Edward instinctively checked her fuel gauge, but it was obviously broken, the needle way to the left of empty.

Horace wavered. There was a long pause. "Well, you could ride with me, Edna."

"That's mighty nice of you, Horace, but I was gonna suggest that you come on over to the restaurant and have yourself a nice big barbecue sandwich."

"Well, Edna, I don't know . . ."

"C'mon, I know you're tired. Your chief would understand. Besides, you'd just have to drive me back here. I'll even give you a sandwich you can take back to him. Now, wouldn't you rather get a nice meal and a cold beer than do all the driving this late at night. Your wife is probably waiting for you to get off duty right now. Ain't she?"

Horace knew that Edna spelled trouble. He wasn't too sure his superiors would be smiling when they looked up and saw Edna standing there. Over the years, Edna had reached the status that only powerful black women can achieve in a Jim Crow world—namely, she knew the secrets and the desires of all the powerful white men. "Well, it is gettin' late and we ain't had supper yet." Horace rubbed his chin, looked at his partner, who was already getting into the squad car. "Can you give me a sandwich to bring home to my wife?"

Edna's face broke free in a rolling grin. "Now, Horace, how could I send you home empty-handed? Y'all follow me on over to the restaurant."

A few minutes later the two-car procession turned into Edna's driveway as a crowd of neighbors and waiting party goers wondered among themselves how she had managed to get a police escort for her weekly trip to the dairy for milk.

Edna patted Edward's hand before she turned the car off and winked at him. "Barbecue done got me out of so many tight jams I'm thinking about getting me a bigger hog pen." This time when she smiled, Edward saw only pleasure.

4

Edward quickly settled into his summer routine. In the morning he and Sarah would have breakfast in Edna's large kitchen. The guests who were staying with her and anyone who was paying for their meals sat in the dining room. Edna always had a number of people who were staying at her place and who expected her to prepare their first meal before heading out to work. Every day during the summer months, when her rooms were full and there were plenty of folks in and around West Rehoboth, Edna prepared a sumptuous breakfast. There were usually biscuits, bacon, grits, ham, scrambled eggs, pancakes, and fried potatoes. On special mornings there was steak and gravy as well.

After breakfast, there were always a list of chores. Sarah had to help Edna in the kitchen and with the few chickens she had in the yard, the garden, and with the preparation of lunch and dinner. But Edna really didn't depend on Sarah. If one of her little friends happened by and asked if Sarah could play, she was out of the house in an instant. And she stayed out all day, coming back to Edna's for meals dirty and exhausted. During the day, Edward would see her running down the road to get the mail, playing mindlessly with her friends, chasing butterflies and hummingbirds, making mud pies (if there was mud), filling every day with the sweet emptiness of idleness. Ennui. The singular moments of childhood. That was why they were there in the first place. No gangs here. No urban threat.

Oh, but there was violence aplenty. At night the small, black community would fairly ripple with the slow-burning rage of poverty, of sweat and frustration. You could feel it loping along in the night air. Behind the Do Drop at the crap game. In the yard of the Hall boys down the street from the bar. And sometimes you could even feel it at Edna's.

When the sun dipped into the Atlantic most folks in West Rehoboth grabbed a seat in their yards and gardens or huddled around the few television sets scattered about in houses. In the early sixties, having a television meant your house was a meeting place. Edna, of course, had one in the dining room, eight feet off the ground, perched on its platform, and another in her parlor.

At the end of the workday, folks would drag themselves wearily home, the darkening sky fluttering with sighs. But after the early hours of evening television were exhausted, most people would somehow find just enough energy to venture out and head straight for the Do Drop Inn or Edna's.

Edward loved nighttime in Rehoboth. He and his sister could stay up late, even be outside in Edna's yard until nine or ten o'clock at night. And then, when Edna insisted they come in the house, they were shuttled to their little rooms while Edna's filled with people who came to play music on the jukebox, dance, and eat barbecue.

It was foregone that his mother would go back to the Supper

Bell Inn as a waitress. She had worked there three previous summers, and so when the owner saw her walk in the door, he simply headed for the storeroom to get another uniform.

Edward and Sarah would always try to be around the house when his mother left to go to work around eleven-thirty. Sometimes she would come home between lunch and dinner, but most times they would not see her again until the next morning. And when they saw her she was usually dressed in her baby-blue waitress uniform—its white lace collar like flowers strung around her neck—the white handkerchief in her breast pocket, a boutonniere.

Every black person who resided in Rehoboth, was visiting, or just passing through could get a job in the summer months. Indeed, the Rehoboth seashore drew folks from all around: Baltimore, New York, Wilmington, New Jersey, Atlanta, Washington. Black people searching for money, for the feeling of gainfulness. The juke-joint sway that permeated West Rehoboth. The brush-scrubbed ruby faces of white people who wanted luxury, holiday, and would pay a colored person to watch their children, cook their food, wait tables, mow lawns, anything. There was so much work there. And it wasn't restricted only to adults. Many children began work at eleven. By fourteen, a kid could have developed a long-term relationship with a particular summer employer that would last until they died or decided not to return to Rehoboth for the vacation season.

Edward loved that part of being there. He could go crabbing and before he got home sell all of his crabs. Without even trying. White people on vacation will buy anything. Everything.

Rehoboth was sandy muddy life when it rained. Nothing was right. When it rained, the water was choppy and dangerous, the beach a pit for the filthy, and the boardwalk unappealing. It reflected the life and times of Eisenhower and before him Harry

S. Truman. It reflected the welfare state that functioned through paternalistic racism. Oh, but when it was sunny and the sky was a swirl of cotton candy and bubble gum and the heat drove everyone toward the water's edge where the breeze off the ocean was a mere kiss to the face, then you knew why so many people flocked to Rehoboth in the summer. It was heaven in a carefree time. If you were white. If you were white and had money you could lie back on your beach chair and inhale the sweet life. Rehoboth had a certain purity just like heaven. Everything sparkled with the glint of sunlight.

Edward was not quite aware of the complexities of color and how they played out in Rehoboth. He didn't fully understand why he could only bowl on Tuesdays or sit in the balcony at the theater. But Jim Crow created a place where no white feet trod. No one spoke of their absence. For the black folks, Jim Crow created privacy in a world where white privilege could invade any moment. And for the summer, Edward became a part of it.

Edna's specialty was barbecue, although she could turn out superior pig's feet, too. She embraced capitalism with a fervor. She had figured out a way to turn every square foot of her large country house into some kind of moneymaking venture. Her dance floor was of moderate size and could accommodate fifty black sweaty fast-dancing bodies. And when the music slowed, twice as many could fit in. And yet, bordering this restaurant and dance floor on one side were rooms that she used to rent to visiting relatives. Every year when they returned to Edna's there'd be another addition. She added a room in the back for the pool room. And this year she expanded upward, creating a third story of rooms for rent. But if you were young, the best rooms were on the first floor. Near the dining room. Near the dance floor. Near the heat of the kitchen and the funk.

Edward's room was among these. There outside the door to his room was a dance floor. People swayed on it and he could tell when a fast record played because the floor would shake.

Sometimes he would lie there in the darkness, listening to the large, hard-shelled black bugs smash themselves against the still-warm lightbulb. He would feel his skin crawl up the sides of his limbs in search of false security. Later these same bugs would descend upon his body to suck blood and raise bumps.

There were other sounds. Like the scampering mice. Chilling. Life in the pits. Running for crumbs. They crawled and he languished in dread. Who was scared?

Still more sounds. Crickets leaped in from windowsills, dispersed themselves about the building, and called throughout the night in distressing signals. "Come back, love, come back."

Rehoboth Beach, Delaware, had Edna and Edna in turn played Hank Ballard and James Brown and Fats Domino on the jukebox. These sounds of black funk blasted through the cheap wooden doors and hinted at entrance into the heart of rumored bliss.

On Edna's dance floor things happened. Why else did everyone place such a high value on getting clean and shaking a leg in Edna's?

Hell, he was young. Everything was blue lights to him. He was shut out. Kept in semidarkness. He was close to being there. It was in the next room. But after ten, he was commanded into his room. Banished. He was left to crazy black bugs that played kamikaze harmony as the night drew on. Later, within the barrel of his dreams, he would unconsciously acknowledge their existence as he felt the dancers frantically gyrating on the dance floor.

He was young, yes, but he was not so young that he did not dream warm fantasy about what went on in that room. During the day, he would watch the young girls drift through Edna's, buying sodas and Lance sandwich cookies, playing music on the juke-box and laughing. Their brown elbows would curl neatly on the red-and-white-checkered plastic-coated cloth that topped the table.

The girls would giggle a while, then move on. To another person's house, or outside to play, or even to the Jim Crow beach reserved expressly for those of the darker hue and cry. But their momentary presence made him aware that everything was not the same. There was a graduation from mud pies in store for Edward. The fruits of the respective diploma lay in the hot nights at Edna's.

He was certain some frenetic energy was unleashed in that room, the same place where he ate breakfast in the mornings. Edna's dance floor.

They were out there squirming and rubbing their bodies close up to each other as he lay there alone and disengaged from the earthy life that roared inches from his feet.

He was not so young that his body would not grow hard. He would feel his groin tense and grow larger. Stretching. Urging. Pajamas past. Fantasy glowed in rainbow colors of the spinning and flashing lights on the jukebox. Under the door, through an opening of less than an inch, though quite uneven, he could see the lights of the music box moving. Bouncing off sweat and the kaleidoscope of gospel.

Draped in the darkness of his own thoughts, he moved into his mattress, trying desperately to liberate his frustrations. They grew around him. Outside that door was life, stomping and laughing.

Occasionally during the night, Edna would break her barbe-cue routine to check on him. He would see her slowly open his bedroom door, strain her eyes to see him. Sometimes, in her raspy disintegrating voice, she would faintly call his name.

"No, Aunt Edna, I'm not asleep."

"Well, you should be. Do you know what time it is?"

Even if he had had a watch, it would have been impossible to read it in the dark. No, of course not, he had no idea of time.

Later, when his mother returned from waiting tables in the restaurant where she worked, her pockets crammed full with dollars and change given to her by the customers, she, too, would look in to see if he was breathing. To softly touch her lips to his forehead.

When that door opened and Edna or his mother peered through, behind them flashed a tremendous flood of light. And noise. He was blinded. Although open, the door revealed nothing of what was outside for him. It denied him. Unprepared for the rush of light, his pupils cooperated to blot out his fantasy.

It was right outside. He wanted desperately to reach out and grab maturity. He fumbled with bogeymen and mosquitoes in the darkness. Life was unrich.

Some days, particularly on the weekends, no matter what he did, all he could think about was the night and how it would feel. Every night at Edna's felt different. Sometimes it was filled with pure joy. Laughter. Sometimes it was saturated with anxiety and tension. Sometimes it was sterile and quiet. Others steamy and fast-paced. He couldn't begin to understand what moved the energy one way or the other. There was nothing apparent to him that happened during the light of day that would hint at the mood the night would bring.

And so, each night as he washed up for bed and prepared to dart from the bathroom to his room, he tried to inhale the atmosphere, hoping to decipher its true tone.

Tonight was Saturday night and there had been a crowd of people at Edna's, especially earlier. Edna had cooked barbecue all day and folks were there eating and dancing. He'd been in bed for about two hours when she opened the door to check on him. He was half asleep. Sleeping had always been difficult at Edna's. The black bugs, the noise, Chuck Berry. As she left, she held the knob of the door too long and it did not click shut. There was a crease of light beaming in from the opening. Edward was frightened.

He debated silently. To close or open. It could not stay as it was. As it was, it teased him, infuriated him. He could hear the music, but he couldn't see anyone dancing. And he desperately wanted to do that. He wanted to see.

Edward slid down to the bottom of the bed, reached over, and pulled the door farther open. The space was at least a foot now and he could see the entire dance floor. Unfortunately, people were already beginning to leave and the screen door had begun its nightly serenade of squeaks as it opened and claps as it closed. He was sweating. Was no one going to stay?

There were about ten people left. Some sipping at their beers, others engaged in mild chatter. The jukebox fell silent.

No. Someone must put a quarter in the music machine so he could see firsthand the "shakes" and the "jelly rolls." *Young voyeurs take notice.* He was hungry.

Someone finally fed the machine. He heard the machinery moving. The lights flashed frantically as it sought to find the right number. Would it be D7 or B1?

Finally the music began to trickle out. It was slow. He hadn't thought of it being slow. He had figured for sure that people only wanted to shake their things and whatever on fast records. What was the purpose in seeing two people hold fast to each other?

He watched a tall, very dark man, with coal black hair conked flat on the sides with just the slightest pomp over his forehead— and eyes glowing through the glare of the jukebox lights and the smoke—approach a table of three women. They must have all known each other, Edward thought. The man's teeth and his large smile brought more light. He had a toothpick in his mouth, and as he leaned forward to ask one of the women to dance, he took it from his mouth, slipped it into his shirt pocket.

He offered his other hand to one of the women at the table. She smiled, winked at one of her friends, and then slowly stood, gently laying her hand in his. She was at least six inches shorter than him, her straightened hair holding strong at her shoulders in a flip. Her round face had a soft orange glow. Edward was sure they knew each other. Maybe they worked at the same job and had been waiting for this moment all summer. Maybe the man had been eyeing her for weeks, finally getting up his nerve now. Right now. Just for Edward.

They moved to the dance floor, but no one joined them there.

The others seemed content to sit and watch. The song was a down-home soul stewer by James Brown. "There's Something on Your Mind."

I can tell by the way you look at me . . .

They locked together and became immediate sweat. The heat. The song. They smashed into each other. His hands roving her back, causing her to shudder. He wanted to turn away. But she responded by cuddling closer.

Their groins played to each other. The material of their clothes merged, sending glimpses of her soft upper thigh across the room as the man pressed so hard, her skirt rose. Then his hand touched her buttocks. She refused not. Simply melted.

There's something on your mind, pretty baby . . .

Her legs opened. And he fit neatly, swaying to the slow cadence. He sank inside her. Then emerged in rhythm. He was sweating. As her legs spread, he broke the rigid shape of his right knee, sinking lower still, and pushed up into her pelvis from a better angle. And every time she accepted. He moved lower. Until after three drops, they straightened up to start again. It was a miracle. To these who never knew ballet. They danced on each other's skin as if it were a main-stage premiere.

I can tell by the way you look at me . . .

She shuddered. They were oblivious to the others around them, and on noticing this, Edward realized that no one was much concerned with them. Only him. He was seeing the Grind for the first time. He watched a fantasy made real; a sweet embrace that was perhaps the spark and the ignition of the young fluttering flame of love.

And then suddenly Edward could not see. Only a whirling swirl of color. He heard a moan. It was him. His body was fevered and arced. His mind tripping over itself. Had Edna heard? Had anyone noticed him? No. No. He tried to calm himself, but fantasy had struck with smooth quick blows in the shrouded light of his room as the funk of J.B. and two new lovers showered him in special knowledge.

Later, just before he was seduced to sleep, his eyelids heavy, his body softer, Edward noticed another couple on the dance floor.

Instantly he was curious. There was something strange about the picture that formed in his eyes. Yes, there were two people, close together, swaying to the music. Every so often they shared something from a little silver bottle. That wasn't the problem. Just to the left of the couple sat a woman who was stiff with rage. He could tell. She just stared at them, her teeth bared, eyes squinted. The picture of anger.

Edward quickly surmised that the man must have come with

the woman who waited. There was a cigarette burning in the ash-tray before her. The smoke twined its way along her chin and into her face, covering it like a veil. But even through the smoke her dark skin fairly glowed.

The woman who danced had skin the color of sand. She was tall and full-figured. Her smile never wavered. She occasionally even looked at the other woman, the one who waited, with the same devilish smile. Edward could feel the tension flowing from that part of the room.

And then the record ended and Edward breathed. This was how life was. The slow rise of tension, the sudden relief. The anticipation. And what was anticipated was met by fate. Edward watched in near disbelief as the man made no move toward the table. Made no movement which suggested he even knew the woman who waited. It made Edward think that he had surmised too much. Maybe they hadn't come together. He watched as the man hugged his dance partner and whispered something in her ear. And then, again the temptation of life resumed as another song dropped into place and pushed a sweet sounding Fats Domino piece into the air.

Edward watched as the woman who waited broke her pose. She slowly, very deliberately extended her arm across the table and grabbed a half-filled bottle of beer and then, with a kind of mindless movement, brought the bottle to her mouth.

I found my thrill. On blueberry hill.

And now the couple held each other close again. The man, with his short-cropped, hustler haircut and his red silk shirt with black buttons, his chocolate face, his glinting gold crowns, pulled his partner tight. And still she smiled. Edward could feel the sweat rising on his face.

And then he looked on the woman who waited. And now he

saw something in her eyes. When the woman who danced smiled at her, Edward saw it flash in her eyes. She would not wait any longer. He watched her rise up from her chair. She still clutched the bottle in her right hand.

The man now had his arms draped diagonally around the woman's waist, softly touching her buttocks. Edward wanted to believe the woman was on her way out the door. That she would walk by them. But instead the woman who no longer waited grabbed the woman who danced and tore her out of the arms of the man. And then she brought the bottle with a great swing across the man's head. He only screamed once and it only started loud because he was unconscious before his scream could reach its full measure.

The woman who had been dancing shrank back like a deflated balloon. Edward watched her disappear out of his limited view as a crowd of people circled the man. The woman who waited no longer and who had broken a bottle upside the man's head had a handkerchief to her eye to catch the tears.

And then Edna was at the door. She looked at Edward and held his gaze for a long five-second count and then, with a heavy shrug, closed the door. Edward lay back and closed his eyes. It was suddenly incredibly quiet out there. Someone had unplugged the jukebox. People were leaving. Somebody probably dragged the man out of Edna's. The woman who danced went home. And so did the woman who would wait no more.

And into the night Edward fled to his dreams. What brought people together?

.   .   .

No matter what Edward went to bed dreaming, he always awoke thinking about Rufus. Where was he? Why didn't anyone talk about him? He made a point to ask Anthony—or Antny as he was called.

Antny was a year older than Edward. He was a skinny mischievous kid in a way totally alien to Edward. There was no city in Antny. He was all country. Barefooted. Ragged. Sand and dirt-caked. Always just a slight trace of dried snot around his nose. His head was like a coconut with peas pasted on it. But Edward liked him almost for these same reasons. Antny was completely oblivious to his own appearance. He never seemed the slightest bit concerned about anything. His summers were for fishing and crabbing and mowing lawns.

They were early to their special place on the pier. The waxing early-day sun beamed down. They sat on a rickety pier, directly across from the private piers on the other side of the canal, and let the water lick at their feet. They sat there, their hands softly holding the string which was tied around a piece of rotten raw chicken (which they used as bait) waiting for the crabs to tug on it, making fun of the rich white people opposing them across the narrow channel of water. Occasionally a slick boat or cabin cruiser would slice its way by them, waving at them as if Edward and Antny were actually neighbors.

Just as Edward was about to ask Antny about Rufus, Antny nonchalantly leaned back on his elbows, looking up at the sun. "Hey, Eddie, is it true that yo' aunt Edna locks the door on yo' uncle Rufus at night?"

"Where did you hear that?" It was precisely what Edward wanted to talk about. Even though he expected Antny to have more answers than questions.

"Heard old lady Mosley talkin' to Miss Beatrice. She said that Rufus was crazy, and if'n yo' aunt Edna didn't keep him locked up at night, there ain't no tellin' what he'd do."

Antny would squint his eyes as he talked. Even though it was in fun, Edward could tell that Antny believed what he was saying. He straightened up and asked him, "Ain't you scared stayin' there at night?"

"Why should I be scared?"

"I'd be scared if I was you. Don't you know about Mr. Rufus?"

"Well . . ." Edward considered how he should handle this. He really didn't know anything about Rufus. But Antny would probably tell him more if he didn't seem so ignorant. "I know a little about him."

"Like what?"

"I know he used to be married to my aunt Edna."

"Yeah, that ain't nothing. Everybody knows about that."

"Well, you're so smart, what do *you* know?"

"I know he's crazy. And that he kilt somebody. And that he can make hisself disappear."

Edward was struck stiff. "Disappear? Really? I don't believe you. How do you know?"

"I just do. Everybody 'round here knows that. Rufus is scary, boy."

Edward had no comeback. He was both angry and even more intrigued. He was angry at something that stirred deep inside him when Antny started talking about Rufus. Edward's suspicions and curiosity about Rufus were personal, not of the same superstitious stuff as Antny's. Indeed it agitated him that Antny would even be talking about his uncle like that to his face. Obviously Antny had never read Agatha Christie or Conan Doyle. Otherwise he would have known that the assumptions people jump to are nearly always wrong. They are fueled by their own guilt or their own insecurities. Their own fears. No. Rufus might be many things, but he could not be all the things people wanted to believe about him. Edward's interest in Rufus was growing.

"I wonder where he is now." Edward couldn't help himself. He decided to take a chance that Antny might reveal something meaningful.

"Yeah, I wonder. He ain't been around much this summer."

"When's the last time he was here?"

"Couple of weeks ago. I seen him sitting on the steps of his shack. Drunk."

"How do you know he was drunk?"

Antny looked at Edward like he was a five-year-old and said, "He couldn't hold his daggone head up. I know what a drunk man looks like. There's drunk people all around here. You see them every night staggering home from the Do Drop. Rufus was juiced, I swear for God."

"Well, I don't think you can automatically say that my uncle was drunk like that unless you know for sure." No matter how low on the pecking order he was in North Philly, he wasn't about to let some country boy take such liberties. That was the thing about being from the city when you were around country folk, he thought. All you had to do was give your voice a little edge and they'd usually back off. They always thought city kids were tougher. But Edward wasn't so sure. When he thought about it, Antny, and the rest of the kids around Rehobeth, lived much harder lives than he did. They fended off drunks and dodged fights all the time. Still, he wanted to let Antny know that he would not take too much of this disrespectful stuff, he was talking about someone whom he was supposed to be related to.

Antny was still staring. "Where you say you live?" he said finally, with an air of bewilderment.

"You know I live in Philly."

"They don't have no drunk people in Philly?"

Obviously Antny wasn't intimidated by his ghetto history. "Yeah, I know, but all I'm saying, Antny, is that you have to be precise in your observations. I want to know the truth about Rufus."

"You sure is funny. You talk funny. And you sound funny. I don't know about no observations, but I know what a drunk man looks like. Anyway, you weren't here. Me and Junior, that boy who live down the road in that white house . . ."

Edward nodded his head. He remembered Junior, another husky eleven-year-old with knotty hair. Troublemaker. Bully. He remembered he didn't like Junior too much. Particularly because last summer he wouldn't stop calling him "fat boy" even though Junior was just a little slimmer than him.

"Well, we was throwing cans at him. And he was like dancing. Hopping, you know. We hid behind those bushes over there." Antny pointed to a clump of purple sage. "And when he wasn't looking, we tried to hit his feet. You shoulda been here. It was the funniest thing you ever saw."

Edward was angry again. "Why would you do that? He wasn't doing anything to you."

Antny smiled. "You wait. You'll see. It's fun. We always do that to drunk people. It's really funny at night because they can't tell where those cans are coming from."

"Didn't he know it was you?"

"He was drunk, Edward. D-R-U-N-K. Do you know what that means? Anyway, later on he just got crazy. Screaming and hollering back there like he was killing somebody. He kept a racket going all night."

Edward was silent. "What do you expect him to act like with y'all treating him like that?"

Antny just looked at him. "You jus' mad cause he's yo' uncle and you don't want to admit that he's crazy."

"Well, anyway, I'm not scared of him."

"I am. Unless I catch him drunk. Then his magic don't work."

"Antny, what are you talking about? Magic?" How many ridiculous things could be said about one man? Edward wondered. Yet, the more he heard or guessed, the more excited he became.

"I'm telling you, that Rufus ain't right. You have to be careful around him." And then Antny lowered his voice and leaned into Edward's ear. "Know what some people say?"

"What?"

"Some people say . . ." Edward could feel Antny's lips almost touching his ear. "Some people say that Edna done *already* killed him some ten years ago and that Rufus is actually a ghost." He pulled his head back and looked directly into Edward's eyes. "Now, what do you think about that? Huh? People wouldn't be saying all that stuff if it wasn't true. That's what I say."

Edward was silent again. He let the subject drift into air. He was fully engaged. Trying to find out information about Rufus was difficult. And he felt like he couldn't even get started in his investigation until he actually got a chance to *see* Rufus. He prayed it would happen before the summer was over. Suddenly he felt a tug at the line he held in his hand. At the other end was a crab. He slowly led it closer and closer to the surface. And then, when it was visible, he reached for Antny's net and scooped it up. The first of the day. Six inches from point to point. Maryland blue. The sweetest crab swimming.

. . .

Just two days later Edward had his prayers answered. Rufus had evidently reappeared, because after breakfast, Edna had given him a basket of clean clothes and pointed to Rufus's shack through the back door. Edward gulped.

Goldenrod spit itself into the air, staining it with a brilliant yellow-soft essence. Like strands of golden thread, the pollen laced the heavy atmosphere. But the Atlantic Ocean was close enough to move the air and make its breeze feel like a soft leather glove—even in the late July sun. Edward was just outside Edna's back door. His round, fluid, cinnamon body stood completely still. He pondered his dilemma. He could bend down, pick up the basket of laundry, which smelled of sun-dried soap and hot-iron creases, turn around, and take it back to Edna. Or he could do what she had told him to do: take the clothes out to Rufus.

He had a feeling that Edna would not understand if he brought the laundry back undelivered. She might even punish him. Edward didn't trust the look in her eyes when she told him what to do. He was sure she'd not appreciate insubordination.

He stared at the fading whitewashed shack fifty feet from the back of the house. That was where Rufus lived. And it was Rufus's laundry he had at his feet. He had never met Rufus in the way two people normally meet each other.

But last summer, with the Mr. Peabody incident, Rufus intruded into Edward's consciousness in a way that he never had done before. Now he was someone who was driving Edward crazy.

And Edward also knew that his lack of information about Rufus was by design. Some discussed and agreed-upon pact between his mother and Edna and anyone else who had charge over him and Sarah during the summer. It was the only answer.

Then why now? Why was Edna so nonchalantly sending him into the teeth of the thing they feared most? Edward's body quaked. On one hand, his curiosity was beyond control; on the other, he was scared to stone. Rufus's reputation struck fear deep inside him.

When Rufus *was* in West Rehoboth, he lived in his shack, in Edna's backyard. She'd wash his clothes and make sure someone brought him food. The only thing that Edward knew for sure was that Edna didn't allow him in the house.

Hay fever danced in Edward's nose and triggered explosion. Twelve times he sneezed. And after the twelfth, he watched a curtain of blue-and-yellow worms squiggle in front of Rufus's shack. They slowly squirmed in the air, rising from the ground up and out into space. They always visited when he sneezed so violently. After the attack, Edward felt weak and wanted to go back to get a candy bar from the candy store on Edna's porch. Instead he waited for the worms to work their way to heaven. Eventually they disappeared. He felt stronger.

But he could not go forward. Perhaps this was why Poirot's approach rarely led him into confrontations and messy investigations. He thought about things. About the crime and its suspects. He used his little gray cells. But what was the crime?

There was, of course, the Mr. Peabody Affair that needed clarifying. There was that. But this was much bigger than turtle soup. He knew he was involved in the biggest case of his life, but he didn't know what it was.

And here he was afraid. Suddenly he didn't want to meet Rufus. He wanted to go the beach. Maybe he could get his mother to take him to the beach before she went to work.

He turned around and headed back into the kitchen. Edna had her back to him, which he ignored. "Aunt Edna, you know, ah . . . I don't know him very well. Actually I never even met him. Maybe you could do it." Edward stared at her back, his eyes pleading just in case she turned around.

Which she didn't. Nothing surprised her. Nothing disturbed the seeming serene forward flow of her life. So she continued with her work. Edward was not all that much in a hurry anyway, so he wasn't that uncomfortable with her deliberate pause.

She was dicing potatoes for the potato salad that would accompany her locally famous ribs. After a few moments of silence, she slowly turned around.

"Eddie, now can't you see I'm busy. You're wasting time. Just go on out there. You hear? I declare, you kids is so lazy nowadays." She was back to her potatoes. "I'm not asking you to slaughter a pig or clean no fish." She looked up again. "Will you just get goin'? Take them clothes on out there."

He stood there, losing weight through confusion. Why now? he wondered. They'd shielded him from Rufus all this time. Why was it different now? Yes, he wanted to meet the man, but . . . not today. Not this way. And then, as if she could read his mind, she said, "You're old enough to take care of yourself now. And I'm gettin' old. I can't be running all around the place when I got a boy 'round here like you who can do it for me." She paused and smiled. "Git goin' now. I don't want to have to sling you out of this house."

Defiance fit him worse than his snug shorts. His thick thighs slid out of the madras Bermuda shorts like brown butter when he moved. Edward grabbed the basket and headed for the back door. Again he stood just beyond the back door trying to make himself go forward.

He looked closely at the shack. It was nothing more than a plywood box with square holes cut into it that sat atop six sets of gray rectangular cinderblocks. It was elevated to keep the rodents and the water out. There was a thin coat of whitewash that was anxiously peeling. It was as if Edna had constructed the building so that it looked as frail as it actually was. She wanted it to look as if it would fall over in the first spring rainstorm.

Inside this building, Rufus had only a bed, a caneback chair, a dresser, a small pinewood stool, and a hot plate with a frayed black cord.

Edward forced himself to head in Rufus's direction and leave the safety of Edna's. It was hot. He felt the sweat on the underside of his butt. He held the basket in both hands, its bottom rest-ing roughly against his stomach. His thin white sleeveless undershirt was riding up, encouraged by the basket of clothes. In front of Rufus's shack there was a small patch of sand. He planted his feet in the sand and put the basket down. Uncomfortable barefoot, Edward nonetheless stood there without shoes or socks. Edna had dared him to put his city shoes away for the summer, especially when he was around the house.

The door was already wide open. And even though the sun was screaming, Rufus's shack was nearly black inside. Impenetrable. Edward stood staring into the darkness. He hesitated then reached in and knocked on the open door.

.   .   .

Rufus heard the soft clatter of the boy's small hand on the door. He didn't move. He had to constantly fend off the ceaseless teasing and taunting by the children. They threw cans at his house. Dared each other to sneak a look inside. They had no notion of privacy.

Rufus was deep into his rye whiskey. The pint bottle was almost gone. But he was feeling no pain. Besides, he had two other bottles stashed away. He heard the knock again. He tossed his voice into the open space. "Yeah? Who the hell is it?" It was sharp like a shucking knife. He always wanted to make the first sound of his voice cause hesitation, caution. He wanted it to sound like he had expected the interruption. That he could not be threatened. If you wanted trouble, he wanted you to know that he would be there from the beginning. His agitated voice pierced Edward's thin protection.

Edward's thighs quivered. Suppose Rufus was crazy and killed little boys? Suppose he *was* a ghost?

"Aunt Edna gimme something to give you, Uncle Rufus." Edward spoke to the sun, which smiled at him over the roof of Rufus's shack.

Rufus's head jerked up when he heard the words "Uncle Rufus." He puffed harder on the stogie that hung from his mouth like an appendage. Rufus stroked his fishing knife. He had traveled great distances but never been separated from his knife. It was his only proof of manhood and he valued it greatly. After a short pause, he shouted from deep within the shallow shack. "Who's that?"

Edward hadn't rehearsed. How was he going to identify himself? He didn't know whom Rufus would know that he knew. After all he was only twelve. The pressure quickened his pulse. Thoughts poured into his head like sand rolling in with the waves. How had he let himself be pulled into this situation? He didn't like being in Rehoboth and he didn't like meeting old men for the first time. The pressure inside him rose. He wondered about heart attacks in twelve-year-old boys.

Finally he said the only thing he could think of: "I'm Angela's boy."

Rufus didn't hear him. Didn't want to. "Tell 'em I don't want none. Hear me? Tell those bastards out there I ain't got no more money. Nothin' in here but me. And I know good and well you don't want me." Edward heard the moan of the caneback chair.

Money? Edna hadn't mentioned anything about money. Edward had no idea what Rufus was talking about. But the threat in his voice petrified him.

"Hey out there," Rufus screamed. "You still out there?"

"Yes, sir, I'm still standing here." His voice trembled. Edward drew in a bodyful of air. He felt unstable, as if he would fall over. Suddenly his thick legs didn't feel so solid, so substantial.

Rufus tried to focus his mind. But it was a wild thing, hopping around like a bead of butter fat on a hot skillet. "Well, git, goddammit. What the hell you still out there for?" Rufus's voice was like car tires on a bridge grating. It worked its way into Edward and made his bones tremble.

Edward looked down at the basket of laundry and thought again about going back to the house. His fear of Edna was diminishing as he negotiated with Rufus. What if some or all of those rumors were true?

Edward pumped himself, his chest rising. "Aunt Edna gimme these clothes to bring you." He heard Rufus moving around inside.

"Edna? Is Edna out there?" Rufus labored himself out of his chair. He slid his knife into its carved leather sheath, which was always attached to his belt. Rufus had carefully selected the soft tan cowhide. He had cured and stained it. He had painstakingly carved his initials in it. A fancy *R* and an even fancier *B*. Rufus Brown.

As Rufus got up from the chair he immediately began looking for another pint of rye, his favorite tonic. He checked his dresser, a slightly burned oak piece he had dragged out of the smoldering piles of discarded objects and trash at the county dump.

"No, sir. Just me." Edward looked around just to make sure. If only someone else had come with him.

"Well who the hell are you?" There was a break in the anger. There was something in the boy's voice which acted like a crowbar in Rufus's mind. It pried open a thin sliver of light.

Edward felt it and pressed forward into new territory. "Aunt Edna sent me out here with this basket of clothes to give you and she said you had a bag to give me." He reasoned that if he could be specific maybe Rufus would understand why he was there. After all, he was actually doing the man a favor.

"Edna give you my clothes?" Rufus asked in a distant, vulnerable voice. Then, in a sudden burst, he blurted, "Damn, that woman even give my clothes away. She locks me out here where ain't nobody at. Won't even let me in the house to play pool in the pool room no more. What in Christ's name she gonna leave for me to do?" Rufus jerked his body around as he talked and looked for the liquor.

Edward was coated in bronze. He stood quiet and motionless, thinking about what Rufus had said. Slowly his fear of Rufus was turning more to panic. He struggled to get a handle on the conversation.

"But, Uncle Rufus"—Edward talked to the dark space in the center of Rufus's shack—"Aunt Edna didn't gimme these clothes to keep. She told me to bring them out here for you, because she said you was probably running out of clean clothes."

Satisfied with his explanation, Edward waited for Rufus to respond. He heard the noises of broken glass as Rufus, wearing heavy work shoes, moved to the doorway.

The sunlight frightened Rufus's eyes. They tried to turn around and hide in the darkness. They screamed and threatened him. But now that he had gotten up and found his bottle and was standing in the door, he would not comply. He trained his hurting eyes on the boy in front of him. "That them?" he asked.

Rufus was a tall, square-shouldered, rough-skinned man. So dark he was like an overripe California plum. He wore a short-sleeved T-shirt that had originally been white. Now it was dark gray in places, brown in others. His pants were a massive pair of unhemmed light blue pin-striped railroad overalls. On his head was an engineer's cap of the same material. A burning cigar was clenched between his brown teeth.

Edward could only nod his head and hand him the basket. Rufus swung it up with one hand and tossed it into the shack.

Then he reached into the darkness and pulled out a brown paper shopping bag with twine handles. He held it out to Edward. The boy tried his best not to look in Rufus's eyes. He couldn't explain what he felt. But he could definitely feel something rising between them.

He fixed his eyes on the bag of dirty clothes. After a second of hesitation, Rufus pulled it out of the air and held it close to his chest. As if it were a little body pressed against his own. With this movement Edward was forced to look up into the man's eyes.

Suddenly it was hard to see light. Even in the middle of the day, with the sun screaming at them, all Edward saw was shadow. And two little dark red lights: Rufus's eyes. And in those eyes, he saw nothing. It was clear that Rufus wasn't even looking at him.

Deep inside, Edward could hear his own voice. It was cursing. Just one swearword after another. "Shit. Damn. Fuck. Shit. Damn. Fuck." Words he'd never say in front of any grown-up. Words he'd only speak in his room when no one was home or hanging out with Sonny. Words his father would backhand him for before they even settled on the ear. "Shit. Damn. Fuck."

He knew something strange was happening. Or was about to happen. And then . . . then it happened. It was coming toward him like a brown boulder flying through the air. He could see the creases in the paper as it neared him. The grimy paisley-print boxer shorts ejecting a foot before impact and taking flight on their own separate course.

And then it plastered him right in the chest with a small explosion as more clothes flew out like shrapnel. But there was enough force in the moment of impact to send an unsuspecting Edward backward. In his bare feet, his heels caught a clump of grass in the sand and sent him down hard on his butt, still holding the bag of clothes that by now had released a stench unlike anything he'd ever smelled.

He dropped the bag and scrambled to his feet. He was angry. He wanted to say, "What the hell is wrong with you? You think I wanted to do this?"

Instead he just stood there trying not to sneeze. Not to cry. Right now, he didn't even want to breathe.

"What you starin' at?" Rufus spat the words at him. Then, in a twinkle, there was a slight grin. "You said you wanted my clothes, didn't you?"

"Yes, but I'm just doin' what Aunt Edna told me to. I didn't do nothing to you."

"And I gave 'em to you, didn't I? Heavy as you is, I didn't 'spect I'd knock you over doin' it." He paused. "I didn't hurt you, did I?"

Edward's anger began to subside. His mind was a jumble. "No," he said too quickly. And then, "I guess not."

Rufus looked away from Edward, drew in smoke from the cigar, and blew it out over his shoulder, back into his shack. Then he stared directly at Edward, fixing his glare so that the force from his eyes began to move the boy. After a moment Rufus threw the cigar away.

"I bet you think I'm some sort of goddamned ghost or something. They must of told you all about me by now."

"No, sir. I don't know anything." Edward tried to remember he was standing on sand. That his legs still worked.

Rufus squinted, wiped his forehead with his open palm. "You got to put my black ass on your shoulders to know what I know, boy. And that ain't no little thing."

Edward could think of nothing to say. He was sweating like a Thoroughbred. After a moment of completely awkward silence, he turned to go.

"What you say yo' name is?"

"Edward, or, ah . . . some people call me Eddie," he said, turning back to Rufus.

"Angela's boy, huh?" Rufus paused, rubbing the coarse mixture of salt-and-pepper-colored hair which lightly covered the creases of his face.

"Yes, sir." Edward watched Rufus's face grimace when he heard the "sir."

"Come here, boy." Rufus seemed like he was going to walk back into his shack. Edward was uncertain whether he had been invited in or not. If he had been, he wasn't sure he could accommodate. Once he'd gotten back on his feet, he'd screwed them into the sand. Now they, his feet, seemed to rule his body. And they seemed to be saying they would only release their grip of the ground if he was bound in the opposite direction, namely back to the safety of Edna's house.

But instead Rufus twisted off the cap of the bottle of whiskey and plopped down on the top step of a group of three rough-cut stairs.

Rufus's mind was slowing down. He hated interruptions. He had planned to sit in the dark all day thinking. So, when Edward had disrupted his peace, he had lost control of himself. But now he was catching up. "You like it here?" Rufus looked at him and brought the bottle up to his mouth at the same time.

"I just got here a few days ago."

"That's not what I asked you, is it?"

"No, sir."

"Well, then goddammit, boy, when I ask you something don't give me no roundabout."

"Yes, sir."

"Are you gonna sit and talk to me or are you gonna dig yourself a water well?" Rufus said as he pulled the bottle from his mouth and planted it between his legs. Edward's round body was still twisted. His feet going away from Rufus, his head and shoulders trying to lie.

Edward let his body realign itself. If this was how he would die, he would go bravely. He faced his uncle.

"Sit down, boy, you make me nervous. Sit right on down there." Rufus pointed to the bottom step. "I guess I could get you a chair, but you don't need one. You just a boy." The bottle was in his mouth again. Edward sat quietly, watching, listening.

"I don't like people who ask a lot of questions, know what I mean?" Rufus didn't wait for Edward's answer, which would have expressed agreement. "People think they got a right to just jump in your life and take things from you. What you know is something, too. You can't just take stuff and not pay for it or even say thank you."

Rufus took a long swig from his bottle and looked up, trying to find a spot that had not been overwhelmed by the sun. He couldn't help it. He hated the notion of conversation. Every time he tried to talk to someone, he could never tell what was going on. If he talked to himself, everything was fine, but when he tried to talk to others, regardless of who they were, he had to struggle.

Edward had only been sitting down for a few moments and already he was fighting the urge to rise. He didn't like sitting below Rufus like that. The man was already too big. From where Edward was, Rufus now looked more like a talking black marble sculpture. He found himself standing.

Rufus watched as Edward stood. He started to say something about that, but another subject pushed that one away in a blink. Rufus looked into Edward's eyes just as the boy was coming up to man's level.

"Do you know what love is?" Rufus said, holding his stare.

"Yeah. I mean, I think so."

"You don't know nothing 'bout love, Eddie. Not a god-damned thing." Rufus sat still, moved only his mouth. "I'm gonna tell you something about love. Yup, that's what we gonna do today."

Edward's heart suddenly leaped to the outside of his body. He quickly caught it and tried to hold it down. He had thought about Edna standing in the kitchen, now probably slicing cabbage for coleslaw, or whipping sweet potatoes for pie, wondering why it was taking him so long. She had told him to exchange the laundry and get back to the house. She wanted him to help her in the kitchen. He wanted to leave, but Rufus hadn't exactly asked him a question. It was foregone.

Rufus surveyed the yard his shack shared with Edna's. On one side was a clamshell driveway for the cars, and between his front door and Edna's back door was a sizable vegetable garden and a small pigpen, although there were currently no pigs. Edna had had them all slaughtered.

He wanted Edward to know about love. He wanted Edward to stay. But, now, he was having trouble getting a handle on what he wanted to say. "Well, ah . . . you know, ah . . . love is this spirited overpowering thing that comes crashing out of nowhere, hell-bent on tearing everything up and leaving you empty-handed and all scratched up . . ."

Edward stared out toward the Atlantic Ocean, which was beyond the woods and railroad tracks that separated West Rehoboth from Rehoboth Beach. As he listened something washed over him. Suddenly his fear fell away like dirt. This was what he wanted. He wanted to sit down and listen to Rufus talk. If Rufus wanted to talk about love, then fine. He'd listen to that. He wanted to know his story. He wanted to know him.

So he found himself retaking his seat on the lower step. He liked the sound of Rufus's voice. He liked the way Rufus just talked to him. No formalities, no protocol.

It was hot and Rufus smelled like under the house, but suddenly sitting there made Edward feel good. After a while Rufus looked down at him. Their eyes met again. Edward nearly fell in.

All thought of leaving left Edward. He had been seduced. Something held him there, passionately silent.

"Love is like a burst of air that comes on you all a sudden and changes everything." He whisked his arms in the air in jerky motion. "Sometimes it's good, but most times it just kicks you square in the old behind. Then it's gone, flying off into somebody else's life."

Edward didn't know what to say. He understood what Rufus was talking about, but how could he say anything back? What could he say? Love flew away. Flew away.

"Well, sir, where does it go?" Almost immediately Edward regretted having said it.

Rufus interrupted his train of thought. "Boy where is you from? How old are you?" Rufus placed his red eyes on him.

"Twelve."

Rufus wrapped his thick lips around the opening of the bottle. He squinted as the liquor reached into his brain and plucked a string. "Sheee. You sound like you five asking me a question like that. Where does it go? How the hell I know where it goes? But you better believe me, boy, it definitely goes."

Then, as his eyes cleared, he wiped his mouth with the back of his hand, he repeated, "I'll be damned if I know where the hell it goes. It just does. Love is one son of a bitch."

Edward smiled when he heard 'son of a bitch.' He always wanted to laugh when people cursed in front of him. And Rufus was so good at it.

Rufus caught the reflection of amusement in Edward's eyes and turned away. He grappled with the different strains of conversation running in his head. He rarely talked to anyone. For Rufus this was a long conversation. And suddenly he was tired of trying to make sense. Tired of trying to find entertainment in a stupid twelve-year-old boy. "Get the hell out of here."

"Sir?"

"I said get the hell off of my steps. She sent you out here to spy on me, didn't she? I know what's goin' on. I'm not stupid, you know."

"I'm not spying on you."

Rufus put a blade in his voice. "I said git. Now git."

Edward was up like a splinter had shot up from the step. He grabbed the bag of clothes and stumbled away. As he wobbled back through the path to Edna's back door, he kept twisting around to see if Rufus was still there staring at him. He was. But just as he reached the door and looked back, he saw Rufus standing, weaving, trying to get back into his shack. "Oh, hey, boy." It was Rufus screaming at him. "Don't be a goddamned stranger. You hear?"

Edward didn't move.

Rufus turned to face him and screamed again, "Don't make me say it again, goddammit. Did you hear me?"

"Yes, sir," Edward said weakly. Now *he* felt drunk, dizzy, disoriented. What had just happened? He dropped the bag near the washing machine and ran to his room.

. . .

The next day Rufus was gone. His front door padlocked. Edward had casually walked back to his shack after breakfast. When he saw the rusted Master lock hanging from the door, he turned on his heels and ran back into the kitchen.

Edna was still sitting at the breakfast table with a toothpick hanging from her mouth. This struck Edward as weird since she openly kept her teeth on the sink in a glass at night. But this was a minor discrepancy. He was interested in only one thing.

"Aunt Edna." He was slightly out of breath. She looked up at him and then went back to staring out of the window which looked onto her driveway. "Where's Uncle Rufus?"

Edward waited patiently for her to respond. He was becoming accustomed to Edna and her ways. He could not rush her. He realized that. But after at least thirty seconds, he realized she wasn't going to say anything at all.

Why did she treat him like that? Why couldn't she just say, "I'm not going to answer your question?" Or go ahead and answer it or something. Why did she have to completely ignore him as if he wasn't even standing there? But he was tired of waiting. "He was here yesterday. Is he gone?"

"Was his door locked?" She sucked her teeth.

"Yes."

"Then he's gone."

"Where? When will he be back?"

"Eddie." There was surprising tenderness in her voice. "Now listen to me, son. You don't need to be worrying about Rufus. You hear me. He comes and he goes. I don't try to keep up with him and neither should you."

Edward sighed. Just as he was beginning to think that she would finally open up and talk to him like a person, she was pulling back. "But why not?" he said, hoping to lure her into deeper conversation.

"Because I told you not to, that's why. I don't want to have to talk to your mother about this. You just do like I tell you. Rufus is nobody to be messing with. He's a drunk. Sometimes he gets out of control, and I don't want to have to worry about you. We've managed to deal with this up to now, and I don't want to have to think about you out there messing around Rufus." She paused for effect. "Now, do you understand me?" She grabbed his shirt and pulled him closer. "Do you understand me? I don't want you back there. Do you hear?"

"Yes, I hear you." Edward stifled the bubbling desire to ask more questions. To press her for specifics.

Edna shook her head. "I should never have sent you out there." She paused and began gathering up things to put in her pocketbook. "Okay now, do you and Sarah want to ride with me to Milford? I got to get some eggs."

"Well, I was hoping Mom could take us to the beach. She doesn't have to go to work until two o'clock today. She said we might go."

"You ain't been to the beach this year, have you?"

"No."

"Well, have fun, and if you go be sure to bring me some caramel corn from Dolle's."

And that morning, Edward and Sarah went to the beach. At ten-thirty it was already over seventy-five degrees, and even though there were a few clouds in the sky, it promised to swelter. Edward sat in the back with his sister as his mother and Dottie, a friend of hers, sat in the front. It was Dottie's car. The ride from Edna's to the beach was one of Edward's most favorite journeys.

First there was the slow, gravelly ride past the Do Drop. Now, on a workday morning, the Do Drop was like a whitewashed barn, with a clamshell-and-shale-rock lawn all around it. In the daylight, the huge building, if you put a cross on the roof, might have been a church. But Edward knew better. There were running horror stories about the Do Drop. People being shot. People being stabbed. People gambling. Fights. Everyone knew the Do Drop was dangerous. It didn't matter how it looked with a smiling sun beaming down on it.

And then they turned onto Hebron Road, which would take them to that proverbial fork. They passed the Hall house, where the family of six brothers, ages fourteen to thirty lived. In the small scraggly yard that surrounded a wounded, scarred, and battered house were a gaggle of chickens, and on the side a lone droopy brown cow. Edward stared at the animal.

He heard his mother talking to Dottie. "What's the news about the Halls?"

"Nothing much. Just the usual. They've been pretty quiet this summer so far. Two 'em are in jail, though." Dottie was a tall, slender woman of about the same age as Angela.

"It's terrible what happened to them." Edward's interest was piqued. His mother was talking now without restraint. "I knew their father, you know. He was a rough customer."

"You don't have to tell me." Dottie was now turning into Rehoboth Beach proper. "I remember that crazy fool."

"Ol' T Hall. Rufus sure took care of him." Edward heard the laughter in his mother's voice and watched as Dottie burst into a rolling chuckle. But the laughter stopped when Angela added, "And then Shirley started drinking and—"

"Yes, chile," Dottie cut in. "You don't know how that woman could drink. And when she got drunk she was meaner than a horde of wasps. I *knew* she wasn't going to make it. Didn't take long either. Less than a year after T Hall died, somebody shot her."

"Lord have mercy." Angela breathed heavily. "And just like that six young men were loose on the world. Angry, ignorant, and parentless."

Edward was immediately torn. They were passing his favorite landmarks. Places he liked to acknowledge simply because they were still there. He had been coming to Rehoboth for five years and it amazed him that so many things stayed the same. The sub shop they were passing now and the open-air food market that was just ahead. The hardware store, the bridge over the canal that they crabbed in. The railroad tracks which cut across the street and trailed off into the woods. The beach shops, the boutiques, the Thunderbird shop where you could buy souvenirs of the seashore variety and various Native American artifacts, the five-and-ten, the police station, and finally, at the foot of this street which roped its way from the highway, was the boardwalk and the Atlantic Ocean.

He wanted to stick his head out of the window and take it all in, but he couldn't. And it wasn't Sarah in her usual role as major distraction. His sister was actually quiet, lost, really in some daydream. Or maybe she was thinking the same thing he was. The scenes that were passing outside the car were familiar and yet exotic. They were at "the beach." This was what they did every summer. But he couldn't concentrate on all this. He wanted to hear more about Rufus.

"Mom?"

She turned back to face him, interrupting her conversation with Dottie, which had shifted to whether they brought enough towels. Edward stared at her, trying to discern whether he could ask his question directly. He couldn't read her face and was immediately confused. "Yes?" Edward realized he only had another second to speak before she would shift her attention back to Dottie.

"What did he do?" It hadn't come out right. It was what he wanted to know, but he knew as soon as he said it, his mother would never answer such a loaded question.

"Who, Eddie?"

"Uncle Rufus. You know, what you were saying back there."

"I didn't say nothing about Rufus."

"Yes, you did. You said he whittled somebody down."

"Oh, you mean that Hall mess." He watched his mother turn back to face the road. They were pulling into the parking area. She pointed to an empty slot and said to Dottie, "We can park there."

Edward looked at his sister, who was now tapping him with her foot. "Cut that out." She had joined them back in reality. His relationship with his sister was quite awkward. He didn't know how to deal with her. She was too young for . . . for just about everything. He couldn't tell her secrets. She couldn't help him with his homework. And yet she was always bothering him. Distracting him. Always wanting him to take her somewhere or get something for her. But she could do nothing for him. Just give him a big pain.

"Make me," she said.

"I'll make you all right." He lowered his voice. "You wait till we get back home. I'll scare you so good tonight you won't sleep for a week." It was his primary way of dealing with Sarah. Sometimes, back in Philly, when she was aggravating him, he'd sneak into her room and hide in the closet. There he'd make little noises until she was buried deep under her covers. And then, before he got sleepy himself, he'd burst out of the closet, a sheet or coat over him, run to her bed, and scare what little sense of safety she had left right out of her.

But he had been distracted. "Mom." He groaned. "Aren't you going to tell me?"

"Tell you what, Edward?"

He knew she was messing with him. What was it about the women in this family? They lorded over everything. If it was important to know, they knew it. And they decided who else would know and then only as much as they thought appropriate. But he was a detective. An investigator. How dare they withhold information from him? This was why no one ever wrote about a detective *and* his mother. She'd never let him do what he had to do.

"Tell me about Uncle Rufus."

"I don't think it's something you need to know."

"But I do, Mom. I'm conducting an investigation. I need information."

"What type of investigation, Eddie?" It wasn't the first time she'd heard that from her son.

"There's some kind of mystery here. Nobody wants to tell me anything about him."

"If it is, it's only a mystery to you. And have you ever thought about the fact that maybe you don't need to know? You're a child. You can't know everything the adults know."

"But I just want to know more about Uncle Rufus."

The car came to a stop and Dottie slowly got out. She opened the door for Sarah and they moved to the back to get the umbrella and ice chest. But Edward was still inside, leaning on the front seats pleading with his mother.

"And just what is it you want to know?"

"Is he Aunt Edna's husband? Why don't they live in the same house? Is he crazy? Did he really kill somebody?"

His mother sighed and looked out the window. "Listen, sweetheart. People have their lives. They live them. Some people mess up their lives. Some people drink too much or gamble too much or get into too much trouble. You can't always figure out what happened. Or why. Sometimes it *is* a mystery. Now, I know you're curious about Rufus. But I'm not going to answer those questions. It's none of your business. And I want you to let it go. You need to start reading some books other than those silly mysteries you always got in your hand. Have you read that Langston Hughes book I gave you?"

"No." Although he was definitely looking forward to it. But he still had two Poirot mysteries to read before he returned to the jazzy world that Langston wrote about.

"Well, read that for a change."

"But, Mom . . ."

"That's it, Edward. You understand me. No more questions about Rufus. It's nothing you need to worry about."

And so that was that. Edward nodded and got out of the car. He had hit a nerve. There was definitely something to worry about. Maybe there was no crime, no threat, but there was enough uneasiness about any talk of Rufus to stimulate his gray cells to no end. He had to focus his investigation. He wanted another crack at Rufus. *Précisément.* He needed to talk to Rufus again.

· · ·

The beach was amazing. Brilliant sun. A happy ocean, flexing its softness five feet into the air, lowering itself into sensuous valleys, flowing white and blue and green with swirls and sweetness. Edward and Sarah dodged waves and made a very shaky and very impatient sandcastle. It was gone before they could finish, crumbled back into its natural state.

The five miles of beach rimmed with an active huckster-filled boardwalk presented its black visitors with a curious situation. They could enjoy it. Yes, Lord, the Atlantic was for them, too. God had created the ocean and sand enough to cover its shores, but God only gave up a hundred yards or so for the darker folks of Rehoboth. They were remanded to the Crow's Nest. Partitioned on each side by an ugly weather-beaten jetty. Separated from the throngs of pale skins who slowly turned on the beautiful sand. No Coppertone in the Crow's Nest. No designer swimsuits.

But Edward barely realized he waded in segregated waters. Sarah was completely oblivious. Angela and Dottie had both come from the South, where Jim Crow was born, and were capable of living above it. In the Crow's Nest they were on the shores of Marseilles, perhaps. Colorful umbrella, fancy beach chairs, pretty towels, incredible food. Their pinkie fingers floated upward as they sipped Kool-Aid.

After a while Edward was sitting by himself, watching Sarah, who had found a playmate among the sparse crowd of black folks. Now that he was at the beach, he wanted only two things: to go to Dolle's for caramel popcorn and saltwater taffy and to get back to Edna's and see if he could talk to Rufus again.

When they got back to Edna's, Edward quickly checked to see if the door to Rufus's shack was still padlocked. It was. He then ran through the yard and into the kitchen, where he found Edna standing over five naked chickens without heads, which lay like babies waiting to be changed on the drainboard of her sink.

"Aunt Edna, where did Rufus go?"

"I declare, Eddie, you gonna just about drive me crazy with this Rufus stuff. He's gone. That's all I know. He got new, clean clothes on and he's gone."

Edward wanted more but stopped himself.

For two days Edward waited for Rufus. At night he played in Edna's yard with his sister and Antny and the other children. Every one of them, including Edward and Sarah, was a ragamuffin, dirty and giddy from an overabundance of summer pleasure. Their skin, an array of colors, all essentially brown, was coated with the thinnest veneer of sand. Brown on brown.

But at night, with the mosquitoes nibbling and the moths caught in a mindless dance with heat and light, these children played. Mother may I? Red light, green light. Hide-and-seek. Five-ten ringo.

While the adults fussed and primped before walking up to the Do Drop Inn or settled in a dark room with the flickering television staining the still July nights with images of Ed Sullivan or Lawrence Welk, the voices of the children rang through the pines, mixed with the dark smoke that still wafted from Edna's brick barbecue pit and permeated the atmosphere.

But Edward was a passive participant. Yes he was there with them but Rufus had nearly all of his attention. He didn't understand why he was so intent on finding out more about his wayward uncle. It might have started with the demise of Mr. Peabody, but now it was something more, something about his brief contact with Rufus which was drawing him in. There was a story there. So while the younger children made mud pies and chased lightning bugs, and Edward's peers huddled together, boys in one group, girls in the other, he was only marginally interested in what they were doing.

Antny was busy trying to describe his idea about sex to Edward, Junior (who was usually called "Dunor" because that's what his little sister sounded like she was saying when she called his name), and a rust-colored boy with hair almost the same color named Jasper. Antny was talking almost in a whisper. "I sure would like to do it with her," he said, pointing to Theresa. Theresa was fourteen, her chest doing battle with her prepubescent attire. Edward blushed. Junior nearly drooled.

"And I know how to do it, too."

"How you know?" Jasper had a feather-soft voice.

"Don't worry about how I know. I just do. And you want to know the secret?"

Edward looked up. "What secret?"

Antny broke into a wide grin. "You got to know how to do the nasty the right way or else she'll get a baby."

Edward smiled, too. He suspected that Antny didn't know any more than they did but could tell that Jasper and Junior were totally enthralled by the lesson they were about to be given. "So how do you do it?"

"Well, the main thing is . . . when it feels good, you have to say 'soooot ahhh, sooot ahh.' " Edward couldn't believe his ears. Antny sounded like Edward's mother when she slurped her morning coffee from a teaspoon. The coffee whistling through her pursed lips, the pause, the obligatory "ah" as its warmth and sweetness reached her palate. Then he watched Antny, in a moment of complete animated frenzy, run to an inoperative well that sat in a corner of Edna's yard, wrap his arms around one of the posts, and begin grinding his pelvis against the wood. All the time saying, "Sooooot ahhh. Soooot ahh."

"This is how you do it. You got to keep saying it or she'll get pregnant."

"Who told you that, Antny?" Edward couldn't take it anymore. In North Philly it wasn't uncommon for boys his age to already be having sex. He was still a virgin, but he knew enough to know that what a person was moaning while it was happening had nothing to do with whether a girl got pregnant or not.

"My cousin told me. And he knows. He's done it." Antny was stone serious.

Edward just shook his head and let the conversation continue. But the words passed over his head like salt spray skimming over the rolling ocean. From where he was standing, he could see the outline of Rufus's shack. The moon was thin, so there was just the slightest glow around the whitewashed building. Suddenly Edward heard the crickets and the toads all around him. Behind Rufus's shack fireflies lit up the woods. Music from the Do Drop was also a part of the air, as was the sweet smell of honeysuckle and rose.

And then, at about nine-thirty, there was Rufus, standing on the cinderblock steps, a sack on his back, fumbling with the padlock on the door. Edward watched as the door eventually swung open. He watched as Rufus turned his one light on. A solitary bulb hanging from a nail in the ceiling, now swinging from Rufus's rough touch.

Edward started toward the light. He heard Antny's voice flickering over his shoulder. "Eddie . . ." Antny had the strongest Southern sound in Delaware. "Where ya think you goin'?"

"I'll be right back."

"You better watch yo'self with Mr. Rufus. 'Specially at night, dark like it is. We gonna have to go home pretty soon." Edward was moving out of hearing range. "You comin' back?"

"Yeah, I'll be back in a few minutes." Edward wasn't sure Antny heard him, but he didn't stop moving, deliberate but without a clear sense of why, toward Rufus's shack. Before he realized it, he was standing in a deep darkness, just on the periphery of the light that flowed from the doorway.

He just stood there. After a minute or two he realized he was standing in exactly the same place as he'd stood during his last visit. And he felt just as incapable of going forward or retreating. After about three or four minutes, Rufus appeared in the doorway with a bottle in his hands. Edward had heard nothing from within the shack before Rufus materialized. And even now, with him standing six feet away, it seemed as though Rufus was looking right over him.

He coughed.

"What's the matter, boy?"

"Sir?"

"Goddammit, you little snotty-nosed land crab, I know ain't
nothing wrong with my goddamned voice. You heard what I said."

"I'm fine, Uncle Rufus."

"You don't look fine."

Edward decided to take the advantage. "You been away?"

"Away?" Rufus sat down, took a swig. Edward watched him
turn inward. To some memory, some journey. "You know what?"

"What?"

"I'm gonna take your behind to school tonight. I can look
inside you, boy. You know that? I can see right into your goddamned brain. I know what you're thinking. You want to know,
don't you? You want to ask me all kinds of crazy-ass questions.
Satisfy yourself. Right? Goddammit . . ."

Edward didn't know what to say. Rufus was obviously working
himself into some kind of frenzy. Why was it that when Rufus was
away all Edward thought about was talking to him, and when he
was there all he wanted to do was get away.

Rufus began patting his pants pocket. "When I met that aunt
of yours . . ."

"You mean Aunt Edna?" Edward finally had a shred of understanding about what was happening.

Rufus stopped frozen. He stared at Edward. He invaded
Edward's line of defense and marched at will throughout the
boy's body. "Now, what other goddamned aunt you think I'm talking about? Huh?"

"I'm sorry. I've just got a lot of aunts, that's all."

"Far as I'm concerned Edward, you only got one."

"Yes, sir."

Rufus backtracked in his mind, trying to recover his original
intent. After a few seconds it was again within grasp. "Like I was
about to say. When I looked into those pretty brown eyes, I said to
myself, 'This here girl is the girl I gots to marry. Listen to me, son,

hear what I'm tellin' you. That lady was as fine as any lady you ever did see."

As he talked, Edward tried to create a picture of Edna in his mind. The Edna image that formed was that of an old and cranky woman. He couldn't imagine that Edna had once been attractive. In *his* picture Edna had tiny dark spots on her face and cream-colored splotches on her arm. Her skin was dull and fit her loosely. No. Edna had never been attractive. He was sure of it.

"Was she really that pretty, Uncle Rufus?" he asked, in spite of a feeling inside him which urged him to silence.

Rufus was flying now. He was safe within the crease of his knowledge and the subject of this discussion. He stood up. "Pretty? Boy, you don't know what pretty is till you see a picture of Edna back in the old days." He reached into his pants pocket.

While he fumbled and shifted his weight around to extract his wallet, Edward continued his mind drawing. He tried to capture a young Edna. But it was difficult to achieve. Edna wore brown opaque stockings that hid everything and caused her whole body to glow tan.

"Yes, sirree. That girl was fine." Rufus whistled, still struggling with his wallet, which was stuck diagonally in his pants. He was suddenly full of bounding excitement.

Finally his wallet popped out of his pants. He pulled from it a stack of cards, pictures, and trash that had accumulated throughout the years. He began to peel them off, one by one, looking at each as if for the first time. He wanted to stop at each paper and explain it to Edward. He would have pointed out his expired Merchant Marine ID. His expired driver's license. The title to his truck.

Within his shanty, there were no plaques, no degrees, or cita-
tions that were framed and capable of identifying a time or a feat
he had accomplished. Whatever he had done, he carried the
proof of it in his wallet.

Finally Rufus found what he was looking for: Edna's picture.
He sighed. He sat back down and put the bottle back to his mouth.
Edward watched him hold it to his lips for mountains of time.

"My Lord, that woman still takes my breath away. To this
day, if somebody asks me why I ain't worth a plugged nickel,
Edward, I say it's because I was caught up in the beauty of that
woman."

Edward had wondered about that. How did a man get so
turned around? What kind of man lived in a shack in the yard
behind the house of the woman he had once married? Why did he
put the blame on Edna?

"Can't blame her," Edward heard himself saying. He couldn't
believe he had said it. He hoped Rufus hadn't heard. Unfortunately, he could tell by Rufus's cold eyes that he had.

Edward had surprised Rufus again. He hadn't expected the
boy to be so bold. He could feel Edward's fear, and yet the boy
kept saying things that might have provoked him. But the way
Edward said it worked its way around Rufus's defenses. He suddenly felt weak, vulnerable. "Guess not, boy. Guess you right
about that." His voice was distant.

"Is that her picture?" Edward wanted to change the subject.

"What? What picture?" Rufus wanted to go back in his house.
Back into the haze of his self-contained world. Where he knew
the details about everything and didn't have to explain them to
anyone else.

"That one—Edna's," Edward said, pointing. "Ain't that her
picture?"

"Oh yeah, yeah, that's her." He handed it to the boy.

It was Edward's turn to be surprised. The only available light came from the shack. But in the abject darkness it was like a torch in a tunnel. "What kind of picture is this?" Edward asked.

"What the devil you mean by that?"

"It don't look like no picture I ever seen," he said.

"It's jus' old, that's all. 'Course it ain't like them new pictures they takin' now."

Edward looked at it again. The photograph was so brown and cracked that Edna's face was like a small tan circle in an amalgamation of creases amid the sepia fog that enveloped the image. But beneath the splashes of discoloration, Edward could see a beauty trying to radiate. Her hair was flowing full and her face displayed seemingly sharp features. Like those chiseled by a steady hand. The longer Edward looked at it the more he was stunned at how striking her face was. Edward was captivated, in particular by her smile. It was a smile which challenged him. Edward knew Edna. The Edna he knew had false teeth. He had seen them in the bathroom. This was not his aunt Edna's face. "This ain't Aunt Edna," Edward said.

"Who do you think it is? Jayne Mansfield?" With a violent jerk, Rufus lunged out at Edward, who was frozen by the sudden movement. He wasn't sure what Rufus was about to do, but this time he would not let himself be caught so completely by surprise. In that moment Edward considered the possibility that he might have to defend himself.

If his uncle Rufus thought he was a punk, he would find out different. Yes, he dodged the gang violence and the gangs. Yes, he knew how to maneuver through the dangers of the neighborhood. But he also knew how to, as they said on Whither Street, "hold his hands." He was not a punk. If he had to knock Uncle Rufus out to keep him from doing something to him, he would.

In Philly, if you weren't prepared to do at least that much to defend yourself, you became a prisoner to your own stoop. Even if you were a chubby little boy like Edward. Even if almost every other boy could beat you into a pulp, you still had to know enough to put up a good fight.

But when Rufus lunged forward he wasn't coming for Edward. Instead he snatched the picture from Edward's hands and held it up to the moonlight.

Edward felt his heart thumping. This was worse than the roller coaster at Willow Grove Park. Not the Wild Mouse, but the big one. He swallowed hard and tried to settle himself as he kept his eyes on Rufus.

This was one strange man, Edward thought. One minute Rufus was treating him like a little kid, the next his drinking buddy. He had no idea who Jayne Mansfield was or what she had to do with Edna's picture. "All I'm saying is that this doesn't look like Aunt Edna," Edward said.

"Boy I'ma get mad if you don't shut up. That's your aunt Edna, sho' nuff. But I can tell you one thing, she don't look nothing what like she used to." He drank again, then held the picture out to the boy once again.

Edward hesitated. He was caught in a chaos of fear and curiosity. He looked away as he raised his hand. Rufus leaned forward and extended the picture farther.

Edward slowly turned his head away from the back of Edna's house and met Rufus's eyes. He could see Rufus now as a face two feet away from him. One of Edna's back-porch lights providing just enough illumination to feel Rufus's clarity. To see him.

And then Rufus did something which completely and utterly seduced Edward. He smiled. A beautiful, sweet, welcoming, lucid smile devoid of snarl or sneer.

For a moment the man and the boy both held the photo. The man smiling. The boy stunned by the face of the smiling man. When Rufus let the picture go, he turned back to his shack and sat down again.

Edward looked at the picture again. It was plain to see. Edna had changed dramatically. He couldn't help thinking that if that face was really hers, life was the cruelest friend anyone could ever have. To have once seen a face like that turn into what was now her was downright depressing.

As he stood there he felt something sweep over him. The night breeze riddled with the chirps of nocturnal insects. A salt air kiss from the ocean. Some unspecified power. He felt Rufus moving through time. He saw Rufus holding Edna. He felt Rufus swooning into the whirlwind of beauty that was once his one and only love.

He looked up at Rufus now, sitting staring at his bottle, and could almost see the shadow of experience dance on his face. He became aware of himself slipping a little out of or perhaps into Rufus. Like a dream in which he was both himself and Rufus. He couldn't see what Rufus saw—the only picture in his mind was that of Rufus staring at the bottle, slowly shaking his head—but it was like he could feel what Rufus felt. Suddenly he felt his stomach quivering and a deep fatigue creep over him. A haze of sunlight and dust and shadow draped.

And then Rufus disturbed this moment by bringing the bottle back to his lips. The light disappeared and brought them back to the Delaware night. The uneasiness left. The sense of tiredness evaporated. Edward watched the man take a long swig. So long it made him think that the liquor Rufus drank must have been as sweet as a Nehi soda.

Rufus finally pulled the bottle away, and again ran the back of his left hand across his face, watching Edward as the boy looked again at the photograph.

"Two days after I made her take that picture—she didn't like picture takin', you know—some pretty nigger come diddy-bopping 'round her house. Talkin' 'bout how he come to ask her out on a date." He wiped the top of the liquor bottle with the palm of his hand.

"Now, I don't know if'n you know much of anything, much less bein' a man. But whatever that bastard was doin' over to Edna's that day, I knew it wasn't up to no good. I asked Edna, 'You tell this here nigger to come by and take you onna date?' She looked at me, this little shit-eatin' smile on her face. Didn't say nothin'. 'Woman,' I said, 'this here man walk all the way over here to see you and you can't even tell me whether or not you knew about it ahead of time? I guess he just decided out the clear blue sky that he was gonna take you out, huh?'

"Then I turned around and faced this guy. Hell, he was at least twice my size." Rufus was totally absorbed in his story. As he talked, he would inch the bottle closer and closer to his lips. Then, in the moment of passion during a particular sentence or point, the bottle would return to the cradle of his lap. The liquor had not reached his lips even after three or four attempts.

Edward had a thought that if someone could keep him talking, perhaps his drinking problem would be cured. The thought was punctuated by Rufus bringing the bottle to his lips.

There was a pause in the conversation. And pauses were like starting guns at the races to Rufus. The bottle would jump to his mouth. His head would tilt backward. His eyes would open wide and he would pose that way, with the whiskey flowing down his throat. Abruptly his head would snap forward and he would slam the bottle down on the wooden step between his legs.

Rufus could see the man and Edna as clear as gray ridges on the broken white clamshells that Edna used to pave the driveway. "So I told him to stay away from my woman. I must have been drunk or something because he nearly broke my damned neck. He picked me up and threw me clean through Edna's front window and over the porch. Edna started screamin' and cryin' and I guess he just got tired of kickin' my ass, 'cause all a sudden, he just stopped hittin' on me and walked away.

"It's awful to get your ass kicked like that, Eddie. I was just layin' there in the goddamned sand trying to get my mind together. I should of cut his fuckin' throat. That's what I should of done. I had my trusty friend right here, too." He lifted the pointed end of his knife sheath. "I should of cut his ass too short to shit. I promised myself right then and there that nobody was ever gonna do that to me again without knowin' they had tangled with Rufus Brown. That son of a bitch got away clean. Yessir, got away clean."

Rufus paused, his eyes focused backward. "And he wasn't the only one neither. All my life shit been happ'nin' to me that way. I just be mindin' my own goddamned business, and wham. Only so much of that a man can take."

He looked softly at Edward, "Then, to make matters worse, Edna comes over to me and sees me layin' out there, broken up into little pieces, and she says, 'Rufus, why you pick a fight with that man, huh? Did I say I needed you 'round here to protect me?'

"Now, what was I supposed to say? Hell, I couldn't tell her the truth. I *had* to fight that boy. That's what a man is supposed to do. He's got to defend his honor. He didn't have no business over there to see Edna. You just got to do it. Even if you get your ass kicked tryin'. Shit."

Rufus listened to the last of what he had just said and couldn't help but laugh. He knew a lot about getting his ass kicked. He squinted to see more clearly in the light that rested against the darkness as he searched for Edward. He scoured the boy's face for confirmation that he had just told a story. Suddenly he wasn't sure he had actually said anything. He almost panicked as he waited for some response from Edward. What if he had just thought the whole thing up in his mind and hadn't really said anything?

Edward let his eyes be picked up by Rufus. He felt first the amusement and then a surprising fear. But he let the amusement take over and found himself chuckling at the scene of Rufus lying in the sand.

Rufus was enlivened by Edward's response. He tried to grab the hesitant joy in the boy's laugh and merge it with his own. He tried. But like a canal eel it was slippery. It slid right through his hands. In an instant he started to cry. He tried to hold it back, but it wouldn't wait.

That man, whose name Rufus could not recall, had broken a little piece of him. And no matter how often Rufus had replayed images of himself cowering at the hand of some citified dandy, it always ended in him feeling like he had lost something valuable that day. He just wanted to remember the man's name. You should know the name of the person who takes something from you. This is someone you want to remember. But Rufus couldn't and he'd never ask Edna. His struggle to remember always ended in sobs. Suddenly something so small became very important. His cry, which had begun slowly, quickly escalated into a babbling, drunken cry.

Edward trembled a little as he watched Rufus cover his rough face with his rough hands. He had never seen a man cry before. His father would never cry. Never. Definitely not from some old fight with somebody whose name he couldn't even remember.

Everything about Rufus challenged him. A smile. Tears. The atmosphere around him. Around them. A weird convoluted mixture of melancholy and spirit.

Edward was tired of standing; his knees felt rubbery one moment and stiff the next, causing him to weave slightly as if caught in the breeze. But weaving or not, he stood there, anchored in the ground, watching Rufus—the bottle wedged between his knees—as he struggled to wipe his eyes with a dirty handkerchief.

"But, Uncle Rufus, that was a long time ago. I bet he couldn't beat you now."

Rufus didn't move his hands, which rested like a tent over his face. His voice emanating from within. "It's not now. I'm talkin' about then. The way it shoulda been."

Both he and Edward knew the truth. Neither one of them could change history. The pain of it was that history had changed him. His past haunted.

"Like I told you, boy, love is a son of a bitch."

Edward lost a chuckle before he choked it off. Profanity brought reflexive glee to him. It almost didn't matter what the words were being used to say. His curses were always secret. Indeed, he felt that was one of the differences between him and some of his other friends. Curse words had found their way into the language of his "boys" to such an extent that there were many who couldn't put a sentence together that didn't contain at least one profane word. It was weird for him to be around an adult who cursed so freely, and was at the same time oddly funny.

But Edward had noticed that the great writers used profanity in a most special way. If words were rocks which the writer hurled, then profane words were bigger rocks, to be used when real damage was intended. Yet, no matter the context, when

Edward came into contact with profanity, it always brought a smile to his face.

"It ain't funny," Rufus said, wiping the sweat from his forehead, putting his handkerchief away, pushing the tears aside, jumping ahead. "When somebody tells you that something is a son of a bitch, that don't always mean it's funny. We could be talking about serious pain." He looked up at Edward again, his eyes so dark they were like jade. "Anyway, forget it, it don't mean nothing. Just don't you tell Edna what I was talking about. 'Specially my saying 'son of a bitch.' She'd probably run me out of here."

He took another drink. The smoky liquid snuck out the corner of his mouth and dribbled onto his shirt.

Edward was swimming in what Rufus was saying. But the last thing, the idea that Edna might chase him away, triggered something. "Don't you live here?" he asked.

Rufus took a few more swallows of rye, got up, stood in the open door of the shack, towering above Edward. He was trying to make up his mind about the boy. Could he trust him? Would he go? "I do now, but tomorrow, well—tomorrow could be a son of a bitch."

Edward was still breathing, even enjoying the dangerous talk with Rufus, so he pushed further. "How come you ain't living in the house with the rest of us anyway?"

Rufus nearly kicked Edward with his big black work boots as he stomped down the steps and into the sand. He whirled around in front of Edward and bent his face down so that their broad brown noses were only two inches apart.

He wanted to stir the boy up again. He didn't want the edge to leave their relationship. He could tell Edward so much about life.

Heart palpitations reminded Edward that he could still die. His breathing shrank. Rufus glowered at him. "I don't know who sent you out here, and for what, but you ain't gonna get nothing from me. Why don't you just go fetch yourself something else to do, instead of pickin' on me all the time. Ain't it past your goddamned bedtime?"

"But, Uncle Rufus, I was just asking—"

"Get out my face, boy." His stare smoldered. The air became like swells at the beach; you had to wade through.

Edward got up. It was time to go. His gray cells were all shot to hell.

5

Edward awoke the next morning to find his mother sitting on his bed. After leaving Rufus, he'd come into the kitchen and saw the stacks of barbecued ribs in Edna's huge blue oval roasting pot. He had begged Edna for a sandwich, which he had shared with his sister. Edna had warned them not to eat such a heavy meal so late, but who could resist barbecue when you've smelled it all night? When the kitchen reeked of it and the outdoor pit still smoldered even as the children played in the dark? How could anyone not want to gnaw on the charred bones or suck the sweet spiciness of Edna's sauce? She made a mild sauce for those who preferred it, but the real prize was the hot sauce daubed by a small mop head on the grilling ribs.

At any rate, Edna had been right. He didn't know about Sarah, but he had a terrible time sleeping. He kept seeing Rufus standing at his shack door, waving to him, beckoning to him. But every time he approached the door, Rufus would pull out his knife and jump at him. Throughout the night both Sarah and Edward had screamed and cried. It had caused Edna some anxiety. She didn't have time to keep checking on them. She had people to serve, hostessing to do.

When Angela came home from waiting tables, Edna had alerted her to the troubles Edward in particular was having.

"I know I shouldn't have given him that sandwich, but they begged me so."

"I know how they can be." Angela was exhausted. The only time she had during the summer to relax and enjoy herself was after work and mid-mornings, before lunch. She didn't feel like she had abandoned her children. The way she saw it, it was good for them to have time when they were essentially responsible for themselves. It wasn't like they were in the city with the gangs and the violence. This was the country. It was a safe place to leave children on their own.

To that, Edna would not have agreed. Yes, it was true, there were no gangs there. But there *was* the gambling and drinking and carousing that went on in and outside the Do Drop. There was the rage—there was no other better-suited word—that ran like well water through the entire community. And that rage could explode at any moment. Any night. Especially a Friday or Saturday night. But any night. Someone could bump into someone, someone could cut a glance at someone's girlfriend, someone could try to cheat someone, someone could walk across someone's yard one time too many, someone could sit on someone's car without asking. Anything could happen. Any night.

So Edna didn't want Angela to think that when Edward and Sarah were left alone there was nothing to worry about. That simply wasn't true. And this morning Angela wanted to be the first thing Edward saw when he awoke. She had been sitting on his bed for nearly twenty minutes when he opened his eyes and gazed on her.

Edward rubbed his eyes to make sure he wasn't still dreaming. But he knew from his mother's sharply floral perfume which challenged his already aggravated nose that he was awake. She was smiling at him and leaning into his face, her lips red pursed. He let her lips reach his forehead.

"How's my man this morning? Did you have a hard night?"

"I don't know. I guess so. I was dreaming a lot."

"Yes, I know. Bad dreams?"

"Yeah." Edward sat up. He was only wearing the bottoms of his pajamas and so his chubby chest jiggled as he situated himself. "I was dreaming about—" Suddenly sanity overtook his waking vulnerability and he stopped. He didn't want her or Edna to know he was dreaming about Rufus. He had to play it cool. And actually, even as he was in the middle of the sentence, his dream was dissipating like dew. "About, something . . . I'm not sure."

"Edna tells me you were out by Rufus's shack last night. Is that true?"

He was just a bit stunned and looked quickly out the window, which offered a view of Edna's front yard and the road beyond. He could even see the very corner of the Do Drop Inn in the distance. "Yes."

"What were you doing out there?"

"Well, um . . . at first I was just walking over there. I was playing with Antny and them, and then I just . . . um . . . I just wanted to go over there."

"Edward, don't play with me."

"I'm not. I saw a light on and I just went over there."

"Have you been talking to Rufus? Now tell me the truth, Eddie."

"Well, he was standing outside."

"What did he say?"

"Nothing. We were just talking."

"About what?"

"I don't remember, Mom. Just hello and stuff." Edward knew he couldn't tell the truth. There was something they didn't want him to know, and if he admitted to already having conversations with Rufus there would be a new set of rules. He had learned from the great Hercule Poirot that restricting the scope of an investigation too early could be a devastating limitation. One must follow the clues, wherever they led. So, how could he possibly tell her the full truth? She would certainly prevent him from continuing his blossoming summer passion.

It was obvious that his mother was losing interest in her interrogation. He could see it in her eyes. She wanted to hug him. To find out what he wanted to eat for breakfast. Whether or not he and his sister wanted to go to the beach. He could see right through her.

"Listen, Eddie, and I'm only gonna tell you this one more time." She put a hand on each shoulder and tightened her grip, pulling him forward at the same time. It was clear that he had totally miscalculated. She was more than a little interested. She was bordering on angry. "I don't want you back there. I don't want you talking to him. At all. Period. You got that?"

Edward was nearly catatonic. Thrown completely off balance. She was serious. Spanking serious about this. But what was he to do about it? Rufus was almost all he thought about. Last night, he had even asked God in his prayers for another chance to talk to Rufus. Edward only prayed when he really wanted something. Now what was he supposed to do?

"Do you hear me? I asked you if you understand what I'm saying to you."

"Yes, Mom, I heard you."

"Your aunt Edna and I know what's best here. You just have to trust me. Rufus is a strange man. There's a reason we don't want you out there with him."

"What reason, Mom? Nobody wants to tell me anything." Now Edward felt the best thing to do was to come clean. "He don't seem all that bad to me." And as soon as he said it, he realized he shouldn't have.

Edna, who had been standing just outside the door the whole time, took a step inside. Angela stood up from the bed, now towering over Edward. "What has he said to you?"

"Nothing, Mom. Really. We just talked, that's all."

"No more, Eddie. No more. If I catch you out there or get a report that you've been out there, I'm going to be very mad."

"I promise."

Angela sighed and broke a smile. "Get yourself dressed and join us for breakfast."

Edward looked out the window as his mother and Edna left the room. He was struck stiff with anxiety as he saw Rufus walking through the yard. The man looked crazy. He wore big, thigh-high black rubber boots with a thick yellow band around the top. His gait was very slow. Almost stumbling.

Instinctively Edward jumped out of bed and started putting his clothes on. For the moment his mother's threat already vapor. As he laced up his Chuck Taylor sneakers, he calculated his chances of escaping the house without someone stopping him.

When the bow was tied he was up out of his crouch and heading for the door. But before he could make it to the porch an arm reached out and snagged him.

"Edward, where were you going?" His mother had a light trace of sweat on her brow.

"Nowhere." He hoped Rufus wouldn't go far before he was

released. But as he looked at his mother's face, he knew he would be confined at least until she went to work. "I just wanted to see what the weather was like."

"It's hot. That's all you need to know. It's hot and it's going to get a lot hotter if you don't mind me." And with that, she dragged him into the kitchen, where a pot of grits, a platter of sausages and bacon, and a bowl of scrambled eggs awaited.

Edward was hungry, but there was a problem. He had never been able to eat eggs without pouring syrup on them. Not just any syrup. It had to be Log Cabin syrup. And for some strange reason, Edna never had Log Cabin.

"Mom, I can't eat that. Aunt Edna doesn't have the right syrup."

"What is the right syrup?" Edna paused with her mouth full.

Angela sat down across from Edna and sighed. "This boy is so finicky. He only eats Log Cabin."

"I got some syrup up there in that cabinet." Edna was rising slowly from her kitchen table. Edward sat down next to his mother. He had a glimmer of hope that Edna had Log Cabin. But when she turned around, instead of the distinctive bottle, she had a large metal can in her hands. "This is good syrup. It's not even opened yet."

Edward looked at the can Edna sat on the table in front of him. It was a brilliant candy-apple red with a golden crown on the label. KING'S SYRUP. He had never heard of it.

"I don't want that. I want Log Cabin." He couldn't help wondering what was wrong with everybody. Why couldn't they just go to the store or let him go and get a bottle of Log Cabin syrup. Was that too much to ask for?

But Edna found the can opener, punched two holes in the syrup can, and poured some in a cup. "Use this. It's good," she said simply.

Edward looked at his mother, who stared at him without the slightest hint that she would come to his rescue. He looked next to Edna, who had gone back to her breakfast with a clear smugness. He cut up a piece of sausage and planted each piece strategically into his eggs. And then, trying to act as casual as he could, he reached for the syrup and poured just a thin thread on the edge of his makeshift omelette. It was thick, much thicker than his favorite. He hated thick syrup. That was why he couldn't eat Alaga or Karo. This was madness. Didn't anyone understand? Taste. Taste was worth standing up for. Preferences. He thought about his hero, Hercule Poirot. Poirot would never stoop to eat some backwoods, underprocessed, overly sweet sludge. This was unthinkable.

He cautiously slid his fork into the eggs and pulled out the smallest portion and put it in his mouth. Almost immediately he spit it out. The harsh waxy taste of the syrup dissipated instantly, leaving only the blandness of the eggs. "I can't eat this."

Edna looked up, bits of scrambled eggs visible on her tongue. "You eat your breakfast. Ain't nobody rich in here."

"Mom?"

Angela smiled at him and said gently, "I think you should eat your food. I'll get some Log Cabin for you later on."

Edward took a deep breath and stuffed the eggs into his mouth. One day no one would tell him what he had to eat. After he was done he asked if he could go outside. But his mother suggested instead that he help Edna out by sweeping all of the hallways and public rooms. He was filled with heavy sighs as he grabbed the broom and went to work.

At eleven his mother left for work and Edward put the broom down. He had been slowly, just barely sweeping the pool room, where the three tables sat like sculptures in a museum. He had been marking time. Waiting for his mother to leave. As soon as he heard the front screen door slam shut and the car that picked his mother up turned out of Edna's driveway—kicking up clamshells in the process—Edward headed for the back door.

As he walked into the sunlight, he could feel the sweat between his thighs and couldn't help thinking about the stain it would make on his khaki shorts. He headed directly for Rufus's shack. If he was lucky Rufus would still be around. He had made too much progress to be confined by Edna or his mother's skittishness. What was the danger anyway? Sure Rufus was strange, but Edward had seen glimpses of true tenderness. Of vulnerability. What intrigued him most was the stark contrasts. The fire-hot anger, the rage, and the flickering softness.

As he came up to Rufus's shack he could see that the door was locked from the outside. Disappointment marked his face as he stood once again in the dirt outside Rufus's lean-to. But in the air he heard a harsh voice, just below the sound of a lawn mower running somewhere up the road and the sound of children playing in Edna's yard. He knew instantly it was Rufus. But where was he?

"I ain't sorry for a goddamned thing. 'Cept maybe the stuff with Edna. But everything else is my goddamned life. What you want me to do? Get on my goddamned knees and beg you like a dog? Be your goddamned pet?"

Edward tried to gauge where the voice was coming from. He slowly and quietly inched his way around the shack, moving toward the back. Rufus's voice floated all around him.

"Shit. I mean, what else you gonna do to me? Huh? You think I'm afraid of you? Guess again. You can throw me around all you want. You done took everything. This is hell. Right here. Right here. This is hell. Trapped here in this life. Nothing to live for. All you let me do is go backward. I'm tired of going backward."

Edward slowly approached the corner of the building and peered around it. He saw Rufus sitting in the middle of a small patch of grass which led to the woods just beyond Edna's property. Edward could see three or four *Playboy* magazines lying on the ground beside the man, their distinctive, glossy covers glowing in the reflection of the sun.

"I could die. Yes. That's right. You damn sure got that right. I could die any goddamned time I get ready and you couldn't stop me. That's the only power I got. But I know I got it." Edward watched as Rufus, now laughing softly, revealed a bottle in his left hand. He wiped the mouth of the bottle with his right palm and took a long swig.

"You damn skippy. I get to die when I want. I choose that. You done did your dirty work and the only thing you left for me to do is go backward or die." Edward looked carefully all around. Maybe there was someone standing in the woods. But after a minute or two, he realized that Rufus wasn't talking to anyone that Edward would be able to see.

"Uncle Rufus?" Patience had never been a solid strength for Edward.

Rufus didn't flinch. "I'm not going to do it anymore. I'm going forward. Yeah, well, I wanna see you do it." Edward took a deep breath. Maybe Rufus hadn't heard him. "A gift? You call this a gift. You're crazier than me. You got me going in circles and you call that a gift. I don't know what goddamned day it is. Is it Friday? Saturday? I don't have the slightest goddamned idea. You did that."

"Uncle Rufus?"

This time Edward could tell that Rufus heard him because he abruptly stopped talking. But he didn't turn in Edward's direction. He just kept staring into the woods.

"Should I go away?" Edward couldn't believe how quickly he could be terrorized by Rufus. No matter how excited Edward was to talk to him, every time he ended up frightened.

"No, you stay where you are. Who told you to sneak out here and spy on me?"

"Nobody."

"Nobody, huh?" Rufus took another drink. "What day is it?"

"It's Wednesday."

"Wednesday, huh? Where you been?"

"I haven't been anywhere. Just in the house."

"You ain't been out here in so long I was beginning to think you wasn't coming back out here." Rufus paused, then let out a hearty laugh. "I was beginning to think that Edna had tied you up and locked you up upstairs in one of those rooms she got up there with curtains in the window."

"Sir?"

"Who the fuck you callin' sir? Don't you say that to me." Now Rufus struggled to get up from the ground and started walking toward Edward. "I ain't no goddamned sir."

"I'm sorry."

"Don't be sorry either. I don't want that. You just watch your step around me. You understand?"

Rufus was now standing right in front of Edward. The boy looked up into his bloodshot eyes and thought, No, I don't understand. That's what I'm trying to do. I'm trying to understand. Instead he just nodded his head.

But Edward did think of something to say. "Uncle Rufus, I was just here last night."

"Baloney. I know when you was here. I been all over the goddamned place since I seen you. I been to France. Did you know that? I was in Paris."

"No sir, I—"

"What I tell you about that? I'm already Uncle Rufus. Don't make it any worst."

"But that's the way my parents make me talk. I always say 'yes sir' and 'no sir.' It's hard not to say it." Edward swallowed. Rufus went back to the spot where Edward had first found him and sat down on the grass again. Edward let time pass and then, as steadily as he could, he asked again, "Ahhh, Uncle Rufus, who were you talking to?"

"Why should I tell you? You ain't nothing but a little sand dab, don't know your butt from a hole in the ground."

"But I heard you talking to somebody."

"I know what the hell I was doing. I was the one doing it. Yeah, I was talking to somebody. What of it?"

"But I didn't see anyone."

"Shit, boy. You keep saying things I already know. You stuck on the obvious."

"Were you just talking to yourself? My mom does it all the time. My father says it's okay long as you don't answer." Edward felt suddenly like he was actually in a conversation. That Rufus was listening and considering what he was saying.

"You think I'm crazy, don't you? That I just sit here on the goddamned ground and talk to myself." Rufus paused, took a sip, wiped his mouth, and then in a completely startling moment of gentleness he said, "There's something there, Eddie. I don't know what it is, but there's something there. I can hear it saying stuff to me. It's like a teacher who just keeps going over the same lessons over and over."

Edward started getting nervous again. What teacher?

"One thing about it, though. I do be moving around quite a bit. Even if I just keep going to places I already been. Living backward is what they got me doing."

Edward was standing speechless. Whatever was going on

ALEX S D. PATE

rivaled any case Poirot had ever had. "So you wasn't talking to
nobody?"

"That ain't what I said, goddammit. I told you it is somebody
or something. I just don't know who or what."

"And so where do you go?" Edward tried to appear nonchalant.
Rufus paused again. "Come here."

Edward walked slowly over and sat down two feet away from
Rufus. Rufus looked at him. His eyes already dancing with
liquor. Red lanterns flickering. He motioned with his rough
crusty hands, hands that Edward now saw clearly for the first
time. Edward leaned in. "If I told you you would think I was
nuts."

"No, I wouldn't."

"Things that happened. People I've known. The whole thing is
like a place. You know what I mean? It's like a city. Or a street. In
one house I'm sucking a teat. In another house I'm visitin' somebody I don't even know down there in North Kackalacka or
somewhere like that."

"Where?"

"North Carolina, boy. You don't know shit, do you? Anyway I
could be sitting here taking my nips on this here bottle and suddenly I'm there. Sometimes there's a voice talking shit in the
background. Sometimes I'm just wandering around, opening
doors, and watching the way things happened. And the dang-
edest thing about it is that when I open my eyes or wake up or
whatever I do to come back to this hellhole, people say I been
gone. I'm thinking I just took a nap. But time passes. Sometimes
minutes, sometimes hours, even days. So there. You want to know
so all fired much. Now you know something."

Edward felt his eyes blink. He actually heard them close and
open again. He also heard just the slightest rustle in the leaves
on the trees in the woods just behind him. His mind was a jumble

112

of thoughts. What was Rufus talking about? Where was this place?

"You ever been to the county dump?"

"No, sir." Edward was confused again. It seemed an odd question.

Rufus glared at him but lost his anger in an instant. "I go there every few days. That's the one thing I *can* do for Edna. She don't make me. I just do it. You know?" Edward stared at him. "Yeah, I get all the trash cans out back there and load them up in the back of my pickup and take them to the dump. Sometime I spend the whole day there. Just sitting on the front of my truck, watching the dark gray smoke. Watching those seagulls there. They must think the smoke coming up from the piles of burning trash is water or something. They're always there. Hundreds of them. Edna don't really like me to take so much time, you know. 'Cause while I'm gone, she ain't got nowhere to put the trash." Rufus chuckled, then took another drink.

Edward found himself wondering how Rufus could drink so much. How could he do that and still keep talking?

"I feel like goin' right now. What about you?"

"Where? The dump?" Edward swallowed hard. "Where is that?"

"If I told you, would you know any more than you know now?"

"But I'd better ask Aunt Edna for permission."

Rufus grabbed the boy's arm. "Do you want to go?" There was nothing but fire in Rufus's head. If he had to wait for Edna's okay he might as well forget the whole thing.

"But"—Edward started to tremble—"don't you think I should ask?"

"I don't tell people what to do. Other people do that. That's why you got mothers and fathers and aunts and other people like that. I'm just Rufus. I won't tell you you got to do a goddamn thing."

Edward looked at him.

Rufus pushed his face once again into Edward's space, threatening. His red eyes blinked like Christmas lights in the seashore sun.

"You goin'?"

Edward wanted to go. "I guess so."

He silently followed Rufus to his gray '54 Ford pickup truck. Edward couldn't help but wonder why everybody black in Rehoboth seemed to drive raggedy, beat-up vehicles. Rufus's truck looked to be in worse shape than Edna's Olds.

His father drove a Cadillac. Both Rooster and Sonny's fathers drove Cadillacs. It was what set their families apart from the other families in the neighborhood. On certain Saturday mornings (Edward could never discern the precise schedule), their fathers would park end to end on Whither Street in front of the Goodmans' house or on Seybert in front of his house and wash, vacuum, and sometimes wax their cars long into the afternoon.

They'd preen and strut, spray each other with the water hose, and usually end up huddled in one of the three cars talking about God knows what. Edward had tried on several occasions to gain entrance to the host car, but they would always shoo him away.

He wondered what they talked about. It always looked like so much fun. They'd be laughing so hard their eyes would look like they'd been crying. Edward would sit on the stoop and just watch them. Sometimes he'd find himself laughing just because they were laughing. Their muted guffaws rolling out of the car windows like some intoxicating gas that instantly infected him.

But Rufus's truck, its gray paint flaking in some spots, worn to the natural gray of steel in others—creased, dented, and de-cromed—was so far away from the standards exhibited by his father that it appeared to him like an amusement-park ride. It beckoned him.

Still, he knew, with every step he took toward the truck, that he was about to do something stupid. He knew he should at least ask Edna for permission. But that would have been an obvious surrender. There was no way that she'd let him go anywhere with Rufus. In fact, she'd probably tell his mother, and that would provide its own consequences. Still, he wanted to follow the trail of vapor that emanated from Rufus. He was captivated. All of his skills as a detective, an investigator, were being tested. How could he not go with him?

He didn't even know what exactly he was investigating. The death of Mr. Peabody? Yes . . . but more than that. A man who talks to people other people can't see. A man who "lives backward"? A killer? An astral traveler? All these things were probably true. Or at least possible. He believed in the magic of life. Things unexplainable. Yet everything he was thinking only pointed to the real mystery. And that was Rufus. What kind of man was Rufus?

Edward pushed aside the knowledge that he was breaking his mother's rule. Leaving the yard without telling Edna. Pushed aside that it was Rufus he was going somewhere with. Pushed it all aside to let excitement overwhelm his body.

As he climbed into the passenger's side of the truck, he could barely contain himself. The truck was, in fact, in terrible condition. Much worse than Edna's car. The dashboard had virtually rotted out, as had the floor. The seats were worn through, straw, springs, and cotton everywhere. And the smell in the truck was so particular, so specific. A mix of age and distance. Of sweat and overexposure to sun. To all the elements. Edward would never forget how Rufus's truck smelled. As he settled into the passenger seat, he couldn't wait to feel the rush of the open air.

Rufus looked at him, his eyes drooping and, even in the bright seashore sunlight, deeply shadowed. "You sure you want to go, now?"

"I'm sure."

"Now, if you really want to we can go on in there and ask Edna if she minds or not." Rufus smiled slyly. He wanted Edward to make this decision himself.

It was Edward's turn to be irritated. He'd pushed all obstacles to the side. "No, that's okay. Let's just go."

Rufus threw the truck into first gear and drove out of the driveway, past the Do Drop Inn and on to Hebron Road, which would lead them to the highway. There, Edward's excitement quickly faded into fear.

Rufus was clearly loaded to the point that his vision and reflexes were just remnants. And yet he sped the rusted pickup down the highway, laughing and swerving. Edward held on to the dented door of the truck tightly.

After about a mile, Rufus became even wilder. Every so often he would drive up onto the median and into the grass. He would straddle the asphalt and the grass for a while then bring the truck back into its proper lane.

He was having fun.

He pushed the gas pedal into the rotting floor of the truck. When Edward looked to see how fast they were traveling, he saw that the speedometer was broken.

During that drive, Rufus became young again, screamed into the flowing air. His face beamed. He drove both Edward and himself through a tunnel of adventure. Teetering precariously on the brink of disaster. Scaring the devil out of Edward as he went along.

He turned to Edward. He liked him. "You know, boy, something bad happened to me a while back. Messed everything up.

Sho' did. I mean messed it up big time." Rufus looked back at the road. His driving was calmer now.

"Now, I can't tell you about it. I don't talk about it, so don't ask me no questions about it. You hear?"

"Yes."

"Anyway, I had to leave Rehoboth real goddamned quick. Had to leave everything and everybody, including Edna." Rufus had never told this story to anyone.

Edward couldn't decide whether he should act like he wasn't interested or press Rufus to open up. He knew he was close to satisfying his curiosity about Rufus. But Rufus had stopped talking and was now singing a song that Edward had never heard before and looking out the window.

> *where is my home*
> *on the sea on the sea*
> *where will you go*
> *we'll see we'll see*
> *where is my home*
> *on the sea on the sea*
> *where will you go*
> *we'll see we'll see*

Rufus sang this ditty over and over. Sometimes he'd do it in a low tone, sometimes nearly screaming. But after a while Edward found the nonsensical singing hard to take, so finally he asked, "Where'd you go? When you left Rehoboth back then?"

"Went to sea," Rufus answered, almost shouting against the hot wind that now took up residence within the cab of the truck. "Sailed across the Atlantic a couple of times and went places a colored man could never hope to get to."

"Was you in the navy?"

"Naw, the Merchants. The Merchant Marines. I wasn't cut out for the BS you have to take in the navy. Besides, all a black man could be in the navy was a steward, and I don't like servin' nothing to white folks."

"Did you like it?"

"Like it? Boy, I *had* to be there. I had to be somewhere. I worked like a goddamned dog. I'd do anything. I pumped the goddamned bilges. I swabbed the goddamned decks. I did anything. Do you know why?"

Edward shook his head, but he was distracted. Rufus was driving wildly again. Edward suddenly realized his arms were virtually fully extended and his round body was almost levitating, moving upward in an involuntary bracing reflex.

Rufus abruptly turned off the highway and swerved onto a two-lane paved road. The truck was weaving again, running onto the shoulder and back into the lane.

"I said, do you want to goddamned know why?"

Edward couldn't speak. But he nodded his head violently.

Rufus was trying to calm himself down, but he couldn't. He just wanted Edward to understand. He wasn't trying to scare him anymore. He wasn't going to hurt him. He just wanted him to understand.

"I worked like a slave for five years so I could come back to Rehoboth. I saved every dime I could get my hands on so that when I got back I'd walk into Edna's and she'd drop whatever she was doing and throw her arms around my neck and everything would be perfect—forever. That's why."

Edward was genuinely interested in the story, but its competition was strong. Rufus was out of control. The truck was barely on the asphalt at all. The trees from the woods on the right danced ever closer to the car.

Rufus could see the trees. It was like they were daring him by sticking out their legs to trip him. He could dodge a bunch of trees. He had dodged worse. He had escaped death more than once. He had stood the test of time.

"Uncle Rufus . . ." Edward couldn't stand it anymore. He was terrified. He let his terror reign over him. "Stop. Stop. You're going to kill us. Slow down."

Rufus turned his head to reassure the boy that he wasn't going to hurt him.

Edward sensed Rufus's eyes on him as he saw the deer peek out from behind a tree. His arm shot up to point at the animal. Rufus turned his head just in time and steered the truck around the anxious buck. But the ground sloped dramatically into a ravine and the car slid into it.

Traveling at the speed it was, the car defied gravity for a moment and rode the wall of the ravine. But quickly the tires let go, and the truck, still being propelled forward, rolled over sideways and slid for another twenty feet.

Edward had closed his eyes right after he saw the deer. He had opened them once to see mud and the ceiling of the truck's cab. Rufus's head had hit the back of the truck when it slid into the ravine.

Suddenly everything came to a stop. The truck, upside down in a deep ditch surrounded by high brush, almost shuddered. It had slid down the sloped highway, into a drainage ditch and behind a small bridge And then suddenly there was a kind of stillness that settled around them. The wheels were still turning and there was a dusty acrid smell softly fluttering about them. Edward slowly opened his eyes. Rufus's face was five inches from his. It was like the truck had gently folded over them, trapping them both between a cushion of metal and the seats of the vehicle. They were like pigs in a steel blanket. Edward could see that Rufus was moving his mouth, but couldn't hear what he was saying.

When Edward tried to move he felt a screaming pain travel through his body like an electric current. He opened his mouth and agony flew out.

Rufus was still talking to him. But now Edward wasn't sure whether he couldn't hear him because he couldn't hear or because his own scream was so loud. And then the tears flooded as dizziness engulfed him.

"Eddie. Can you hear me? Can you hear me?"

It was like Rufus was far away. Edward could hear the cars passing up and over the rim of the ditch. He stifled his heaving tears. Every time he breathed, pain shot all over his body.

"Can you hear me talking to you?"

"Yes. I can hear you, Uncle Rufus."

"Are you all right?"

"I don't think so. I can't move and it hurts so bad."

Rufus closed his eyes. "I guess I did this, Eddie. I did this."

"Help me, Uncle Rufus. Help me." Edward had lost everything he knew about being a man. At this moment he was a little boy. A hurt little boy who wanted someone to take care of him. He didn't need to see Rufus's tears. He didn't need to hear uncontrolled self-pity. Not now. "Owwwww," he moaned.

"I can't move either, Eddie. I'm stuck. I think I'm okay, though. Not too much pain. But you. You ain't looking too good. How bad is it?"

Edward was starting to float away. He only heard parts of what Rufus was saying. "It hurts all over. I can't take it, Uncle Rufus. I'm scared."

"I know. I know. Now just . . . ah . . . take a deep breath. Breathe deep. Just try to stay calm. Somebody'll find us." They were so close, he and the boy. Breathing the same disturbed air. Him fighting intoxication, Edward pain. "You just have to stay strong until they get here. Can you do that?"

Edward closed his eyes.

"No. No. Eddie. Don't go to sleep. Try to stay awake."

"I can't. . . . I'm . . ."

"Eddie, now, you got to hold it together. Be strong. Keep those eyes open." But Rufus could clearly see that Edward was wavering between oblivion and panic. It was too much for his body to accommodate. Rufus felt Edward's life unraveling like rope coming off a forecastle-deck winch.

"Please, son, please. Hold on. Damn." Rufus wished he could wipe his eyes or reach out and stroke the boy's brow. "I should've known better. This is my life, Eddie. You shoulda never come out to my house. You shoulda did like they told you." And then he was crying. His mind unanchored now more than ever before. He felt himself slipping away, too. But he knew where he was going. He knew he would be saved. He only wished he could take Edward with him.

And why couldn't he take Edward with him? What if he could scoop the boy's spirit, his soul, whatever it was that saw things before the eyes did, knew things before the mind, and felt things even before the heart could. Whatever that was that needed protecting. Needed shelter. But he'd never shared that space with anyone else. Never taken someone across the threshold that divided his life between the now and the then. Where history was a thing of the moment. Where it kept happening over and over and where they could stay until someone came to rescue them. At least come and get Edward. Rufus was sure there was no real rescue for himself. He believed he was destined always into the past. But Edward . . . if he could survive this, he had a chance.

"Can you come with me, boy? Can you grab on and come with me? I won't leave without you. I promise. Besides, you said you wanted to know shit about me. You said that, didn't you? That's what you wanted, wasn't it? Well, where we're goin' you're gonna learn more than you wanted. I can betcha that. But you got to come with me or you ain't gonna make it."

Edward opened his eyes and through a veil of pain and tears saw Rufus talking to him. Saw his lips moving. And felt his whole body disappear right out from under his mind. Poof. Suddenly he was with Rufus. Not just lying beside him. But *with* him with him.

"It's the story you wanted to know. You just got to hold on to hear it," Rufus whispered.

6

Edna had indeed been one of the prettiest girls in her school, a small one-room building on the edge of Johnny Giles's property, built by one of his more benevolent slavemaster ancestors. For many years it was the only school in Stoney Grove's vicinity where black children could go. But she wasn't a particularly good student. She had very little interest in memorizing the Declaration of Independence or the Preamble to the Constitution. Didn't like math that much. She could count her way through grocery shopping. And most importantly, she hated having to sit still for that long. In fact, to someone who didn't know her, it would seem that Edna could hardly keep her mind on one subject long enough to absorb her lessons. But the truth, as those around her knew, was that she already had too much on her mind. By the time Edna was thirteen, her father had suffered three strokes in two years.

Her father, Spencer Grand, the source of the weight on her

shoulders for the past two years, waited at home for when she returned from school. Her mother waited, too. Because when Edna got home she was expected to immediately change her clothes and pick up the task of taking care of her father. This included emptying his bedpan, washing him, occasionally cooking and feeding him, and most especially reading the Bible to him.

Spencer's body was dead on the right side. He'd lost his ability to speak, and whether the paralysis was the cause or not, he would not even try to walk. There was a wheelchair in the bedroom and sometimes she and her mother would lift him into it so that Edna could roll him onto the porch. But even this attempt to get him outside met with a rather strong resistance from Spencer. He'd shake his head and grunt when he saw the two of them at the bedroom door.

On this day in early spring, when most farmers were thinking of planting, Spencer lay motionless in his bed as Edna entered. The room smelled lightly of liniment, a sign that her mother had been there earlier, and the hint of strong urine, proof that it had probably been much earlier.

"Hi, Daddy. How are you?" Edna began to straighten the bed linens around him. There were countless pillows on the bed and on the floor. When she spoke her father had opened his eyes briefly.

"I'm telling you. I'll be glad when school is finished this year. I'm wasting my time there." She bent down and paused long enough to kiss him on the forehead. He opened his eyes again.

"God didn't mean for me to spend all my time in school. I need to be here helpin' you and Momma. But I know, I know. I'm supposed to finish school because that's what us colored people got to do now. I remember. Finish school. Finish school. Jesus. That's what you always used to say." She stopped talking and sat down on the caneback chair by the bed. It creaked loudly as she settled her thin frame into it.

She did this every afternoon. Before her two younger sisters got home and disrupted the quiet of the house, she always took time out to talk to him. She still remembered his voice so well. She could still fill in the blanks. Still hear him say things exactly the same way he always did.

"But why do I have to go to school? Just because I'm colored? That don't make sense to me. Anyway, I was gonna tell you about this boy who's been trying to court me. He's nice. And he—"

But just as she was about to launch into a description of her latest heartthrob, her father opened his eyes and began moving his lips. She'd seen him do this many times. It would be as if he didn't care whether he could be heard or not, he was still going to try.

"What, Daddy? Do you want some water?"

He slowly shook his head no, but he held her gaze. Edna moved closer to him. She smelled the sour breath flow intermittently from his mouth. But within the heat of his mouth she could swear she heard a whisper. She looked up into his eyes and felt her heart flutter.

"Momma . . ." she said just above her normal voice. "Momma."

There was a sound that had come from his mouth. Not the normal grunts she was accustomed to. But a soft sound. The beginning or the end of a word.

"What you want, Daddy?" Her growing anxiety put the edge of desperation in her voice. Through the open window she heard her mother's voice. Edna could tell that her mother was all the way out by the road, probably talking to one of their neighbors. This time, when she called her, she screamed out the window.

"Momma." She heard her mother's feet heading back down the driveway toward the house.

Edna turned her attention back to her father. "What is it, Daddy? Can I get you something?"

Spencer still staring at her, leaned his head even closer to her. "Haaa . . ."

She'd heard it. "What? Haaa . . . what? What, Daddy?"

"Happ . . . e . . ." His eyes closed and his head instantly flopped back onto the pillow. Edna reached her hand out to touch his face and it felt immediately odd. She knew he was dead. She could feel his spirit rise right up out of his body.

Her mother rushed in. "What's wrong, Edna? What's wrong? Spencer? Spencer?" And then she erupted in sobs and flung herself on Spencer's body. Edna got up from her chair, and as she went to help her mother, she collapsed on the floor.

Two days before the funeral Edna told her mother what had happened. "I know he said it. I couldn't believe it, but I know he said it."

"I believe you, sugar." Her mother, Lula, was a rather small muscular woman. Two or three shades darker than Edna, Lula had always embodied the unusual mixture of gregariousness and sternness. She could laugh the loudest and the longest. But she could cuss you out or smack you just as quick. And you didn't want to be hit by Lula when she was mad. Edna and her two sisters had the marks to prove it.

They sat at the kitchen table over hot tea. "So you said he was sayin' 'happy'?"

"Yes." Edna paused. "What do you think he was tryin' to say?"

"I think he said it, Edna. Happy." Lula sipped the sassafras tea. Death was a time for sassafras.

"When I try to sleep nowadays I keep hearin' him say it.

'Happ . . . e.' And sometimes it sounds like somethin' else. Not like happy at all. Like 'harpy' or 'hopey' or something like that."

"I'm sure it was 'happy.' Your father always talked about one day being happy."

"He wasn't happy?" Edna was a little surprised.

Lula chuckled. "Now, what colored man you know what got a family and a farm and can't walk nor talk, happy?"

"I know. But I mean, before he got sick. He was happy then, wasn't he?"

"Child, I know you sad 'cause your daddy died. God bless him. He's outta his misery now. Maybe he even happy now. But no, baby. Spencer never was happy. I tried. God knows I did. But that's the damn hardest thing you ever got to do."

"What's that, Momma?"

"Help a colored man be happy. All smiles and teeth they are sometimes. Fancy words and easy on the eyes for sure. But that ain't happy, girl. That ain't nowhere near happy."

Edna couldn't think of anything to say that day. But what Spencer had said to her did haunt. Was she supposed to be happy? Had he finally found his happiness? What had he tried to tell her?

When she was seventeen, her aunt Penny visited Lula and brought along her daughter, Felicia. Felicia was a couple of years older than Edna, but they became quick friends. Actually, Edna was awestruck by her witty, sophisticated cousin from Philadelphia. From Felicia's first visit to Stoney Grove, North Carolina, Edna had been consumed with the desire to move to the city.

While their mothers sat on the porch until the wee hours, talking and singing hymns, Edna was sprawled on her bed listening as Felicia told tale after tale of the urban African-American opera.

Felicia took such relish in her role as the sultry guide to the ways of the city and the pleasures it offered to a young black woman such as she. And she set about trying to convince Edna that it could be the same for her.

Felicia lay next to Edna, her beige palm-leaf-print sundress flowing around her, and spun the sweetest stories.

"Girl, I met him about three months ago at a party on this street called Jefferson Street. At a rent party." She paused and held one tan, thin arm aloft. "I was decked out that night, let me tell you. I went with my girlfriends, Sheila and Betsy. We strolled into that joint at about eight-thirty, and no sooner had I taken my jacket off when I felt these eyes on me."

"Eyes? What eyes?"

"The sweetest brown eyes. Doe eyes. Mmm-mmm."

Edna had never traveled out of North Carolina. She hadn't really thought much about it. She figured she'd eventually marry Joshua, the son of her church's principal deacon. He usually asked her to whatever dance or function occurred in their little town. Joshua was a hardworking man who was one of the top hands on old man Barkley's tobacco farm just outside of town during the summer. In the winter, after the tobacco was carted off to market, he did odd jobs wherever he could find them. In fact, one of the problems with Joshua was that he worked all the time. He and Edna hardly ever sat on the porch and watched the moon like other lovers.

And she was growing tired of that. She was attracted to him because he seemed to care about himself and his future, but all he could get were little low-paying jobs. Which meant he was always working. She never saw "happy" in him really. But she never mentioned her frustrations to Joshua. He was a year younger than her anyway. She figured he'd eventually realize that wives couldn't be bought at the grocery store. That he had to do more than sit beside a woman in a church pew and stroke her hand. Had to do more than gently put his arm around her waist when they stood to sing hymns. Even more than occasionally giving her a box of chocolates.

So she listened to Felicia's stories with rising curiosity. "What you say his name was?" Edna asked mindlessly. She didn't really care what his name was, but she wanted to prolong the story in every way she could. She had a feeling it would be more interesting than anything she could read in *Sepia* magazine. Even at twenty, she still didn't quite believe in love. At least not in the kind of love Felicia talked about. Hers was a heart-stopping, heavy-breathing music-in-the-background kind of love.

To Edna it seemed that each new story introduced a new boyfriend. And each time she had to interrupt and ask what had happened to the old one. Felicia would almost always respond by casually waving her hand in the air and saying, "I just got tired of that Negro."

Now, as Felicia had finally arrived at her latest love, Edna savored every detail just to keep her talking. And what a voice Felicia had. It was as clear as crystal and yet laced with the thickness of a woman enraptured. Edna thought, This here is a woman who knows about love. She could just tell. So she believed Felicia implicitly. Besides, Felicia talked about sex like no other woman Edna had ever known. None of her friends in Stoney Grove would ever say "clitoris" the way Felicia did.

And Felicia said that word every few minutes. "Chile, he pinched my clitoris so hard I liked to kicked him where his brains is," she said once. Or, "Brother Franklin knows a little about this clitoris. He really does." Or about another man she said, "Edna, I swear I don't think that man even knew I had a clitoris the way he was acting."

The first time Edna heard it, she must have struck a pose of shock and apoplexy because Felicia stopped talking and stared at her. After at least thirty seconds, Felicia asked, "What's wrong with you? You got a clitoris, don't you? You know what that is, don't you?"

"Yes," Edna sputtered. "I got one and I know what it is."

"Then why you lookin' at me like that?"

"Because you ain't supposed to be sayin' stuff like that." Edna stopped and then, "Are you?"

Felicia broke a big smile. In Edna's face she saw the fire. She knew Edna liked it. Liked her talking the way she did. Wanted more. She could tell. "I'm free, colored, and over twenty-one, honey child. I can say whatever I want. If I want to talk about my clitoris I can do just that. Now, is that okay with you, country girl?"

Edna felt a wave of embarrassment caress her. She was a country girl. She was a virgin. And she'd probably only said the word "clitoris" three or four times in her whole conscious life.

"It's okay, I reckon."

Now Edna stared at the ceiling waiting for Felicia to properly introduce her to her latest beau.

"His name is Rutherford."

Edna giggled. "Rutherford. Yeah, it's funnier the second time."

Felicia turned to face Edna. "What's funny about it?"

And Edna turned to Felicia. "Rutherford. That's what, city girl. What good is a colored man named Rutherford. That ain't right. But it's darn sure a funny name."

"I think it's cute. He's so tall and handsome. And nice."

"I didn't say he wasn't," Edna said softly. "I just think that name has got to go."

"Well, it's not. Rutherford B. Smith. Who knows, one day I might be Mrs. Rutherford B. Smith."

Edna sat up. "Wait, Felicia, don't skip ahead so much. What happened at the party when you met him?"

"Well, I felt these eyes on me and I just slowly turned around, expecting to see some broke Negro with bowlegs grinning at me, but what I saw was the prettiest set of eyes I had ever seen. And this smile that just melted my heart. Right there I felt like I went to water. Right there, chile."

Felicia curled up and hugged one of the pillows. "He comes over to me," she continued, half speaking into the pillow, "and he gets right up on me. I mean I could see everything about him. His eyes, his smile, his teeth, that black skin. Lord, Rutherford is dark, girl. I mean black like he come from right here. Like he been picking tobacco in the hot sun all his life. But this black man has got him a head full of curly hair. Soft as I don't know what. But I can't keep my fingers out of it. I mean, right there, I thought this man is near perfect. He must can't talk."

Edna laughed again. "Can't talk? You mean Rutherford can't talk?"

"Hush now and just listen. He just stood there in front of me. Not saying nothing. Just stood there. My friend Sheila asked him if he was all right. If he was sick or something. But he still didn't say a word. So she grabbed my arm and tried to pull me away so we could dance or something, but just then he leaned even closer to me and said, 'Girl, I don't know what your name is. I don't know where you stay at. I don't know if you got a man or nothin'. But before my momma died she gave me this here necklace,' and then he opens his shirt two buttons and I see that black skin like satin in those party lights and I almost fainted. But he shows me this necklace." With this, Felicia dipped her shoulders and shook loose the necklace she was wearing.

"And then he says, 'She gave me this and she said when you meet the woman you goin' to marry you give this to her.' I swear

131

that's exactly what he said and then he pulls it off and put it around my neck.

Edna swooned back into the bed with a flop and a short scream. "Lord, Lord. He just gave it to you. Just like that?"

"Just like that. Here it is. He wouldn't take it back."

"Then what happened?"

"Well, then, he grabbed my jacket and put it back on me and then he asked if I would take a walk with him."

"And you did?"

"Yessiree Bob I did. Turned myself right around and walked out of that joint with Rutherford B. Smith. Felt good about it, too."

"I don't believe you," Edna said, but she did. She could see the joy in Felicia's face.

"Now, that was a magical night, Edna. We walked all around North Philly that night. And nobody bothered us either. He is the sweetest man I ever met. I even kissed him that first night."

"Wow. So, is he the one?"

"I think so. I'm wearing this necklace, ain't I?" Felicia smiled. "There's all kinds of guys in Philly. You pretty enough to have your pick, Edna. If you come to live up there, you'll see what I mean. Men that got money and cars and know how to treat a woman like a lady. I mean, we have our share of fools, but it's not like here, where these men ain't got nothin'."

"The men down here ain't so bad." Edna felt like she had to speak up for North Carolina men. "They're respectful, mostly. And they make good family men. Good church men, too. They ain't so bad."

"But in Philly, Edna, there are men who drive buses and taxis, men who work in big buildings. Men who own their own businesses. Teachers. There's all kinds of men. There's just more different kinds. And they're not all rough with dirt and the smell of cows and pigs all up in their skin."

"I could move up there, couldn't I?" Edna blurted. It had been coming all night. The loves, parties, the promise of love for her. The promise of the unknown.

"Edna, you could be workin' in no time flat. Find yourself a man, get a house and everything. Just like in a magazine. Wear pretty clothes and have five, even ten pairs of shoes. You can do anything you want. And white people pretty much leave you alone. Sometimes I go days without seeing white people, unless I go to the store or something."

Edna was mostly silent the rest of the night. But she listened and later she dreamed. The next morning she made up her mind. It was time for her to go.

Two years later Edna was in Philadelphia. At nineteen, she had come North with a country girl's glazed eyes. They were glazed from day and night dreaming. From flipping through glossy pages. From imagining herself walking down a street with scores of people standing around and music in the air.

Felicia and Rutherford (who appeared a little chubbier and a little older than Felicia had led her to believe) picked her up at the bus station downtown. And from there they carried her deep into the heart of urban blackness.

She was immediately impressed by the loud red bricks and cement sidewalks. She brought with her the high hopes that Felicia had stoked and, of course, a kind of innocent purity. A Southern black woman's innocent purity, which showed up in the lightness of her voice, in the sheen and blaze of her eyes.

It wasn't long after she arrived in Philadelphia that she met Richard, a thin, maple-skinned man. Philly was full of available black men, just as Felicia had promised. Men whose voices sounded more like music than any she'd ever heard. Indeed, there was music in the words of her Carolina men, but it was different. Bluesier. Almost languid in its rhythm.

But Philly men talked with a rhythm that flowed in the wake of Cab Calloway. Zoot-suited rhythms. Cool beats. It was the 1920s and colored folks in the city defined coolness. Music was in the air, everywhere. She felt the excitement of being colored as the people around her flexed their freedom muscles.

It was true that black men were still being lynched. And Garvey was raising a ruckus in New York. But there was a feeling of optimism pulsing through the North Philadelphia community she lived in which worked its way under her skin. You could hear it in the way people talked. You could almost dance to it.

Richard's voice was like that.

Edna had taken a job working at a small restaurant on Ridge Avenue, not far from her apartment. It was the first real job of her life. She'd worked her father's farm, tended the animals, sold produce roadside, mended, darned, washed, ironed, and cooked nearly every day of life as the daughter of a farmer. But never worked for anyone else.

Almost instantly she realized that she didn't like it. From the very first day on the job she began dreaming of opening her own restaurant. Maybe it was the optimism in the air. The apparent prosperity of even the poor people around her; their willingness to buy pork chops and fish sandwiches made by other people. Whatever it was, Edna knew that she wanted her own business. She liked the idea of feeding people. She enjoyed the boisterous energy that filled the restaurant at lunch and again at dinner. She liked the immediate familiarity the customers showed the people who fed them.

Determined to make a good impression and also to make as much money as she could, Edna worked hard. She helped in the kitchen and waited tables. She would get to work early and stay until the doors were locked after dinner.

She met Richard late one early September Tuesday as she

walked home. He had been watching her. He had noted the times she passed him as he sat on a milk crate playing checkers with his friends.

Richard was a musician who played weekends at a nightclub on Fifty-second Street, the West Philly strip. On the days when he wasn't practicing his saxophone, he hung out on the corner playing checkers and watching the women. He had been meaning to stop Edna for days, but she had breezed by him so quickly he had sat frozen with his mouth open on a couple of occasions.

Edna was oblivious to people as she walked. She took in the smells, the sounds, the energy—from the greengrocers to the fishmongers to the hawkers of used furniture—of Ridge Avenue. But on this day she had stopped at the corner where Richard sat, trying to remember if she had left her keys in the hot kitchen of the restaurant. She searched her pocketbook.

"What you looking for, sweetie?" Richard's smooth face beamed at her.

She nearly panicked. She was already worried about her keys. She wasn't sure what to do. And even though she was ignited by the play of men and women that routinely described her world, even though she had her eyes opened to the possibility of love, she did not consider herself naive. With coolness and music came danger. She understood that. The same streets that sang to her could just as quickly consume. She knew that.

And regardless of the songs that emanated from the mouths of men, she was aware that she might simply be prey.

"Can I help you? You want some company?" Richard watched her rummaging through her bag. He got up from the crate. Another man who was standing with him immediately took the seat.

Richard walked right up to her. "Excuse me, miss. Er, um, I couldn't help but see you standing here. Fact of the matter is I been watching you for about a couple, three weeks. You come running through here like cheap whiskey. Where you be going so fast?"

Edna found her keys tucked under a fold in the lining of her bag. She looked up at Richard. "What?"

"Where you headin'?"

"I'm goin' home." She started moving again and stepped out into the street. Richard took up beside her.

"Mind if I walk with you?" He caught her Southern accent.

"It's a free country." It was a phrase often said in the streets of black Philadelphia as if it meant something.

"What's your name?"

She told him. He introduced himself. "Where you from?" he said, smiling. He felt an immediate attraction to women from the South. There was something more native, more animal about them.

"North Carolina."

"I thought so. Just come up?"

"About a month ago." Edna approached her street. She wondered if she could ever get used to the shadows that were present, even in the day, on the streets of Philadelphia.

"You still a gitchee, then." Richard laughed.

"A gitchee? What's that?"

"You know, a bumpkin. A pickaninny, a countrified colored gal."

Edna decided to end the conversation. It was one thing to put up with the lame lines, quite another to be insulted. "Thanks for walkin' me home, Richard."

He grabbed her arm. "Now don't go gettin' upset with me, Edna. I was just funnin' you. You know how we do." His smile entered her eyes and squirmed its way into her heart. "How about a date?"

"I . . . I don't think so." She pulled her arm free. But as she did she met his eyes. Found herself falling in. They were fierce tan eyes set in a flawless, slightly rounded face. Against his dark skin, the lightness of his eyes stood out. And he was tall, strong looking under his blue cotton short-sleeved shirt. His slicked-back hair sparkled like a black diamond.

Yes, Edna thought, she could see how a man like him could penetrate her flimsy defense. She knew he wouldn't quit. He could probably tell that she was just as curious as him. That she had, in fact, come hundreds of miles perhaps just to meet him.

"Come on, Edna, what's the matter? You have a boyfriend?"

"No. I don't have a boyfriend." She smiled at the thought. Yes, she read the black confession magazines and dreamed of love.

"Well, now, if you ain't got a boyfriend you got no excuse. Let me take you out on Friday night. You can come hear me play and then we can go to a party. How about it?"

"I don't think so." It was only fitting that he was a musician.

"Come on, Edna, you don't have nothing to worry about. I won't hurt you. What'ya say, brown sugar?"

"Friday?" Edna wavered. "Okay. Okay, Richard."

"Well, alrooooot. That's the way I like it."

"What?" He streamed words together too fast for her. She knew exactly what he was saying, but it came at her in a jumble.

"Friday, baby cakes, Friday at seven."

Edna watched him head back into the darkening facade of storefronts and standing people. She clutched her purse close to her heart and went into her apartment.

That Friday afternoon Edna couldn't deny her excitement. She had taken the afternoon off and spent the time choosing clothes and preparing for her date.

Richard picked her up right on time. She wore a floral-print dress which flowed from the waist. The bodice was snug and flattered her strong features. Richard's black three-button wide-lapeled suit surprised her.

"Well, alrooot," he said as she left her apartment. "I knew you was sweet, but you gonna drive them boys wild out there tonight. But you just better remember, sister. You're mine tonight. Don't let none of them boys mess with you while I'm onstage or I'm gonna have to come down there and bust me some heads." He grinned at her.

Edna nodded her head, speechless. No one had ever made a fuss over her before.

Richard drove a new 1927 Rambler. Edna couldn't help but caress the leather seats as they cut through the city.

"How you get a car like this?" she asked.

"I wish I could tell you it was mine, sugarplum, but it's my boss's. He just lets me use it now and then. Especially when I got a gal like you to put in it."

At the Bluebird nightclub Richard became an alto saxophone in a jazz quartet. He got Edna a good seat in front of the stage then climbed up to begin his set.

Edna watched him closely. He stood above her spewing flowers into the air. He mimicked birds and shooting stars. He roared like a train and pressed blues into the hands of the outstretched. Edna swooned. Bebop rose like a prairie fire all around her. For someone so skinny, the sound that came from his horn was as thick as honey.

The audience swelled and surrounded her with heat. The smoke and the swirling music dusted her mind with dizziness. She found herself standing and clapping, her body moving to the beat. There were times when Richard was in the middle of a solo and would first look out at Edna, find her eyes, then thrust his hips out as the horn shouted gospel to her. She had to admit that her heart actually skipped.

After the last show Richard left the stage and grabbed her arm. "Come on, sugar, I got plans for you." Edna let him guide her out of the club and into the city air.

"Where we goin'?" she asked.

"Take a little ride. When I play like that, I get all worked up. I need to get out in the air with a pretty girl and get myself together again."

She nodded again. In the car she put her head back onto the seat. This was the city. The movement fast. The lights bright. She felt his hand on her thigh as they turned into Fairmount Park. Her stomach palpitated.

"I'm gonna park right here," he said as he pulled the car off the road.

"Where is this?"

"George's Hill." He broke into a broad smile. "This is the place."

Edna could only see the glint of the faint light on his teeth and the sparkle that flashed in his eyes. "What place?"

"The perfect place, sugar. The perfect place to meet ol' Dick." She couldn't see him yet, but his voice had changed tone.

She giggled. "Who's this ol' Dick?"

Richard grabbed her hand and put it between his legs. Edna immediately went to pull it away, but he held her firm. "Now, sweets, that's ol' Dick. He's hard up to meet you, too."

The laugh left her throat. "That's okay, Richard. I don't want to meet him."

"Sure you do." He was now pulling her to him. When her face was in reach his arm slithered around her neck and pulled her to him. He kissed her. She tried to hold him off, but his arms were like ropes. "The music was for you, sugar. So is this."

"But I don't like this, Richard. Now let me go. I like you, but I don't want no funny business." Edna leaned as far back as she could. Now she could see his face. He appeared like a demon, red-faced and threatening.

"Now come on, sugar, don't go acting like some pickaninny. I thought you was hep. You know the score." He pulled her back. Edna felt his hands on the zipper on the back of her dress. She felt the material give way.

"Stop now, Richard." He kissed her again. She tried to match his energy and pull away. But he seemed irrepressible. Then she felt his hands on her breasts, fumbling with her bra. Then his fingers on her skin. On her nipples. She jumped. "I said stop it, Richard."

"And I told you once, girl, don't act so country. This is the scene. This is it."

"Well, this ain't it for me." She broke free. Edna tried to compose herself. Her body was screaming. It wanted him. It wanted to let go.

Richard leaned back against the driver's door and unzipped his pants. He brought his penis into the night air. "This here is ol' Dick. He wants to say hello. Now come on over here, girl, and give ol' Dick a handshake."

"Why are you doin' this?" Edna was a mass of confusion. She hadn't expected this kind of treatment. Is this what being in the city meant? That men forgot the way in which love is made? Discovered?

"Goddammit, bitch. What do you want? Huh? I spent my money on you. Bought you drinks. Got me a car and you won't even give me a little nooky? Now, I done told you this ain't South Jablip. You in the big city now. That's the way it goes here."

"I can't do it like this, Richard." Edna didn't want to lose him altogether. But she had to explain to him that she had saved herself for the special night. The special man.

"Then get out my car." He zipped his pants up and started the car.

"What?" Edna wanted to talk.

"Get the fuck out of this car. Walk the hell home if you can't give me no drawers. 'Cause that's what I want."

Tears flooded her eyes. It was a dark city. A big city. She opened the door and walked into the pitch. Two hours later she crawled into her bed, tired, angry, and hurt.

Three weeks later she gave herself to a Pullman porter who came into the restaurant. It had been quick and painful. She struggled to understand the nature of her sexual needs and how they never seemed to coincide with the way she was treated. But the Pullman porter was hardly ever around and so their relationship was one of convenience and education. One of the wonderful things he had done for her was to take her to Rehoboth Beach one weekend and show her around West Rehoboth. She had immediately fallen in love with the small town.

And finally, after only a year in Philadelphia, she moved to West Rehoboth. After her experience in the city she came to believe that no one wanted to see her grow and blossom like a mother's dream. No one wanted that for *her* sake. No one she had yet met, cared.

7

Rufus felt the hot swish of a breeze move away the veil that had enshrouded Edward and him. He blinked his eyes deliberately in an attempt to clear his vision enough to find Edward's face, which should have been just in front of him.

Yes. There he was. But the boy's eyes were closed tight. His eyelids in a state of total surrender. Although, just below them, Rufus could see Edward's eyes moving as if the boy were looking first this way and then the other even with his eyelids closed. As if a marble were rolling around under each eyelid.

"Eddie?" Rufus whispered. "Eddie, you still with me?"

Edward didn't respond. But Rufus could see that he was still breathing, although the breaths came intermittent, sometimes light, others heavy and strong.

"I be goddamned. I shoulda figured somethin' like this would happen. They was right, Eddie. You shoulda listened to them."

Suddenly he saw Edward's eyes open. The boy stared at him

for a few seconds and then said, "But you . . . who are you? How did we get here?"

Rufus watched as Edward slowly closed his eyes again. After a few seconds he wasn't sure whether or not Edward had said anything at all. Still the question reverberated. But he didn't need Edward to ask it for him. It was always banging around in his head. It was the thing which led to the thing that haunted him. He was constantly living backward. And in his mind he was trying to sort it all out. Untangle the threads that had wound themselves into a tight ball of confusion.

He started crying again, the alcohol coursing through his body just enough to numb his pain and stir his collapsing mind. Through the tears Edward's face began to transform. Suddenly Rufus saw himself at twelve, lying in his bed in his parents' house.

And then the alarm clock began clanging. His mother had given it to him when he was nine because he was so hard to wake up for school. He grabbed it off the nightstand and depressed the button that snuffed its ringing.

As usual he immediately felt the emptiness of the house. His mother had died of tuberculosis two years before, when he was ten. He was used to getting up and trundling down to the kitchen and preparing his cereal and milk alone. His father was long gone, headed downtown to take up his space at Penn Station, where he shined shoes.

Until the year she died, Rufus's mother would have made breakfast for him. Not cereal either; pancakes and sausage and eggs and toast. And then she, too, would head off to her job at the Blakehursts' family house in Georgetown, where she served as nanny and maid.

She had worked for the Blakehursts since before he was born, and nearly all of his early memories of her were centered on his young years spent riding the bus with her and running loose in the huge Blakehurst house.

Indeed, when Rufus thought of his mother he felt her presence still in their small row house in the Anacostia neighborhood. She had such great hopes for him. But the cough set in and she began to slow down. He'd tended to her, watched her weaken, watched her fade until one day when he came home from school to an empty house, he knew before he even saw the note his father had written that she was dead.

She tried to prepare him. Made him promise to mind his father. To behave himself. To grow up to be a good man. And Rufus had fought the tears and nodded and said, "Yes, Momma. I'll be all right." And, "No, Momma, I won't get into trouble."

And for a while, after she was gone, it *was* all right and he didn't get into trouble. His father seemed to work even longer hours, leaving him alone for long periods. The early years of his isolation were spent with his face pressed against the living-room window watching the life that moved outside, waiting for his father to come home.

His father always promised to be home by the time Rufus returned from school. And sometimes he was. But it was unpredictable. Sometimes he was home at three in the afternoon, and other times he staggered home drunk well after Rufus was asleep. Rufus understood how lonely it was for his father and how hard he had to work to pay all the bills.

Rufus had been close to his mother, but his father had always been a steel drum. Sealed shut. He worked, usually did what he was supposed to do, but he hardly ever talked and laughed even less. He was not cut out to raise Rufus alone, but he rejected any suggestion that he give Rufus up.

Rufus had set the clock for nine-thirty even though it was Saturday morning. The earlier he completed his chores his father

had left in a list taped to the icebox, the quicker he'd get out of
the house. He had a freedom that other boys envied. He could do
whatever he wanted all day long. It had been that way ever since
his mother passed.

But slowly Rufus began testing the limits of his freedom. He
started playing hooky and hanging out with older boys, and by
the time he was twelve, Rufus was well known as a troublemaker.

He was big for his age, stocky and strong. And when he
wanted to he could look mean. He could sound mean, too. And
sometimes, when it called for it, he could be mean. He'd beaten
up enough kids to have garnered a reputation for being good with
his hands.

Ever since he could remember he was the biggest and baddest
kid around.

As he scrubbed the bathroom or swept the living room, or
sprayed for roaches in the kitchen, he made his plan for the day.
First he'd check all of his father's pants pockets and under the
cushions of the couch for any change that might be found. Usually he could rustle up at least a dime. But if he couldn't, he
always knew where he could get some money.

He would just go find Jasper, his friend, and together they'd
walk across town near a movie theater and grab some innocent
unsuspecting white kid and steal his money. This had nearly
become a habit.

He blamed that on his father. He hated the way his father
always walked with his head down. How he only raised his voice
before he was about to hit someone, usually Rufus. How he
became a cube of rapidly melting ice whenever a white man was
around.

Young Rufus could wax eloquent on the details of robbing
other kids. He was intoxicated by the sense of power he felt. How
scared of him they seemed. Most kids just dropped their money

on the ground and took off when confronted with a menacing and threatening Rufus.

The previous year, when he was eleven, he'd stumbled on the idea of filling one of his socks with rocks that he'd wield in a pinch. He'd only used it one time, but that time had created a legend on the streets. Some of the kids called him "Blackjack" after that.

Rufus was already on the street when he remembered he'd left his weapon of choice home. But just as he had decided to go back for it, he saw his friend Jasper. Jasper was taller than Rufus but much thinner. The only problem Rufus had with him was that Jasper would rather play or try to talk to the girls than make money. In a pinch, Rufus wasn't sure he could count on him.

Rufus and Jasper had their own special signal to each other. Rufus had never been able to whistle, which was the way most of the boys signaled each other. So instead he and Jasper sort of scatted. *"Eeeeeeoowwwwkeeeeee,"* they would scream, trying to catch the register of a strong whistle. It sounded like the falsetto of an out-of-control singer.

"Eeeeeeoowwwwkeeeeee," Rufus sang.

"Eeeeeeoowwwwkeeeeee," Jasper returned, and slowly began running in Rufus's direction. Actually Jasper loped, his long legs uncoiling and extending with every stride. He'd been a block away, but in a few blinks, there he was pulling up beside Rufus.

"Hey, Rufe, where you goin'?"

"Where you think I'm goin'? I'm headed down to the Bijou. Almost time for the Saturday matinee. Maybe I'll catch me a little fish."

"I figured that. I knew you was gonna want to go down there."

Jasper paused but kept stride with Rufus. "I don't know, boy, my momma told me not to go more than three blocks away."

"Why?" Rufus didn't like Jasper's mom. She was always interfering in his plans.

"I don't know. 'Cause she's my momma, I guess."

"But you don't have to do what she say all the time." Rufus could tell by the tone of Jasper's voice and the fact that his stride was slowing that they were reaching the boundary limits Jasper's mom had set. He stopped and turned to Jasper. "We can go. It'll be fine. Just like it is every other time. I need to get me some money."

"I know, Rufe. I know. But my momma wasn't playin' and you know how she is. I don't want no whippin' today. Plus she said she wouldn't let me have no ice cream tomorrow. And you know we always get ice cream on Sunday afternoon."

"Aw, boy, you act like a baby."

"I ain't no baby; I just don't want her whippin' my behind, that's all." Jasper paused again and stretched the features of his face to show how hard this decision was for him, "You know how she is, Rufe."

"Yeah, I know. Well . . . I'm still goin'.'"

Jasper looked past Rufus to see a group of girls turn the corner. They were obviously about to play double Dutch jump rope, something he liked to watch. "Okay, well, I gotta head back toward home. She'll be lookin' for me in a minute."

"I'm gonna get me the biggest ice-cream cone you ever seen. In about ten minutes. Triple dip. And a hot sausage, too." He stared at Jasper, who actually licked his lips.

"You gonna get a hot sausage sandwich, too?"

"Yup."

"How you know you can get that much money?"

Rufus waved his right hand in the air. "You watch and see. I might even give you a quarter when I get back."

Jasper couldn't think of anything to say.

Rufus tried one more time to persuade his friend. "You sure now? I'm tellin' you, we could be back here before your momma even know you gone." He could see a glimmer of reconsideration flash in Jasper's eyes. And then they both heard something that sent a shiver through their bodies.

"Jasssperrrr!" It was Jasper's mother. They looked at each other and knew there was no need for further discussion.

"See you later," Jasper said, and began running back toward his house. Rufus shook his head as he heard him scream, "Mom. Mom. I'm comin'. Here I am."

Ten minutes later Rufus approached the block where the movie theater was. It was his favorite spot to find his victims. There were always one or two kids who had somehow gotten permission to go to the movies alone.

Rufus would usually walk past the theater deeper into the white neighborhood, trying not to run into any groups of white kids. A lone colored boy in a white neighborhood was as much a target as the unlucky kid Rufus wanted to find.

And then he saw one. He was a skinny, redheaded boy, probably nine or ten. Perfect. Rufus took a deep breath and puffed his chest. He put a hitch in his walk, what the older gang members called a "stroll," and approached the ruddy-faced boy.

"Where you goin'?" Rufus asked with as much edge as he could muster.

The boy was startled by Rufus. Probably more surprised that a colored boy was in his neighborhood than he was by the question.

"You heard me, white boy. Where you goin'?" Rufus knew

that the message was received. The boy started backing up. "You goin' to the movies, ain't you? Ain't you?"

"Yeah."

"Gimme your money."

"I can't give you my money. I need it to get in."

"You ain't goin' to the movies. Not with that money in yo' pocket. 'Cause that's my money now."

"I'm not giving you my money." Rufus could see tears rising in the boy's eyes. He knew it was almost over.

"White boy, lissen to me. I don't take no stuff. If you don't give me your money, I'm gonna beat you up somethin' bad."

Rufus grabbed the boy's shirt and the boy burst into tears. "Don't hurt me. I didn't do nothin' to you. Why you botherin' me?"

"I told you I want your money. Now give it to me." Rufus was shaking the kid back and forth.

"Okay. Okay." And with that the boy tried to stifle his crying and retrieve the change in his pocket at the same time. "Here it is. Here."

Rufus reached out and grabbed the money, and instantly turned to run away. He took two steps, and just as he was about to accelerate, his adrenaline pulsing, he realized he was about to run into a big white fleshy mass. He tried to veer off to the side, not even sure what it was he was trying to avoid. It didn't matter because the mass, which was actually a much bigger boy, extended an arm and knocked Rufus to the ground.

Another big kid dove on top of him and pinned him to the ground. Rufus went into a fit. He kicked and writhed and squirmed, but he couldn't break free and he couldn't do any damage. At that moment he wished with all his heart that he'd brought the blackjack with him. But he was literally defenseless.

Suddenly the action around him slowed and Rufus could see

that there was a small but growing crowd of white bodies around him. But instead of rage and anger, he heard laughter. Slowly, as his ears attenuated to the rising ruckus, Rufus could hear them.

Hope sat next to him on the ground, a pained smile, a worried look on her face which she angled gently in his direction as if he were the lover she'd always desired. on the other side Despair sat shaking his head. tsk tsk tsk. such a long way from home.

"You a stupid nigger, ain't ya, boy?" one said. "He come over here thinkin' he can just rob and steal."

"But we got you this time. We got you."

And then the huge kid who'd first knocked him down stepped out of the crowd, which now included what looked to Rufus like adults. Rufus looked directly into a woman's face and began pleading.

"Please. I didn't mean it. Please let me go. I won't do it no more. I promise."

But she looked at him like he was a picture she was trying to memorize so that she could write a poem about it when she got home.

and Hope knew no way to intervene in a way that would save him from the shame that awaited.

The big kid bent down. "You're a tough little nigger, huh?" But he didn't wait for Rufus to respond; instead he straightened himself and called for the kid that Rufus had accosted. "Jimmy. Where's Jimmy?"

Someone pushed Jimmy forward. "Get your money." Jimmy reached down and opened Rufus's hands, causing the money to fall out. Three quarters hit the ground. Jimmy picked them up, all the time staring at Rufus with a mix of fear and pity.

"Why don't you pick on someone your own size?" The big kid was now back down in Rufus's face.

Rufus erupted into tears. "I'm sorry. I won't do it no more."

The kid grabbed Jimmy and brought his face down so that the three of them were inches apart. "Look at him, Jimmy. Look at this piece of shit. We can't let these people come in our neighborhood and take our money. We got to teach this bastard a lesson."

eyes closed, Hope rose like smoke and wafted gently before dissipating. the future was for them and not for them.

"Whatcha gonna do, Bailey?" Jimmy asked softly. His voice was barely audible over Rufus's whimpering.

"It's not what I'm gonna do. This is your job. You was the one he robbed. You got to teach him a lesson so he won't ever come over here again."

"I got my money. You can let him go." Jimmy tried to back up.

"No!" Bailey screamed. "No. I'm not lettin' this nigger go until he knows he can't ever come back over here."

Rufus tried to take advantage of Jimmy's reticence. "I promise. I know better. I know now. I'll never come over here again. I won't. I—"

But Bailey smacked him hard on the head. "That's not good enough, blackie."

When Rufus felt the heel of Bailey's hand against his temple, he screamed, hoping someone would come to his rescue. But all he heard from the crowd were guffaws and taunts. Someone even started saying, "Kill that nigger. Kill him."

Bailey caught Jimmy's arm and pulled him closer. "You got to do it, Jimmy."

ALEXS D. PATE

"What you want me to do?"

"I want you to hit him one time for each quarter he tried to
take from you. Three times, hard. Right in the face."

*but Despair slowly patted his extended arm and smirked.
there would be time in the future for love. today was for passion, love would come later.*

Jimmy stared at Bailey, and then at Rufus. "I can't do that."

"You got to, Jimmy. You got to." Rufus heard others pushing
him on.

He cut his eyes to Jimmy, intending to plead one more time,
when he saw Jimmy's little fist heading for his eye. An explosion
of blackness cascaded in his mind. And then he felt another
punch square on the jaw and a third on his nose. He heard someone cheer. He heard them all cheering. Laughing. He felt the
blood from his nose pooling in the ridge between his lips.

"We ought to kill you for comin' over here. But we're gonna let
you go to tell all those other thievin', lyin', lazy niggers never to
come over here bothering us again. Or they'll get the same treatment. You got that, boy?"

Rufus nodded his head and tried to get up. But the boy who
was holding him slammed him down again. "I didn't say you
could go yet, did I, boy? Did I?"

"No," Rufus mumbled. His head throbbed in four places.

"Jimmy, take his pants off."

"Why?"

"Just do it," Bailey barked.

Rufus felt someone taking his shoes off and then sliding his
pants down. There was more laughter. Bailey roughly snatched
his shirt off as well. He lay there, in his sleeveless undershirt and
his slightly dingy white cotton briefs.

"Let him up now." Rufus slowly got up. "Now you can go, nigger. Get out of here."

Rufus quickly scanned the crowd. He could see at least fifteen people standing around him. Almost all of them were smiling. And the ones that weren't looked angry. Like they were sorry Bailey was letting him go.

"What about my clothes?"

"What clothes?" Bailey smiled at him. "If you want these old rags back, then you're gonna have to fight me to get them." With that, he took a step toward Rufus. And this was enough to turn Rufus in the direction of home. He ran so fast despair could only haunt his shadow.

Of course, when he made it back to his neighborhood, Rufus was treated to another full helping of ridicule. Even Jasper laughed at him.

"I told you, boy, about goin' over there. I told you. Them peckerwoods is heartless. They even took your clothes." He couldn't help laughing as he walked Rufus to his house. "Bet you won't do that again," he said to Rufus's back, and then to a closed door. "Bet you won't do that again."

Bruised, bleeding, and in pain, Rufus collapsed on his bed in tears. He would never escape the memory of that Saturday afternoon. Never. He closed his eyes and cried himself to sleep, hoping his mother would materialize out of the air and bring with her a whole new life for him. But she didn't.

Rufus saw himself in Edward's unconscious face and remembered how his father did come home early that evening and took care of his wounds. Rufus told him that he'd gotten jumped by a group of white boys when he tried to go to the library. But he knew he didn't believe him because his father slowly began to lecture him. He asked Rufus to look at how his behavior had brought all this trouble on himself. How his mother would not be happy with the way he was living. He threatened to beat him, but he didn't.

Altogether it had been a horrible day. It had marked him. From that day on, Rufus always felt something, something which was like a weight draped around his body. Dragging him down. Holding him back. Drowning him.

Rufus called to Edward again. "Eddie? Eddie?" But the boy was out. Rufus once again felt himself slipping away. "Eddie." Was on his lips as he passed into time.

8

Edna was more at home in Rehoboth Beach. It was nothing like the city. In many ways it was a rural town peopled by refugee city dwellers. Things were slower and smaller in this vacation hideaway. From the beginning she felt stronger there.

She'd been working as a cook at the Supper Bell Inn, an expensive seafood restaurant in downtown Rehoboth, for two years when she met Rufus.

Some nights during her break she would sit on a stool and eat expensive lobster, sweet white lump crabmeat, or Delaware's fine softshell crabs. She could eat the food as long as she stayed in the kitchen. No black person had ever eaten in the dining room. But Edna would sit there and dream of the day when she would own her own restaurant. And in that restaurant she would offer the best food a black person could buy in West Rehoboth.

Rufus appeared one evening, led by Edna's portly boss into the kitchen. Edna quickly discovered by listening to their conversation that Rufus worked for a family-owned fish company in Lewes. He delivered and took orders for freshly caught fish. On this particular occasion, he was displaying the quality of the newest delivery.

Back then, Rufus always dressed in starched and pressed railroad overalls with a crisp white T-shirt underneath. He wore a blue baseball cap with a *B* on it to celebrate Jackie Robinson's Brooklyn Dodgers. Hanging low on his hip was a long sheath for his fishing knife. His shoes sparkled under his overalls.

Edna was immediately curious.

She watched him out of the corner of her eye as she brought a piece of a lightly sautéed crab cake to her mouth. Rufus noticed and turned from the white man and focused his eyes on her, hoisting a tremendous smile across his face.

She saw this cute little boy in a man's body. It wasn't, she thought, like he looked so good or prosperous or happy or anything like that; but like he was fighting to keep from being sad.

She felt the same much of the time. Some people went around talking about being happy and all, but she almost didn't believe it. Who was happy? The white people who owned the restaurant she worked in? Their kids out on the beach in the middle of the night drunk and doing God knows what? And their marriages all messed up. Were they happy? She'd spent nearly all of her time in Rehoboth working for white people and she hadn't seen much happiness. And she definitely didn't know a Negro who she thought was happy. Of course there were plenty of people trying to act like they were. But if they got to drinking you'd find out different real quick. Some people were just good at hiding their pain. Fighting against sadness. That was a part of what it meant to be colored.

Yes. She saw that in Rufus from the get-go. And she appreciated somebody who was at least trying not to fall apart altogether.

She could see the scars, little marks on his hands that told her he had not had an easy life. But there he was. Standing right over there beaming at her as if she couldn't see right through him.

Her boss seemed stunned that Rufus would turn his back on him. He grunted a couple of times and Rufus returned his attention to his work. But ten minutes after the white man had shown him out of the back door, Rufus was back.

"And who is this fine woman who's forced to eat in the kitchen? They should be waiting on you." He nearly sauntered in the door, easing the screen door closed.

Edna smiled, but her mouth was too full to respond. She tried to keep the food in her mouth. Rufus rescued her by saying, "No . . . don't say a word. Lordy, is this my lucky day or has I died and moved upstairs? Naw, baby, don't say a thing. Let me introduce myself. Rufus C. Brown, captain of my own boat, and if I'm lyin' I'm flyin', you the prettiest gal I ever seen in this whole state of Delaware."

Edna covered her mouth. She watched him wave his arms outlandishly as he talked. She cleared her mouth to say something like, "Aw shucks, go on with that stuff," when he said, "What's your name, baby?"

She looked away. He was full of the game. But it had been a while since she'd been intrigued by a man, and everyone was always trying to fix her up with someone. So she found her lips moving. "Edna."

"And where can I find you when I want you?" Rufus tried his best to keep his voice strong. He'd never been good with women. It was something he'd never learned. He'd moved around too much. Drunk too much. He'd already done a couple of tours in the Merchant Marines and all he knew was what he could pay for.

"I'm staying over cross the bridge; I'm stayin' at Beatrice Parker's place."

But Rufus knew how to sound sharp. "Oh yeah? Now I know it's my lucky day. I know that gal. She lives back over there in nigger town. Tell you what, sugarplum, I'll be back in about a week, and when I comes to Rehoboth I want my first mate standin' by." With that and a parting "good-bye," Rufus turned and walked out of the kitchen entrance.

In the following days, Edna sought information about the curious Mr. Brown from a host of sources, not the least of whom was her new best friend, Beatrice Parker, who had a rather large house and had rented out a room to her. But Beatrice, who knew Rufus through a girlfriend, could only tell Edna that he was originally from Washington, D.C., and little else. Even without specifics Edna knew Rufus's story was complicated. When she thought about it, every colored man she'd ever met had a story to beat the band. Still Edna was waiting with a thumping chest when Rufus came to the restaurant the next time.

He brought flowers and a Whitman's Sampler. Although Joshua back in Stoney Grove had brought her candy once or twice, when she saw Rufus standing there with his arms full of things for her, it felt like the first time it had ever happened. She swooned under his gaze in the wet-floored kitchen. There was something about Rufus which worked itself into her. In her heart she knew better, but he smiled so easily, could light up so brightly. Amid the crabs and the shrimps they smiled at each other and made promises to meet again.

On their first date, he brought her a bushel of clams and a newspaper-wrapped "mess" of fish. They sat in Bea's living room, looking at pictures and talking about the places he had traveled. Later that night, after Bea came in from work, had eaten dinner, and gone to bed, they held hands on the porch.

"Gal, if this ain't a strange thing. First time I come over here and you feed me some good food and give me such good company. And you ain't once asked me for nothing. Every woman I ever came to see has gotten around to askin' me for something."

She looked at the fried fish on the table between them and said, "I guess I don't have to ask, huh? Besides, if you want me to ask you for something, I ain't had a proper chance at it yet." Edna smiled. Even then Edna could feel tension under the surface. But when she looked at his face, all she felt was his growing affection for her. He seemed so sincere.

Rufus saw his future in her. He'd stumbled around for too many years.

For three consecutive weekends, Rufus drove the ten miles from Lewes to visit Edna. On the third Sunday he suggested she move to Lewes so they could spend more time together.

She'd listened to his stumbling suggestion with mild surprise. "To Lewes? Go back with you to Lewes?" Edna asked. "What I got in Lewes?"

"You'd have me." Rufus had no real style. It was all superficial, the jive lingo and all. He just wanted someone to be with.

"I got you in Rehoboth Beach, what I need to go to Lewes for?"

" 'Cause that's where I am."

"Why don't you just move to Rehoboth if you want to be close by. Lewes is just up the road anyway. We don't need to change nothin', Rufus. Things are just fine the way they are."

"So you won't come?"

"There ain't no reason for it, Rufus. Besides, this is where I want to open my restaurant. I don't want to live in Lewes. All the black folks live right around here."

At first, Rufus thought that Edna would give in. Actually he wasn't even sure why he wanted her in Lewes so much. But the more she protested, the more the idea grew on him. But after a few days, she refused to even talk about it. For the next two weeks, he couldn't make himself do anything. He stopped going to work. Stopped doing anything. Within a month, Rufus did the only thing he could think of. He moved to Rehoboth.

"I quit my job," he told her, full of hope and excitement. "I'm gonna find something in Rehoboth to tide me over until we work things out."

"What things, Rufus?"

"Well, I got some things in mind for us, Edna. You just wait and see. When I'm done with you, you gonna love yourself too much Rufus Brown."

"I don't know what you're expecting, Rufus. But I'm no Do Drop hussy. You just remember that."

"How could I forget it, Edna?"

"How come you like me anyway?" Edna stared at him, looking for some sign to help her understand him.

" 'Cause you got spunk, woman. You ain't afraid to speak your mind and you're tough. I like that. Besides, you cook the best goddamn ribs I ever ate." He grinned.

But Rufus had his dark side, which Edna soon found out. He had a hard time holding on to a job. She discovered later that he had been fired from his job in Lewes.

Rufus had a temper that he sometimes could not control. He would zip off into a fit if things didn't work out for him. That was his history. He'd been fired from one job after another, usually for fighting. It was the same in the Merchants. Rufus was constantly in trouble. And nothing really changed even after he moved to Rehoboth.

He had only been in Rehoboth a month when he tangled with one of Edna's old boyfriends who had come by unexpectedly. She had been embarrassed by Rufus's bold assumption that he had to protect her. To make matters worse, Rufus almost never won any of his fights. He was always the one with swollen purple eyes and split lips. He was always the one lying in the road.

Once, as Bud, the local iceman, passed Edna and Rufus on the road to Beatrice's house, he mumbled something and tipped his hat. Edna felt Rufus's ugly energy rise instantaneously.

"What you say?" Rufus stopped in the road and turned back to the horse-drawn wagon.

Bud reined his horse, Billy, to a stop. "Nice day to y'all."

"Naw, Bud, I want to know what you said." Rufus walked toward the older man. "I heard you say something about my woman. What did you say?"

"Fine day is all. Fine day ahead and behind you. That's all." Bud smiled.

"I'm gonna kick your ass, you nasty old son of a bitch." Rufus started for the wagon. Edna came up on him quickly, though, and grabbed his arm.

"What's wrong with you, man? He ain't done nothin' to me. You neither."

"He's talkin' 'bout you."

"He ain't doing nothing of the sort. Just let him be. Now you come on."

Rufus looked up at the still-smiling Bud and grimaced. "If I hear you say somethin' about my woman again, I'm gonna kill you."

Bud looked down at him with seeming disinterest. "You want a block of ice, Mr. Rufus? Give it to you real cheap. Ain't gonna do nothin' but melt anyway."

"I don't want your goddamned ice. You just better watch your step."

Edna dragged him away. It was like that constantly. Rufus puffing out his chest and accusing people of cheating him, talking behind his back, of trying to make fun of him. He seemed ready to die on a dime. This was what she'd feared. Something was eating him up, tearing away at that ability he'd had to fight against the sadness. She saw it overtake him. She couldn't help thinking that she'd contributed to it, but she couldn't figure out what it was. She hadn't even known him that long. In the end, she decided that this *was* the way he was and everything else had been an act. The fact was that he was already drowning in sadness.

And yet Rufus was oblivious to his faults. He pursued Edna as if he were a prince. From the day he came to town, and nearly every time he visited her, which was almost daily, Rufus would ask Edna to marry him. Edna had already seen enough. She liked him but didn't want to marry him. So she always rebuffed him on the grounds that they had a good friendship and needn't complicate it with marriage. But Rufus was persistent.

Even when he started drinking, as he did after many fruitless winter weeks of looking for a job, he dedicated himself to making Edna his wife. He was obsessed with her. No matter what he did, every day ended with Rufus coming to Edna's for a late-night cup of coffee. If he was lucky she would invite him to stay the night.

On those nights, if he was sober enough to manage it, he would try to pound her into submission with his sex. He would throw everything in himself into her. But Edna knew how to take it without giving herself away. The next day he had no more control over her than he'd had the day before. It both frustrated him and kept him coming back.

As this routine settled into place, Edna did begin to anticipate his visits. Rufus gave her someone to talk to. Sometimes she didn't care whether he was so drunk that he could only collapse on her couch. She would tell him about expansion plans, new ways to make money, the people she missed in North Carolina. He had become her companion. After about six months of this courtship, such as it was, she was almost ready to say yes to him despite what it might portend.

She had not opened herself to anyone since she had moved

poolroom at night, racking the balls, settling bets, and warding off fights.

But the passion that had momentarily flashed between them had dissipated. Rufus had moved in, but he had his own room on the second floor (hers was on the first) of her new building, where he spent his free time, usually drinking. Sometimes he would slip off to the Do Drop. He had to sneak to do it because Edna had declared the Do Drop Inn off-limits. His weekly forays there were always charged with the confrontation that awaited him when he returned.

The Do Drop Inn was the source of many downfalls. Rufus was just one of many. One night he walked the seventy-five yards to the end of Hebron Avenue, where the Do Drop was just beginning to fill.

It was a Saturday night, nearly ten o'clock. And the roads leading to the Do Drop were streamed with people in fancy clothes, colors flashing, hair pomade scenting the already heavily scented air.

The birds quieted into a whisper and the moist seashore air hung heavy amid the heat and cooled it down to a mild boil. A kind of boil that doesn't bubble but sends rabid dogs running and crying babies into a fitful, sweaty sleep. Throughout the town, young black mothers prayed that their children would find peace within the envelope of night. That they would not call out. The mothers were in search of respite, and crying babies were the only calls to which they were forced to respond. And on a Saturday night in West Rehoboth, responding was meant to be a voluntary act. Especially for young mothers.

In the slow sounds of dusk, one could hear the music of the older children playing and racing in the front yards. They played innocent games with new meanings. Where they did a five-ten ringo or a hide-and-seek with a twist. The girls would hide and the boys would find, and before they lost each other, a kiss was passed, or maybe a caress.

It was the beauty of the moonglow that washed into the minds of those of West Rehoboth. But it was still early. Still very early indeed.

Rufus sat at a table in the corner of the large dark room. The bar stretched the length of the building, which was as long as a barn. He sat there nursing a shot of rye and a nip, a small bottle of Rolling Rock beer.

Sitting at the bar just in front of him was T Hall. T Hall was a dishwasher. His days were endless barrages of baked porcelain, china, and silver passing before his tough black-red hands as they went in and out of burning hot water. And after all the dishes and silverware were clean, the chefs would bring in the pots, sticky with the remnants of lobster thermidor and mashed potatoes and whatever else they cooked for the hungry tourists.

T Hall had a crease across his face. A wound taken in personal combat from unknown opponents many years back. It was a five-inch scar that caused his jawl to smile at you if you stood close to him. There were times when a person could glance quickly at a mumbling T Hall and swear that his scar had talked. It was the way that T Hall gave birth to his words. They dripped noiselessly from the corners of his mouth and stumbled about in the air until they were gone, and fizzled up empty quiet.

Someone once suggested that he try ventriloquism. That statement had cost the brave speaker four crowns and three trips to the white dentist in town.

T Hall was also known to have an uneven disposition. At noon, in the hot sun or in the heat of the restaurant's kitchen, T Hall was easygoing, almost playful. He joked often with the busboys as they heaped more and more dishes into his sink.

Occasionally he would break into fits of animation and joy, throwing shrimp and scallops back and forth at the cooks, cursing freely.

Like Gabriel, the man who never led his rebellion but was hung nevertheless, T Hall's problem was thought. He thought about having things dishwashers should probably never think about. Because, as most people knew, it caused profuse sweating and a deep red glow in the eyes, coupled with a massive distortion of cause and effect.

It was the simple act of thinking which T Hall did once a week at the Do Drop Inn that made him dangerous. One could not find a more volatile place to think in West Rehoboth. The longer he thought, the more he wanted, and the more he wanted, the more he realized how hopeless it was to want. It was at this point that T Hall began to think that if he kicked somebody's ass, things would brighten up. Or, if he could just encircle some woman with his long black arms and sear fire clear through her flailing legs, his whole life would have more meaning, more promise.

The next day, after a night of destructive energy, T Hall was remorseful and loving. It was always on those days that he regretted having thought of all the things he did not have and all the things he wanted. The previous day's madness would have sent him into the streets chasing the rabid dogs. And it was the day after that he loved his family more and worked the hardest around his little three-room house.

The Do Drop Inn was now punishing its neighbors once again with the droning jukebox blaring its music into hard-core fuzz. Chuck Berry was somewhere skipping across a stage, while his record provided an opportunity for the clam shuckers to watch the barmaids curlicue a shimmy or double-stomp a cross fire.

T Hall was downing double Grand-Dads. After sloshing back his fourth double, he broke his reverie and began talking to the bartender. But Gus, the bartender, paid no attention to him at all. He didn't have the time or the interest to listen to every hard-luck story that sat at the bar. He knew T Hall well enough to know it was indeed hard luck. Or no luck at all. Gus didn't want to hear it.

"My goddamn mortgage is two months past due and my boss is talking 'bout not staying open much this winter 'cause ain't been many people 'round this dump after Labor Day." T Hall slammed his hand down on the bar to command another drink from Gus, who stared at him a second or two before going to the bottles.

"Damn, but I'd like to get me that new Ford Clarence is tryin' to sell to somebody. All I'd need would be a little cash to lay on him. Hell, I know Clarence'd cut me a big break on the price." T Hall's voice rose. Yeah, he knew nobody gave a good goddamn. He knew. But to hell with everybody.

"Them kids needs to get a whole new winter outfit. The clothes they're wearin' so small it's pinchin' their nerves together.

"If I only had about two hundred dollars. If somebody just walked up to me downtown and said, 'Young man, you look like a hardworkin' Negro, I know you've got it rough, here's two hundred dollars from a friend of the Negro people.' Lordy, that *would* be something. Play me a number. That's what I'd do. I'd play me a whole bunch of numbers and hit for some big cash and leave the trash burning in this seaside dump. Maybe I'd buy that new car Clarence is tryin' to get rid of."

T Hall was riding high now, planning what he would do with the money he won from playing the numbers. First thing he decided to do after he won was to make a trip to the racetrack and invest his money in a good sound horse that ran fast. In that way, he would win even more money—legitimately. Some people had actually started laughing when he'd talked about somebody just giving him money just because he was black. Now that was real funny. Why should he be the one to get money? Everybody in that room, in West Rehoboth, in the whole damned country who was black was owed something by somebody just for putting up with the crap they had to put up with. Not to mention the crap their parents and those before them had had to survive.

That's what they'd done. Survived. They were still trying to learn how to live. But the Do Drop Inn wasn't the place to be going into all that. So they laughed at T Hall because he was obviously losing it. And then the wise ones lost their laugh. Because they knew once "it" was lost, there might be all hell to pay.

Rufus had listened to the entire monologue and wished T Hall would shut up. He had his own thoughts to think. He struggled within himself to keep from saying something to T Hall. Unfortunately, at that precise moment, T Hall turned around and looked directly at him.

Something happens in bars like the Do Drop when two people who should never be in the same room lock eyes. Everyone knows something has changed. A shadow is cast. Everyone begins to look around to identify the trouble. Now people who were crying in their beers and sleeping on tables picked their heads up and looked around. Jerked back to reality, they were riveted by bad vibrations and the presence of at least one evil disposition.

T Hall stared at Rufus. Rufus would not let go and stared back. The communication between them was fuzzy. Rufus couldn't gauge what was happening. He just knew he wouldn't let a ragged barfly intimidate him.

By now, some had spotted the problem and were watching the two men. Some slid off bar stools and slipped out the side door, heading for Edna's until the clouds blew over.

"You got a problem, boy?" Rufus heard the words but had not actually seen T Hall say them. The shadows and T Hall's scar obfuscated. And it took a second or two for Rufus to realize he was talking to him. He remained silent.

"You sho' is lookin' at me mighty hard." T Hall's eyes blazed in Rufus's direction. And Rufus knew, because he'd been in too many situations like this, that something was about to happen. He could let it happen, and most likely, if he did that, it would happen *to* him. But on this day, Rufus wasn't likely to do it that way.

Still staring directly at him, T Hall began talking again. "Fuck a goddamn Do Drop Inn, goddamn dirty cardboard shanty shit of a building." He held his half-empty glass up in the direction of the bartender, still looking at Rufus, and said, "This fuckin' likker tastes like plastic piss in a shot glass."

No one said anything. In fact, the bartender walked to the other end of the bar, hoping T Hall would not make him use the shotgun that rested on a shelf under the counter.

T Hall knew that the bartender had a shotgun and said nothing more about the liquor. But still, he poked holes in Rufus.

More folks left, some professing a desire to join the perpetual crap game going on outside in the back. Some of these people didn't have any money to gamble away, but instead of being caught in a madman cross fire, they were wont to use any excuse.

T Hall slowly turned back to the bar. He motioned for another drink. "Gimme another one of these Grand-Dads, will ya, Pop?" he shouted at the man behind the counter. He then plunged back into his conversation with the uninterested bartender. Rufus let a sigh leave his body, although he kept staring at T Hall. He wasn't about to let his guard down.

"What the fuck, I'll never hit the goddamn numbers. I won't have bus fare to get to the damn racetrack, much less have enough money to place a stinking bet. The fuckin' cards are stacked against me, that's for sure." T Hall slipped down the last of his drink as the bartender set another glass in front of him. T Hall's eyes were flowing red and his face had wrinkled up.

Again T Hall turned around and singled out Rufus with his eyes. Finally he spoke. "What's eatin' you, houseman?"

Finally, Rufus turned away from the stare and the words. He knew what T Hall was signifying. Signifying was a criminal act among black folks. T Hall was suggesting that Rufus could do no better than maintain the house at Edna's. It was typical to call the man who ran the poolroom a "houseman." Rufus felt the skin on the back of his neck tighten.

"How come you ain't racking them up, houseman? Ain't the poolroom open tonight?" T Hall broke into a tense, mischievous smile.

There was a limit to what Rufus would take from some no-account rummy. "I'm not botherin you, T. Why don't you mind your own fucking business?"

"I guess you ain't got no business. That's why you're the god-damn houseman, houseman."

It was then that Rufus realized that T Hall wasn't going to stop. And if he didn't get up and leave right now, something bad was going to happen. Rufus pushed the table away and got up to leave. T Hall again broke into a grin.

"I guess I was wrong about that, houseman. Actually I guess that bitch Edna must be mindin' your business. Eh, houseman?"

Rufus didn't know why everyone he had ever worked for had turned against him. He didn't know why people picked on him. Why he was the one they fired after fights. Even fights he lost. Now he was with Edna, trying to get himself together. He was try-ing to live up to the Rufus he had dreamed of being. He wanted something for himself. A business, a small fleet of fishing boats.

Something. Rufus's thoughts began to form the same darkness that T Hall's had. They were being pulled into each other. Rufus felt the magnetism and finally let go.

He turned and walked toward T Hall, who was off the stool and heading in his direction. The crap game had stopped and people were frozen at the doors watching the scene unfold, causing a bottleneck at the exit.

"What did you say?" Rufus spoke softly.

"You heard me, you pussy-whipped son of a bitch." T Hall was in Rufus's face. "I said, you let that bitch run your goddamned life. What's the matter, you don't like the truth?" T Hall sized Rufus up and figured he might take out his dissatisfaction with the way he was pinned to a wall of bleak desolation, in a world that ignored his existence, on Rufus.

Rufus looked past T Hall, through him really, at the horde of people by the side door. He wondered what they thought. Were they laughing? He thought he heard someone laughing. He tried to quiet it. Yes, he was angry. Yes, just let this moment pass. Edna would be expecting him soon. He knew he wasn't supposed to be at the Do Drop anyway. "I know you're drunk, T. So if you apologize for callin' my woman a bitch, I'm just gonna walk out of here and we can forget the whole thing."

T Hall rode the wave of his own energy. He couldn't stop himself. Some kind of self-escalating energy moved him. In a cat's breath he crashed Rufus's face with his closed hand. Rufus, taken totally by surprise, was thrown backward into the table he had just left. His head hit the seat of one of the chairs. He felt his mouth fill with blood.

He looked up at a grimacing T Hall. Inside, Rufus began separating into parts. He wanted to cry. Let the tears protect him. Why did this keep happening to him?

T Hall stared down at him. "Get up, houseman. Get the fuck up so I can put your ass back down on the goddamn floor."

Rufus tried to gather himself. He spat out the thick wad of blood that had collected in the bowl of his mouth. Deep inside him there was the desire to run for the door. To hope that he could make it outside before T Hall could grab him and sling him across the bar. A part of him was already up and running. Another part stared back fiercely at his attacker.

As he pulled his hands back to lift himself off the floor, he felt his knife. Now the part of him that had stayed felt a surge of excitement. He would not let this man run him off. He would not be insulted. If there was laughter he would extinguish it. He would put an end to the whole matter. He pushed himself up.

T Hall was there to meet him, and before Rufus could get his balance, T Hall had again hit him. Square on the eye. But this time Rufus rolled over and launched himself quickly, pulling his knife free in the process.

It was about eight inches long with a bone handle and a sliver-sharp serrated edge. As it rested in his hand it flashed and gleamed in the bar light. Stunned, T Hall froze. Rufus, too, was caught in the glint and glimmer. He felt the roller-coaster energy from those who still stood around them. Some were inching even closer. Their smiles full now. Rufus saw the teeth flashing all around him. It was time to put the whole matter to rest.

Another part of Rufus ran out of the bar. The only part that remained, that filled the outline of his body, had now plunged itself into the fight and set about trying to hurt T Hall.

Rufus was a wild flurry, a windmill. He felt the knife slide into T Hall. He felt it. The only feeling he could compare it to was the sensation of biting someone. Sinking into their flesh and wanting to go farther. To make it hurt. To go beyond hurt. What might start out as a playful nibble turns into a tremble of pain and pleasure. Suddenly he didn't want to stop. He was at the center of everyone's attention. T Hall wasn't T Hall, but a wall to be torn down.

T Hall, his mind full of wild noises and colors, could only raise his hands in defense, and then, when they were sliced and hurting with excruciating pain, he brought them down lower and Rufus set upon his face and head, cutting and cursing in the gush of red-black blood puddling up at his feet and in the seat of the chair that T Hall had slumped down in.

T Hall was barely conscious now, but he knew that he was hurt and that he was losing himself to the air. He wanted Rufus to stop. His face was burning as if the fire from Edna Hull's barbecue pit was going full force, down way down, somewhere in the recesses of his jaws. Then his neck went limp and his mouth became unable to serve his words. He thought about the number he should have played and the car he was going to get and . . . oh . . .

T Hall was a moaning memory, lying between the table and the chair, bleeding his life and his hopelessness out into the raw rat-eaten wood that made the floor. His blood dripped through the cracks and onto the ground that lay two feet beneath the floor of the building. When the blood hit the sand, it splashed and beaded up into muddy red globules of deadened life. It would be much later before T Hall was dragged from the Do Drop Inn by the Rehoboth Beach police.

Rufus knew only the movement of his arms, which had started to slow as T Hall fell away. Rufus was intoxicated. T Hall had stopped coming forward. Everyone had stopped breathing. No one was laughing. He didn't look down at T Hall. Couldn't believe that his life was draining away as he stood there. He didn't want to see T Hall ever again. He turned around and pushed through the crowd, which was fast closing in on him. But almost magically the group parted and cleared a way for him into the night. There was only one direction to go. One place to be and one person to be with.

. . .

Whispers traveled like insecticide, heavy and strangling, as quick as two feet and two lips. Rufus had killed T Hall and had escaped the scene.

On the road to Edna's, slugs, slimy crawling moping snail-like creatures, lined the edges. In West Rehoboth the children attacked the slug by throwing salt from some mother's dinner table on the poor snotty stuff's back. And the slug would begin to melt and leave a trail of itself, transformed to liquid goo. Although quite cruel, the first time you saw it happen it was a wondrous sight. Some children enjoyed the power, and even perhaps the cruelty, and so the slug population was held in check by Morton salt.

Lighting the walkways, the fireflies flashed mechanically in phosphorescence. A cold effortless light source. And children, at times, would capture these lightning bugs and pinch out their lights. They would then, using the natural fluids flowing from the bug, stick them to their little-girl ears as earrings. The boys would make rings.

Lightning bugs, slugs, and Rufus were on the road to Edna's. It was the only place he could go. It was the place where the other parts of him were waiting. He needed them.

At Edna's, things were getting off to a wicked pace. James Brown blared from the jukebox and Edna was in the kitchen fixing sandwiches for all the fast-footed shimmy shakers spilling their guts and ounces of water on the plywood floor. She had barbecued the ribs outside and now they were stacked two feet high in a huge, oval roasting pan. The pan was deep blue with white specks. The customers walked up to a window that connected the dance floor with the kitchen and purchased rib sandwiches.

Everyone knew that Edna's barbecue was the best, and what made it the best was the sauce that she wiped on it with the trimmed head of a mop with its handle cut down to about a foot in length. Hot as ten devils cooped up in a steam bath built between a boiler room and a portion of the Sahara Desert, her sauce, as hot as that.

As the song ended, the wet bodies, with sweat dripping down and across their sea-salt-worn faces, were moving to the chairs where they hoped to rest until James Brown or Hank Ballard could move them into the spiritual love medley that dance is to black folk.

Then there was a sigh. Someone had played a slow song by the Chiffons. There was a flurry of activity as people chose their partners.

It was then that Rufus walked into the room, out of breath, hobbling from the bruises he'd incurred in the fight, bleeding from the mouth. The lovers hadn't even gotten started in their effort to grind away each other's middle parts. Time stopped there.

Rufus was in Edna's.

"Edna," Rufus called out loudly. He knew then, knew the moment he'd slipped his knife into T Hall, knew that he was unraveling. He knew it as the scenery whizzed by him on the way to Edna's. His mind was full of colors. Reds and yellows swirling around. Sometimes they took shape as thoughts. But mostly they were just colors which had no connection to consciousness.

"Who the devil is that?" Edna answered from within the protection of her kitchen.

"Come on out here, Edna." Rufus was breathing hard.

Edna moved cautiously from the kitchen. When she saw

Rufus she ran to him. He was shaking. The knife still stuck in his hands.

"What happened?" Edna quickly wiped her hands on her apron before she put a hand to his cheek and pulled his head to her shoulder.

"I don't know. I think I might of killed T Hall. I don't know." Rufus mumbled his words into Edna's neck.

While they stood there, Edna holding Rufus up, everyone fled out the back way through the poolroom, leaving them there alone in the room. Already word had traveled that T Hall was in bad shape. Some speculated he was dead. They all knew that the cops would be there soon.

"Edna," Rufus began, "you gotta help me. I needs me someplace to hide till I can git outta this goddamn shithole of a town. I—"

"Rufus. God. Rufus. Are you all right? Here, come in the kitchen, let me put something on your face," Edna said.

"Edna, I need a place to hide." That's what the colors were saying. Hide. Disappear.

"You can't hide, Rufus. You can't hide from the law." She knew as she said that that whatever dreams she'd had about her and Rufus, as small as they were, would never happen. He was drowning.

"Edna, they gonna be here in any minute now. You know what they'll do to me. I got to get out of here. But I need a place to hide a little while. Just a little while." Rufus was sweating and bleeding and crying all at the same time. He was desperate.

Edna was trying to catch up with him. She didn't know what to do. She never had trouble with the police. She didn't want them in her establishment except to eat. She could hope he survived, but she feared he was lost to sadness and despair and she was powerless to do anything about it.

Rufus pulled away from her and ran up the stairway behind him to the second floor, where his room was.

Edna screamed, "Where you going? Are you crazy, Rufus? Don't make this worse than it already is."

Rufus moved quickly up the steps, sweating and feeling his heart pump double time as his blood marched the retreat against the background of a hangman's noose.

"I ain't got no choice, Edna, no choice. I can't let them jus' come in here an' take me away. I gotta try." Rufus was at the top of the stairs, breathing heavily and facing into his room. The colors now grew bolder. Fight, they said. Fight.

"What the bejesus are you going to do up there against the police when they come? You ain't got no gun. You're already hurt. Rufus"—Edna stopped to catch her breath—"why don't you come on down here and act like you got some sense."

"I can't do that, Edna." Once inside the room, he began pushing the furniture against the door.

Edna reached the second floor. "Don't you know these white folk's police just waitin' for some fool behind black man to lock hisself up in a room, fat-mouthin' 'bout what he can't let them do."

Edna tried to calm herself down. "Listen, Rufus, I know that whatever happened you didn't mean to hurt nobody. I know that."

"You're right, Edna. I didn't want no trouble. But he called you a name."

"But, Rufus, I just don't understand how you can pen yo'self up here like this an' jus' wait for them to come an' git you. It don't make no sense to me."

From behind the wooden door, she heard Rufus breathing hard. "I just don't know what to do."

"The cops are gonna find you here. Somebody had to see you comin' down the road. This town ain't but so big, you know. Besides, everybody knows you been staying here."

Rufus was quiet. Suddenly the colors disappeared and he could see clearly that they had not been thoughts. Edna was right. No doubt someone had seen him coming down the road, and if someone had seen him, they would surely call the cops. And if all of this was true, he was a dead man. Panic flooded his body, making it pulsate. The colors flashed back.

"Shit, goddammit, fuck a goddamn cop. I don't care. I killed somebody, now they gonna come in here and kill me. Well, they ain't if'n I kin help it."

"But you can't do nothin' 'bout it. 'Specially barricaded up here," Edna pleaded.

"I kin make it a lot harder for 'em." Rufus ended the conversation.

Edna could hear the sirens of the police as they came into the darker section of Rehoboth Beach, Delaware. They were just getting to the scene of the crime. T Hall had been dead for at least twenty minutes before the police and ambulance arrived. If T Hall had only been wounded, he would have bled to death waiting for the police. But Edna was thinking about Rufus and how the police would be at her front door in a few minutes. She walked back down the steps and into her kitchen.

Some of the people who had left were slowly moving back into Edna's. They murmured and whispered among themselves. They figured that Rufus had left Edna's for someplace quiet and safe, like a sanitation ditch.

But no one plugged the jukebox in again, and it seemed that they were content in sitting around, waiting for some sign from Edna that they could begin their ritual of fire dance and love that showered the small-town seashore air with the warm glow of black bodies "getting down."

Edna heard the police as they turned into her clamshell-covered driveway. She could hear the tires crush and crackle over the broken shells as the car pivoted, announcing themselves as the turning wheels of white reactionary small-town-cop fate. She peeked through the streaked window and saw Horace and his buddy walking cautiously up to her door. Their guns were drawn, so she dared not run to the door, for they might mistake her for some clay pigeon.

They knocked loudly. Horace screamed out, "Miz Edna, come on out. I knows you home. Come on out, Miz Edna. We don't want no trouble with you."

"I'm sure you don't, Horace." Edna was at the door. "I ain't done nothin' wrong."

"I know, Miz Edna, but we's lookin' for Rufus Brown 'Spect he murdered T Hall a little while ago. Somebody said he come on down here. That so?"

"Well now, Horace, you know I don't coddle no criminals; this here is a respectable business establishment."

"I know that, Edna, but have you seen him?" Horace was growing impatient. His index finger smoothly, gently caressed the trigger of his service revolver.

"Maybe," Edna said softly, hoping he would not hear.

"Now jus' what the hell does 'maybe' mean? I reckon we betta search the place, Henry," he said to his partner as they moved past Edna and went inside.

"He ain't here, Horace," Edna blurted out. She had tried deep down inside to dismiss the importance of Rufus's freedom. He had killed a man. They wanted him for murder. But she knew Rufus and knew it must have been a mistake. And she couldn't countenance the godlike attitude of the peace officers invading her home.

"He ain't here. He was here, but he left about fifteen minutes ago. He went out the back and into the woods out yonder."

This she said with relief, as though the lie lifted a great burden from her aging shoulders. Edna held her head up. "He could be nearly to Lewes by now. You know that's where he lives." She was sure that Horace didn't even know Rufus. Wouldn't know that Rufus had moved in with her.

"He ain't gonna get to no Lewes. The state police'll have him flushed outta them woods by daybreak. He ain't 'bout to get to Lewes. He'd have to hit the highway somewheres, and then we'd get him." Horace smiled to his partner.

"Horace, I got a heap of spareribs in the kitchen and these folks ain't eatin' like they usually do; why don't y'all come on in the kitchen and sit down a spell. Them state troopers will probably catch that Rufus in no time," Edna said, trying to keep Horace from searching the rest of her place. She knew he wasn't about to go into the woods after dark, searching for a colored man. What he could do, however, was sit down at Edna's table until it was time for him to go home. And if he was going to stay, the best place for him to be was in the kitchen, filling his fat belly with barbecue.

"Well now," says Horace, "I must admit that I'm hungry, what with all that's been a-goin' on—I kin smell that barbecue from here. What d'ya think, partner, we got time for some sandwiches?"

Suddenly a surge of people pushed through the back door. Rufus had frightened them on his way out. They weren't sure what he was doing and so they were now running back into Edna's. But they were like an alarm.

"What's goin' on?" Horace shouted at them.

"Rufus just ran out of here like a bat out of hell," someone said.

Horace ran to the window and saw Rufus slipping into the night-dark woods. He turned back to Edna, then to his partner, and back again to Edna. "Thought you said he wasn't here no more, Edna? Thought you said he done left?"

"I . . . I thought so, too, Horace . . . I . . . ah . . ."

Edna slumped into her chair and sat frozen amid her stack of barbecued pork as Horace and his partner ran back out of her front door and got into their car. She didn't know what had just happened or what would happen next. But as she sat there staring at the glazed brilliance of her handmade barbecue sauce, the little specks of black pepper not nearly enough warning for a sensitive palate, she exhaled heavily. And suddenly she heard the sound of her father's bedraggled voice as he lay on the precipice of death. "Happ . . . e," he'd said. She had heard it then as a sign. An encouragement. Look for happiness. Believe in it. It will come to you. Her mother had thought it had more to do with the kind of happiness people are said to have at the moment of death. Rapture. Maybe, but Edna had internalized it as a hope for herself.

Against her own better instincts she'd given Rufus a chance to hurt her. Or to be her happiness. And now, with the sound of sirens shouting all around the seaside country of sand and loblolly pines, with the smell of death and desperation in the air, she knew Rufus had destroyed her last ounce of energy to believe that love would be her happiness. You just couldn't trust a man who'd been beat to death by his own history and the world that gave it to him. You just couldn't. Especially a man who had stopped fighting for his own self. A man who'd just given in. You couldn't put your life on his shoulders. You couldn't lie back and feel like those white women in the moving pictures who could actually tell you how good they felt just by what was in their eyes. You just couldn't.

She heard people settling back into their places in the restaurant. She didn't feel like cutting up the rest of those ribs for four-bone sandwiches. She didn't feel like scooping large spoonfuls of her luscious potato salad or the sweet acrid joy that was her collards. She didn't want to go find Rufus. She didn't want to sit where she was. She wanted instead to disappear. To vanish into nothingness. But it wasn't happening. Her feet were sore. She had a headache. Her body whispered its substance. She was alone in a world of chaos.

And right there, in that instant, she broke from all other things living. If she had to be there, to live her life, then she would do it on her own. She wouldn't wait for Rufus, would never allow him to trick her into believing that her happiness had anything whatsoever to do with him or anyone else. She began to separate into little pieces with tears her only glue. Right there she promised this to herself. She'd live. She'd thrive. Her.

9

Rufus's mind was ablaze as he tore through the woods. It was dense enough to provide cover and yet the trees were far enough apart so that even in the light of a half-moon, he could keep a steady pace. He knew the police would soon be close behind. He could almost feel the gathering energy behind him.

There was a part of him that felt like stopping. Maybe digging a hole or finding a hollow log and simply trying to hide. He was tired already and his flight had just begun. Who knew how far he could go; how far he had to go?

And where? Where was he going? His parents were dead, and even if they weren't he'd never go back home. He'd always been alone anyway. Home or not. He had no idea where he was going. But there really were only two choices: stop or keep going.

His legs answered his mind as he kept pumping them through the brush, dirt, and sand. When he'd tangled with T Hall, Rufus was nearly drunk. But now his mind was clear. The colors gone for good.

He was frightened, confused, and growing tired, but as he ran, the thoughts in his head seemed to come in clusters. One moment he thought about his home back in D.C., the next about what Edna was doing or where T Hall was now (still in the Do Drop or being rushed to the hospital?) or whether he could actually get away or not.

He fought a feeling inside him that this night was the night he could meet his fate. He thought about all the stories he'd listened to of old-timers who could fill an entire night with tales of runaway slaves and the struggles they endured.

For a minute he imagined himself that way. In all the stories he'd heard, there were always puddles or swampland to traverse. The runaways would slosh and stumble and fall and read the signs of the stars as the hounds bayed in the distance.

Every colored man who'd ever done something wrong and had to take flight from the law had probably felt the way those slaves did. Running from the patrolers. Running from the dogs and the curses of white men. From the sound of white men approaching. Terrified. Heart thumping at a frenetic pace like a Scott Joplin tune. Knowing no one would save them if they couldn't save themselves. And knowing, too, that saving oneself was almost impossible. It meant putting meaning to the saying "miles to go before I rest." It meant believing in God or Elegba or something that would provide the place for rest and the energy to take up the run at the next dusk.

But he didn't believe in God or anything beyond the reality of his struggle. Which dropped the chances of survival nearly to chance.

And then he thought about the day when he ran home virtually naked, trying to take back his tears and his begging. He'd never forget how all the way home, as people stared, laughed, and pointed at him, all he could think about was how afraid he'd been at the mercy of those white people. He'd grown to hate that boy who whimpered like a coward in the face of their power. They'd taken something from him.

Never mind that that event began a long list of traumas and tragedies he'd had to live through. Or that most people would have predicted his death way before now. Never mind all of that. What he wanted most was to live that day over. To spit in that big white kid's eye and take whatever punishment was due in the exchange.

And on he ran. Finally he reached the point of his greatest vulnerability as he came to the end of the woods, which opened onto the yard of a tractor sales and lease store. Beyond that the highway. He could already see the flashing lights up and down the road. He held back in the darkness. They were obviously waiting for him to emerge. Occasionally a beam of light would peer into the edge of the woods. From where he stood, he could always see it approach, and hide behind the tree that became his blind.

Suddenly he had an idea. What if he doubled back? They'd never expect him to do that. Carefully he backed away from the waiting officers and slipped quietly into the woods. He turned in the direction of Edna's and began running again. But as he moved deeper into the woods he heard new noises. He stopped, realizing that there was another group of troopers working through the woods, intending to flush him into the waiting grasp of the troopers from whom he'd just turned away. They had indeed anticipated the possibility that he might turn around.

He veered now toward the west, where the highway also abutted the woods. There was a fence running alongside the roadside there and he figured the police had left that side unattended, expecting him to try to make it to Lewes just as Edna had told them.

When he reached the road, he slowly crept up to the fence and felt no other presence there. He quickly scaled the fence and ran as fast as he could all the way across the highway. Once there, he dived into the ditch and waited. Every now and then a state trooper car would fly by. After a while he could see troopers across the road walking alongside the fence. He hoped it was too dark for them to pick up his footprints, which, when the night faded, would be quite visible.

After a bit they moved on. He slowly stood up and began walking along the roadside. He realized he was being a bit brazen, but his only chance now would be to catch a ride from someone who'd already passed the police checkpoint. But who would stop for him? And at this hour, which he figured was about 4:00 A.M., there weren't many cars passing anyway.

He looked behind him. A car was coming. He jumped into the ditch in a crouch. It was another state trooper. The car sped by as if they knew exactly where Rufus was. He chuckled to himself. "Y'all some dumb cracker son of a bitches."

He raised himself up again and continued southward along the road. Two more state troopers passed, one going in each direction. But just as he was sure the last one had passed, and was back to walking, a car pulled up behind him. It was within twenty feet of him before he heard the tires crunching the rocks of the road's shoulder.

Rufus was petrified. How had he not heard the car or seen its lights approaching? He turned his head around even as his body continued to face southward, but the car's lights weren't on. That was why. They'd outsmarted him.

He waited for someone to holler at him, but all he could hear was the purr of the engine. As he strained his eyes to see in the waning night light, he wasn't even sure now it was a state trooper's car.

And then the car lights flashed on for a second before being extinguished again.

"What the hell?" Rufus said out loud. "Who's that?"

From the car a voice, a soft woman's voice floated. "Do you need a ride?"

"Who is that?" Rufus walked in the direction of the car.

"If I were you I wouldn't ask too many questions. Crawl into the backseat and lie down. Stay still. And keep your mouth shut."

Rufus walked by the driver's side, but just as he reached the door, the driver turned away. She was dressed in black, with something like a shawl draped over her head. To Rufus, at that moment she was like the image of death, beckoning him.

"Who the hell are you and why are you doing this?" he said as he slid into the car and closed the door.

"I told you to be still. There's some food in a bag on the floor there, but if I were you I'd wait awhile before I ate it. We've got a long trip ahead of us and you're going to have to make it laying down back there."

And with that, the driver threw the gear into drive and moved forward.

10

The years passed in the rhythm of the rising swells of the Atlantic Ocean. Steady, individual, and yet a part of the life of the water. Four years passed that way. Through the depth of the roaring ocean, Rufus long-marched back to Rehoboth, back to Edna.

But along the way, Rufus turned in on himself. He lived with the face of T Hall, muttering, moaning, bleeding, and hovering just in front of him. He lived that moment every night after he finally climbed into his rack to fall asleep. He sailed aboard the S.S. *Selma*. The steel-gray-and-black freighter was steaming from Venezuela with cargo, bound for Norfolk, Virginia. He had decided to stay aboard six more months, enough for at least one more voyage, probably to Europe. But first they were headed back to the United States to deliver the sugar and wool that they were carrying and to pick up new cargo.

When he was alone, on nights that were quiet and warm, like

those they came upon in May on the shimmering Caribbean, his thoughts strayed to Rehoboth and the death he had fled.

He regretted his flight, especially his life with Edna, which he now romanticized and worshiped. His memory blunted the sense of decay that had decorated his relationship with her, even before T Hall.

He held no fear of the law. He knew that he was probably safe now. There were times when being black had its benefits. The police would only look so long for a black man who had killed another black man. Still, he couldn't wait to find out for sure. To test the air, the water, and the graces of the community.

How had he escaped? He wasn't sure. He'd gotten into that car and everything that happened after was more like a dream— diffuse and confounding—than something he could actually explain. Even to himself. All he really knew was that he had awakened groggily in an alley in Norfolk, Virginia, two days later.

And even though nearly three years had passed since he'd last seen her, Edna was always on his mind. Of course, Rufus expected her to have forgotten all about him. "She probably thinks I steamed away for good. Well, she'll be surprised when I get back there, my pockets full of money." He often said into the night-sea air.

After years of being away from Rehoboth, with many months out on the ocean, Rufus had begun to accept loneliness as a way of life. The only man he talked to was Otis Jessup, a white thirty-four-year-old second-class ship's mate who disbursed the pay chits and monitored the ship's safe.

Otis was on his last cruise. He talked incessantly about moving to Tampa, buying a boat, and water-skiing the rest of his life away.

The other men aboard ship left Rufus alone. He worked in the bilges. He worked hard, and he worked silently. During meals he sat by himself, and only in the night, when he slept in the tight compartments, did he relax among his shipmates. No one was awake when he quietly made his way above deck to his favorite place on the forecastle, where he'd often sit on a chock and think of the night he killed T Hall.

There were many nights when he shivered in the cold salt spray, which stung his body and urged the tears to fall. He cried his sorrow out into the ocean air.

He made promises to a nightly audience of flying fish, sea-gulls, porpoises, and whales. He promised them that he would change. That he would make his way back to Rehoboth and try to make up for what he had done.

He often found himself mired in the crusting salt of the whip-ping ocean spray, talking to his friends and the ever-present face of agony, T Hall. "Killin' somebody just ain't in me. I don't know how I did it. I swear to you. Sometimes I get to thinkin' that there was somebody, maybe even a whole bunch of people who made me kill that boy. That they's the ones who set me up to kill T Hall." The flying fish were silent. They'd glide out of the water, skimming the surface, and propel themselves over the bow. Occasionally one would get caught in a scupper or on deck and lie there. Rufus would run out and fling them back into the water. Still, every morning the bo'sun would have to sweep the deck clear of dead flying fish.

The dolphins were silent, too. Everyone listened but said nothing. "Shit, I didn't go there to the Do Drop Inn to kill nobody. That wasn't why I was there. But there I was. Suddenly I done killed somebody."

T Hall never smiled at him, only glowered in the mist. Rufus was a criminal. He had killed. And, regardless of the inept, unconcerned police, he had turned himself into himself. His punishment was life.

And now, like Otis, he, too, anticipated his journey back

home, back to Rehoboth. For Otis, it would be when they pulled into Norfolk. For Rufus, there were still oceans to cross, new cities to visit, more money to save.

Rufus liked Otis because the white man seemed comfortable with him. Didn't seem afraid of him. Otis asked questions. Personal questions. It was Otis's nature to nose around, pass along information. He was the center of communications on the ship mainly because he handed out the checks. Everyone wanted to be friends with Otis, because if he turned against you he could "misplace" a month's pay.

Rufus would always cash his pay chit into twenty-dollar bills. He'd keep some for spending and stow the rest of it in the ship's safe. He had a small tin box with a lock on it and his name written on tape on the top. He paid a monthly charge to keep the box.

Every day after the bo'sun knocked off ship's work, he'd head down to the bursar's office and ask Otis for his money box.

"How much you got in there by now?" Otis was a large red-faced man from Roanoke, Virginia, who, if he had had a beard, could have played Santa Claus. He was like a red mountain in the tiny office. The door to the room was divided in half. When inside, Otis would open the top and conduct business with the sailors over the small counter.

"Otis, now you know I ain't gonna tell you that," Rufus said, smiling. He produced the key that hung around his neck and opened the box. He pulled the box close to him as he leaned on the counter. "Ain't you got no work to do?"

"No, Rufus, I was just sitting here waiting for your black ass to come down here and count your money."

"This black ass you talkin' to got more money than you'll ever have." Rufus laughed his words out.

"Rufus, I'm getting real short, you know. Don't fuck with me. Look at this." With a big grin Otis pulled out a small chain of brass links from his pants pocket. "Now this here is a short-timer's chain."

Rufus looked up. "I know what it is." He went back to counting his money.

"There's fifteen links left on this sucker, Rufus. Fifteen days and I'm in Tampa, cutting through the water on a pair of skis, bein' pulled by my new boat. I'm talking about the good life."

"You must have quite a nest egg salted away," Rufus said, his head still buried in the box.

"I got enough. But, like you said, boy, I bet I ain't got as much as you. Shit, you don't do shit. If you had as many women as I have, you wouldn't have no money either. You won't even take your horny ass over on the beach and buy no pussy. Don't you like women?"

"You know goddamned well I like women."

"Then how come I never see you with any?"

"I got me a woman back home in Rehoboth." Rufus had finished counting his money. It hadn't changed since payday, but he counted it anyway. Every day.

In the time that he had been in the Merchant Marines this go-around, Rufus had earned a lot of money, saving as much of it as he could. He didn't trust his shipmates, so he rented the money box to keep it safe. As of that moment there was nineteen hundred dollars in that box, in twenty-dollar bills. His goal was to have as close to five thousand dollars as he could before quitting the ship and going home to Edna.

"What you gonna do with all that money?" Otis stared at Rufus.

"Well, Otis, I'm gonna make things right again. This here is my salvation money."

"Don't tell me you gonna give it to the goddamned church?"

"Naw. I got a lot of amends to make. I fucked things up pretty bad back home. This is gonna help me set things right." It was a part of his promise to the flying fish. He would bring home his money and his new self, his repentant self, to Edna and beg her forgiveness.

Otis watched Rufus's eyes carefully. "What kind of amends? What the hell have you ever done? You never do shit around here. Never even seen you get in a fight." He paused. "Shit, Rufus, I don't think I've ever seen you drunk. What kind of a goddamn sailor are you? You're givin' us a bad name."

"I can't drink, Otis. I get all fucked up. I start actin' real crazy."

"Yeah, I know what you mean. When I drink I always like to kick some ass." Otis laughed.

"Naw, man. I don't mean like that. I . . ." Rufus paused. Otis wasn't a flying fish or a pirouetting dolphin. Yet he felt safe. He sighed. "I mean, I start crying and shit like that. Real sloppy shit. I can't drink no more."

"Crying? What kind of shit is that, Rufus? What the fuck has a grown man got to cry about?"

Rufus stared him in the eye. "You ever kill a man, Otis?"

Otis just stared at Rufus. Suddenly he *was* uncomfortable. He saw something in Rufus's eyes which made his back tighten. His stomach grumbled.

"Are you gonna tell me you killed somebody?"

Rufus saw T Hall's face flickering in the space beside Otis. "I didn't mean to."

"You? I don't believe it. What'd you do, bore the son of a bitch to death?" Otis laughed a deep relieving laugh.

T Hall's face began to ooze blood. There was a deep, rough-cut gash just below his jawline which welled up with thick-running blood. There were other cuts about the face.

"You can laugh if you want to." Rufus slid his money box back to Otis. "But it ain't funny. I cut him too short to shit, Otis. Swear to God. Ripped him up good."

Otis froze again. Then, regaining his train of thought, he replaced the lockbox in the back of the small office. Returning to Rufus, he asked softly, "You mean you stabbed somebody?"

"I didn't want to, Otis. I was drunk, confused. He was one of those assholes who just looks for people to fuck with. You know what I mean?" Rufus watched T Hall's image disappear.

Otis stared at Rufus. "Yeah, I know what you mean. But, jeez, did you have to kill him?"

Rufus had never asked himself that question. He was always consumed by the knowledge that he had killed T Hall. He was possessed by the image of it, the gore. He had never considered that he might have stopped short of ending T Hall's life. He was silent as he thought about Otis's question.

"Well, I guess I did. You know how it is aboard ship here. If you get into a fight with someone, you better finish it. You either got to end up shaking hands and having a beer together or somebody has to get hurt. You know that. Otherwise one of them is gonna sneak the other one late at night. Throw a goddamn blanket party or some shit like that." Rufus referred to the seagoing practice of settling scores in which a group of guys would throw a blanket over someone they had a grudge against and beat the person senseless. Not only was the victim helpless, he also could not identify his attackers. Rufus had seen it happen many times.

"I just couldn't stop. I lost control. I wish I could live that day over."

"Yeah, I bet." Otis was speechless. He knew hard-hitting men; he knew drunken, empty men. But he had never talked to anyone who had confessed to murder. "So what you gonna do with the money? You can't bring the guy back."

"That money ain't for him. You're right, Otis. Can't nothing bring T Hall back. Naw, this money is for my sweetheart."

Otis again broke into a smile. "You ain't gonna give this money to no woman, are you?"

"That's what I said."

"No, Rufus. You don't understand shit, do you, boy? You got to take that money and have a good time with it. Don't you go throwing your money away."

"It ain't throwin' it away. Look, Otis, when I left Rehoboth I didn't have a pot to piss in, the cops was on my tail. I had nothing. Edna never saw me when I was at my best. I want to show back on the scene. My pockets full. I want to show her and that whole backwater town that I can make it." Rufus's face hardened with determination.

"But goddammit, Rufus, I know what I'm talking about. Take your money and have some fun. Don't waste your time on 'em. And for God's sake, boy, don't spend your goddamn money on 'em."

Rufus straightened up from the counter. He looked at Otis. "Well, Otis, if everything works out, if I get me a second chance, I'll gladly give up four or five thousand dollars."

Otis's eyes twinkled at the figure. "Boy, you got five thousand dollars?"

"Not yet. But by the time I get back from the next cruise, I'll have it. Almost got half of it now. But don't you tell nobody. 'Bout nothing. The money, my killin' somebody. Nothing, you hear?"

"Don't you worry about that." Otis put both red, sea-worn chubby hands up. "But how did a colored boy like you manage to get all that money?"

Rufus smiled at him and turned to go to dinner. "Like you said, Otis, I don't do shit around here; no women, no booze. You're my only entertainment."

The next two weeks moved slowly as the ship approached Cape Hatteras and prepared to dock in Norfolk. Rufus had spent much of the time that he was not working in the engine room, gathering his things and packing his large canvas seabag.

On the last day out to sea, Rufus went down to count his money, but both halves of the office door were closed. His stomach jumped when he found both locked and the room empty. He knocked a few times, then turned and nearly ran for the mess decks, the most probable place to find Otis.

Relief ran through his body as he saw Otis sitting with a group of his country-music-loving rednecks, a small group of guys from the Ozarks and Appalachia. Six of them were drinking beer, listening to Loretta Lynn and laughing loudly.

Rufus approached the group cautiously. Otis looked up and waved him over. "How you doin', boy?" Otis asked.

"Fine, Otis. How come you not open today?"

"Because this is my last night out to sea, boy. I'm celebrating today." Otis looked around and smiled. They all seemed to suppress laughter. Rufus immediately tensed up. He could tell that Otis had told them about him.

"I want to get my money out, Otis."

"It's not my job anymore, Rufus. The new guy will come aboard tomorrow after we get into port. I already signed over all that shit to the captain. He checked everything out and gave me my fuckin' release. I'm free, Rufus. Tomorrow." Otis lifted his glass. "Tomorrow, I'm gonna be on a bus to Tampa."

"Well, that's fine, Otis. I wish you luck. But I sure wish I could get my money tonight." Rufus was a little confused.

"Now I just told you, Rufus, that that is impossible. The office is locked up till we get into port. Anybody that wanted their money was supposed to come to the office before noon today."

"I didn't know that."

"Well, Rufus, that ain't my problem. There was a sign on the wall outside the office." Otis flashed a wide grin that bordered on a snicker.

"That's bullshit, Otis. I didn't see no goddamn sign. You know I come there every day. I didn't see no goddamn sign."

Otis stiffened. "Now I done tol' you once, boy. You can't get your money until tomorrow. Now you just better let me be."

Rufus felt the mood of the group sour and decided to wait until the next day when they reached Norfolk. He turned and began to leave when one of the other guys said, "Hey, bilge rat. How you get so much money?"

Rufus hated to be called a bilge rat. Even though he cleaned and maintained the bowels of the ship, the place where all of its engine wastes eventually settled, he didn't like the denigrating label. He wasn't a rat. He was a man. He could tolerate the sly use of the word "boy" when the men talked to him because he knew they were partly trying to test his strength. To see if he'd get mad. But "bilge rat" was different.

"I ain't no rat, Jake. Lay off."

"Leave him alone. He's a good old boy, that one. I like Rufus. Leave him be." Being a friend of Otis did have some benefits.

Rufus left the mess decks before he lost his temper. He had nurtured his aloneness. Had grown it like a flower. The incident with Otis and his friends was one reason why. He worked in an environment of white men. He had to watch himself. If he lost his temper and hurt a white man, there would be no escape. His sentence would be certain death. He swallowed as much abuse as he could and he cried into the ocean at night. In the barrel of his sleep, he dodged the horrified gaze of a fiery T Hall.

The bright Southern sun flared over the Virginia shore early the next afternoon. Rufus was on duty down in the engine room, a labyrinth of huffing puffing boilers and steam. He was used to heat. When it was 105 on deck in Southern waters or the Caribbean, it was at least 120 in the engine room. Rufus listened as the tugs came out to meet the ship. He heard the slow turning of the ship's screws as it maneuvered for entry into the harbor. The ship shook as the tug nestled its nose and guided the larger ship in.

After they were tied up and the engines were shut down, Rufus ran up the ladder to his berth to get his bags. He then headed for the quarterdeck to await the new disbursement officer or, failing his arrival, an opportunity to petition the captain. He wanted to be on the quarterdeck before everyone left.

He wanted his money in his own hands and would not be happy until he met Otis's replacement and was sure everything was fine. Slowly the men of the *Selma* filed through the quarterdeck and down the gangway.

Rufus leaned against the bulwark and watched the wives and children waiting for their husbands and fathers. He felt a hand on his shoulder. It was Otis.

"Well, good buddy. This is it. I'm off to the warm good life of sunny Florida."

Rufus grunted. He was preoccupied. He wanted only for someone to open up the office and give him his money.

"Otis, can't you do something about my money?" Rufus turned around and faced the round man.

"Goddamn, Rufus, you got a one-track mind, boy. You need to relax. Money ain't gonna do you no good. You don't even know what to do with it. You need to just settle down and realize that money is only gonna get you into more trouble. Now, that's my advice. Forget the goddamned money. Enjoy your life. I know I am." Otis laughed, signed the logbook, and waved good-bye as he left the ship.

As he watched Otis hail a cab at the end of the pier, Rufus decided to try to find the captain. He climbed the ladder to the bridge. Captain Jacob Sparks generally frowned on the sailors invading his territory. The captain had washed out of Annapolis but had retained the instinct for rigid protocol and discipline.

"Excuse me, Captain?" Rufus was weak with fear.

"Yes?" Captain Sparks was a short thin man with a gaunt face that sometimes looked as if it had been dragged many fathoms in the saltwater.

"Captain, I've been trying to get my money that's in my lockbox for the past two days."

"So why didn't you get your money from Otis? What's your name?" He stared at Rufus.

"Rufus."

"Rufus. Right, yes, I remember your name now. Engine room, right?"

"Yes."

"Well, like I said, why didn't you get your money before Otis Jessup left?"

"I tried to, but he said there was gonna be a new man doin' it and that I should wait for him."

Captain Sparks was instantly interested. "Well, come on, Rufus, let's see if we can get your money." They headed toward the bursar's. "How much did you have in there?"

Rufus hesitated. Why did everyone want to know how much money he had? He had saved it. It was his sweat.

"I'd rather not say, Captain."

"Well, Rufus, you're gonna have to tell me so I can verify the amount."

Rufus pondered, then figured he had nothing to lose. "It was nineteen hundred dollars, Captain." They reached the office and Rufus stood back as the captain unlocked the door.

He pulled Rufus's box out and put it on the counter. Rufus's heart stopped.

"Where's the lock?" Rufus asked.

"What lock? You had a lock on this box?"

Rufus felt everything, all of his anger, his energy, his hope gathering inside him. He felt like he was a boiler about to steam over. "Yes, Captain. Everybody puts a lock on their boxes. I got almost two thousand dollars in there."

Rufus tore the top off the box. He pulled out the contents. The energy transformed to tears and leaked out of his eyes. He counted quickly. There was three hundred dollars and a note.

> Dear Rufus,
>   You'll get over this. I needed the money. Don't worry, I'll have fun with it. You don't deserve this much money. So I took a little of it. No big deal. You're a hardworking nigger, you'll figure out how to make more. Now, if you're thinking about looking for me or telling anybody, forget it. REMEMBER I know what you did back there in Rehoboth Beach. You tell on me, I'll tell on you. Don't worry.

There was no signature. Rufus crumpled the letter into a ball and stuffed it into his pants. The captain had watched him carefully as he read it. He saw the lines in Rufus's brow stretch out over the brown man's face. He saw the tears using those lines like canals.

"What's it say?"

"Nothing, Captain. Nothing."

"That's not all your money, is it, Rufus?"

"It's all I got, Captain. It's all I got." Rufus turned and headed for the quarterdeck. He evaporated as he walked.

. . .

Rufus walked the lonesome Granby Street of Norfolk, Virginia, smoking his cigar and kicking invisible cans. Everything had turned ugly again. He was drinking again, empty. Feeling only a desire for relief. Someone to remove the yoke that had slipped around his shoulders. The *Selma* was scheduled to get under way in the morning and Rufus had no better idea of how to recover his balance, his sense of movement, than when the ship had docked. He was sinking into oblivion. How could he go back to Edna with nothing? The word "failure" was stuck in his throat. He had failed. Was failing. And he knew it. That was the most infuriating thing about it. Most people fail imperceptibly. A little at a time. An expected promotion which goes to someone else. An investment that never pays off. An illness. Life in slow motion. Things happening slowly. And then you look up and time has passed you by. But when you can see it, feel it happening, it can be thoroughly deflating; robbing every ounce of forward-thinking energy. Wasting human spirit.

On this August night he walked, oblivious to everything around him. The blurred colored lights and the fast talk which streamed through the air were as satin ribbons flapping to some unfelt breeze. Red, black, and green. He ignored them. Let them flap. They had no effect on him, except that he knew they were there. Flapping. And he knew he shouldn't touch them. They were sensitive strands, tenuously caught up in the movement of air.

Yet around him, beyond the flapping ribbons, was the backdrop of a darkly painted canvas. Men moved about in hats pulled down across their brows. Women stood here and there, straining to catch an eye.

Rufus licked the coming shadow of tomorrow, feeling at times like a hound dog on the tail of a jackrabbit. Behind him was the creeping pressure of Despair.

Despair. It was there, like the shading of a tree by a Minnesota lake: dark, cool, and always moving.

Sometimes, Rufus would reach out and touch the tentacles of hope and wonder, and from that a smile would erupt across his face like a newly awakened volcano. It was so temporary. And, as he thought about it, he'd not felt hope since he'd opened his eyes in an alley in downtown Norfolk.

Despair, in all its shadowy regalia, now seemed to be his companion. In his mind it was but a hesitant thought that something was wrong. Rufus never knew Despair by its proper name. It visited him in various shapes and visages.

He cracked a faint smile, looking up to face the streets of Norfolk. He was heading for a place where there was lively music and sparkling air. Diversions. Activities that would put Rehoboth and its damaged memories in their proper place, well behind him. Time would slowly lead him to a darkened street where music blared and bodies touched.

Rufus's pulse quickened. He could feel the energy. He moved like a sheet on a clothesline being pulled in before a storm. He headed for the highest of Saturday-night combat zones.

at night, within the belly of sleep, smoke rings languish in crevices where the face of Hope lies panting and grinning—panties half ripped off, breasts exposed, colorless— her skin stared into space. we are sure. Hope has met a lover somewhere in darkness and passed what flows between them. buried herself into him and let his tongue lash inside her. made tender noises in mock refusal. not denial. we feel his presence although he has obviously fled. we sense the rip-

ping of clothes was for passion not violence. for love. Hope
pants at the receding aura of her lover. her lover? who?

Rufus was inevitably bound for Church Street. When the ship was in Norfolk, Rufus gravitated to Church Street. Norfolk, a town with a reputation so ugly only the United States Navy could be proud to call it home. And what a fine home this town made. One could still find little, neatly painted signs which said ugly things like: NIGGERS AND SAILORS KEEP OFF THE GRASS. Norfolk was grimy gulch.

It was rumored that the Norfolk's chamber of commerce had advertised in the newspapers of other cities, inviting its castaways to give Norfolk a try. Therefore, where most large cities have their share of bums, muggers, pimps, shysters, and ugly women, Norfolk exaggerated its commitment to bad atmosphere.

In this picture Church Street had prominence. Church Street was like a three-block-long Do Drop Inn. There were many clubs there, each with its own dark reputation. There it was appropriate to dance and drink and talk loud. It was also where people found themselves dodging bullets and evading sharp objects. Somebody would make a pass at someone else's lover and words would crisscross the air like the fire from a flamethrower's mouth. Soon chairs would take flight and screams would be thrown about like snowballs. And the sound of bottles shattering would provide background music to the festive but deadly melee.

Even more than his experience at the Do Drop, being a sailor, Rufus had had more than his share of bad luck with streets like Church Street and so he came prepared, mentally, for whatever might happen. In fact, one of the reasons things happened was because *everybody* came ready to react to the slightest shove, terse words, or smashed hat. And please do not step on anybody's patent-leather shoes, please.

Nobody ever seemed to ask questions about life on Church Street. What made these people so concerned with such seemingly small things? How could a man kill another man for a scuffed shoe or a stingy brimmed hat that had been smashed? Why violence? It was as if everything existed there to become a part of somebody's novel. Folks born into poverty and disenfranchisement were forced to elevate the smallest things, the most minute and insignificant of things, into major issues of survival. A person's shoes were important to living. One could take pride in the shoeshine. There were so few things to take pride in. The traveling feet that padded over the concrete of Church Street were simply characters in a bad story. A story without endings. No significant protagonists, only flap-mouthed, carpetbagging bigots who often spoke of the Negro question but left the justice to Bull Dogs and other animals of Southern ancestry. So, if you stepped on a spit-shined shoe, you were stepping on somebody's independence, their raison d'être.

The day slowly folded into its shadow, and Rufus sat on a bar stool in the Princess Bar. These situations had lost their irony for him. It was true that nearly everything bad that happened to him had happened in a bar. But so had whatever lightness that found its way into his life. In bars there *were* laughing people. And dancing. There is no accounting for the tremendous power and release that dancing gave. He'd get drunk. Find a woman to dance with and swing himself into oblivion. Any night.

The great thing about the Princess Bar was that a man didn't have to stumble around the room in search of a partner. Rufus knew that if he planted himself on a bar stool, flashed enough money, and had enough drinks, someone would be there next to him. Which was what happened. At some point a woman named Daphne found him and smiled. Rufus had noticed a slight pout as she had said her name the first time, "Daphne," as if she was at once proud and ashamed. She drank the drinks he bought and danced with abandon. They sweated together, and when the music went slow, she put her pressed, greasy hair on his chest and swung her hips into him. As the night moved along, Rufus fought the spinning environment as his hand groped for her soft flesh. She was young, maybe not even twenty-one. She was just a little overweight, but her eyes were sensually magnetic. Her eyes seemed older. She teased him with them when they danced. And when they were at the bar she leaned forward, staring at him. They were like caramel candies. Soft and chewy.

He was sure she wanted him as he leaned over to kiss her. Daphne let his lips barely reach hers before she pushed her dark hands to his chest. "Damn, baby," he said, "I jus' want a little lovin', that's all. What's wrong with a little kiss?"

"You cut that out now, Rufus, you hear?" Finally separated, she moved just beyond his reach.

"What's wrong with me kissing on a pretty woman like you? I'm a man baby. How you expect a man to be actin'?" Although he tried to be very clear, Rufus could hear his slurred words dropping out of his mouth like broken teeth.

"I expect a man to act like he's got some sense. You just be nice, sugar. That's what you do." Daphne tossed her head back as if she expected her hair to follow the motion. Instead, the pomade that held it in place also prevented it from moving. Still, the sweat from the heat of the dark-skinned bodies crushed into such tight quarters made her feel momentarily as if her hair would whip to the back of her head.

She looked past Rufus, to the sea of people moving around her. Occasionally she would catch an eye or a smile from someone. She would linger, smiling back or staring until there was a nonverbal cue to move on. She had small, oval-shaped eyes with eggshell whites surrounding dark brown pupils. Her nose was wide and the nostrils flared out across her face. Rufus stared at her. All he could see was her full red lips, which, every now and then, would poke out at him.

"You just drink that Old Grand-Dad and keep your hands in your lap. It's too soon. Maybe later we can go out someplace. You just be cool." While she was young, Daphne talked with a certain wisdom and confidence that shook Rufus. It was obvious that if he persisted, she would simply get up and sit beside someone else. He decided to sip his drink and wait.

As the club grew more crowded, and the smoke became thicker, Rufus sat mesmerized by the swaying of young behinds as they moved in bossa nova rhythms. His eyes were now drooping slightly as he was partly tranquilized by the whiskey and partly depleted by the exhausting experience of sitting in a place of so much activity. Sitting there, staring at Daphne, he felt paralyzed.

He watched the men pulling the women out of their chairs, dancing them into corners, touching them, kissing them. There were times when he wanted to get up and go back to the dance floor. Times when he wanted to express his sense of oneness with the sounds, but his body would not cooperate and so he was hopelessly bound, stapled to the bar stool. All the while Daphne sat next to him, talking infrequently, nursing a champagne cocktail. He was almost surprised when he felt her hand on his arm. She leaned her head close to him.

"Rufus, sweetheart, will you excuse me? I'll be right back. I see an old friend of mine that's just come in."

Rufus nodded. True enough, as he looked to the door, there was a tall black man standing just inside. His expensive suit fit him too well, Rufus thought. His shoes sparkled and his hat rested with majestic consequence on his head.

Rufus watched as Daphne approached him. He noticed that as she reached him, the man looked at her cautiously. Then he kissed her. The kiss seemed, to Rufus, to speak of a certain knowledge, as if the man knew her a bit too well.

Rufus turned his head so that he could watch them out of the corners of his eyes. It seemed as if she was motioning toward him. The man smiled, then whispered something in her ear. She cut her eyes back into the man's face affectionately. She bared her teeth, grinning. Moments later he watched her approach her seat again. The man had disappeared into the crowd.

Rufus watched as she came near him. He wanted her. He had been out to sea too long. Her short, slightly bowed, but shapely legs beckoned him. She sat down.

"Who was your friend?" he asked.

"Just somebody I know, that's all. You ain't gonna get jealous on me now, are you, sugar?" She was playing with him. He could sense it. She knew he wanted her.

"Naw, I ain't jealous; just wonderin', that's all. Just wonderin'."

"Well, you just stop wondering and drink up."

It was late now and Rufus was drunk. He remembered sticking his hand down Daphne's blouse to find soft smooth breasts that stuck to his fingers. He kneaded them. After a minute or two, she pulled his hand out of her blouse. "Let's go," she sighed.

Hitting the hot Norfolk Church Street air destroyed what was left of Rufus's sense of understanding. The heat mixed with the alcohol to produce an incoherent and confused man. Stumbling about in the darkness, Daphne holding him up, he tried to orient himself. He struggled to remember what was going on, where he was going.

"Edna, Edna, I love you, baby," Rufus moaned out into the night.

"I ain't no Edna. My name's Daphne."

"Yeah, yeah, that's right. You Daphne. Let me fuck you, Daphne. I'll show you a real good time."

As they turned into an alley, two feet walking, two feet stumbling, Rufus reached back and grabbed her behind. "Come on, Daphne, where we goin'? Let me love you, baby."

"Rufus darling, that's just what I got in mind. A little lovin', a little wrestlin', and a whole lot of fun."

"Yeah, yeah, whole lotta fun . . . but when, baby? When we gonna have some fun?" Rufus slobbered on himself.

"In a minute, sugar. You just be patient now, you hear?"

Suddenly Rufus heard something behind him. He turned and met blackness as a thud echoed off the brick walls of the alley. As he hit the ground, he saw the light of an overhead street lamp reflected in the shine of highly polished black shoes. The cuffs of expensive pants brushed his forehead. Then he was asleep.

hurting inside, but glad, the spirit that is Hope tried to make herself presentable after such a rowdy session with this unnamed lover who probed deep and stimulated the crated forces that stood guard over the riches and treasures buried in the mind. a sigh but captures the frustration of not having this lover's love nested within. a sigh simply measures the need for this lover's return. Hope wishes Hope was stronger, but the stains on the grass mark a spot where Hope met a stranger who conquered separation through a physical intercourse that joined the holy waters and the spiritual bodies encased in burning heat. come back goddammit goddammit come the hell back. bring that good thing back with you . . . come back and drive it straight through. you done come by here, touched, seared my flesh, then ran off . . . Hope's spirit crushed . . . lover on the run . . . pick up lover moving swiftly through the bramble . . . Hope's spirit crushed . . . Hope has been loved. screwed . . . Hope's been screwed . . . who screwed Hope? who?

Rufus opened his eyes. The morning light highlighted the dull shine of the galvanized trash cans that surrounded him. He wanted to move but felt a certain safety in remaining motionless. Things should not simply fall apart.

He lay there, among the trash and debris which whispered affectionate and embracing sounds, in a fit of panic and an urgent sense of loss. Somewhere deep in the pit of his thoughts, he remembered Edna smiling at him as he promised his never-ending love.

But quickly the image dissipated and he was thrust into the process of decay and infestation. All around him things—food and discarded triflings—were lifeless like himself and mirrored his momentary attachment to the pursuit of affection and its resounding, almost devastating end.

And, to put a point on this moment, he missed his ship and once again found himself adrift with the wind blowing in one clear direction.

11

"Why is life like that? All those terrible things that happened to you?"

"It is strange, Edward, it really is. But life isn't all like that. I think maybe you've seen too much already. But believe me, there is beauty in it still. Truth. The light of freshness is buried in us and in every moment we breathe. It is there. Sometimes we are so encrusted, so rotted over with misery, bad situations, that we can't see it. Feel it. But it is there."

In this world, a world made just for Rufus, his voice, the sound of it, and the way he talked were all different.

"But it seems that every time you try to do something—at least the stories that I've heard about you—are bad, negative. You drink all the time. You curse. You killed someone. What is good about that? And then on top of it, you are always the one who gets in trouble."

"Yes, what you say is true. It sure does seem like Rufus C.

Brown has lived a wretched life. I guess if you simply take the moments of my life in which I am in my own skin, living in the full open consciousness of this world—in Rehoboth Beach, or Washington or Norfolk or Philadelphia or anywhere, for that matter—you might tsk-tsk me and think my life is all misery. But you would be wrong. And you'd be wrong in many ways. I was once a child, you know. I was once without guilt, shame, anger, hatred, weaknesses, sadness. I was once pure. Just like every living thing. And every day I became more and more dirty. More things were put into my body and my mind than should have been. It has proven, I guess, to be too much. But, Eddie, the mighty fact of the matter is that the man who speaks to you now—in this place which exists who knows where—is innocent. In this place where the stories swirl around us like the wind; a wind which sweeps up whole periods of time and compresses it into a gusting mist which speaks of my past, I am a man who is truly pure."

"What do you mean?"

"I mean that in this place I am innocent. I can tell you a different story, in these minutes or hours we have here between memories. Here, I remember what it was like before my father raised his hand to me. I can see that arena of black-eyed Susans clustered over there and be nearly brought to tears by their brilliance. I can remember running up and down the streets of a sweet chocolate city, where colored people ruled everything that was not official. Washington, D.C. Enough of the South to make it candy. It was a glorious city. We played baseball in the streets, cooled ourselves from the hydrants until the cops, black cops, mind you, made us leave. So even though there is pain and misery all around us, running through our lives like so much water, understand that here, in this crevice, I have discovered truth. Peace. And now you are here. You can see it."

"Where are we?"

"I really don't know, Eddie. I'm just as lost as you are. The only thing I know is that I'm not drinking and I don't need a drink. And I don't feel nothing, certainly not sadness or anything like that. No pain. No pain."

"Is this heaven?"

"That's what I thought, too, the first time I came here. But that can't be because I keep going back. If it was heaven I would have stayed. Besides, *you* might be bound for heaven, but if that whole heaven-and-hell thing really exists, I'm a cooked goose, you might say. By the way, how are you feeling?"

"I'm fine, I guess. What's happening?" For the first time, Edward realized they were sitting in Rufus's truck. It was moving slowly, steadily, and straight down a narrow dirt road. The sun was high, but it wasn't hot, just bright. "We were in an accident, weren't we? It was hurting me so much. My stomach felt like it was going to explode. But now I don't feel anything. Are we dead?"

"No, I told you no, we're not dead. Just relax about where we are. Be happy we're here instead of in that smashed-up truck. Just be happy here, right now."

Edward was suddenly conscious only of his thoughts. He could see through his eyes, hear through his ears, but he wasn't sure he could move his arms. Or stand up should the car stop and its doors open. But his mind was keen. His thoughts were more clear. As if a veil had been lifted from his eyes. "Is this where you disappear to?"

"This is it."

"And you keep seeing the same stories over and over?"

"Yep."

"And sometimes, when that's not happening, you're riding in this truck on this road?"

Rufus nodded. "I know this road like I know the size of my

213

own heart and every feeling it's ever had. Eddie, when I'm on this road, life is so good."

"Are there ever any other people here?"

"Sometimes I see a person walking on the side of the road. But I just wave or they wave at me and we smile at each other and move on."

"This is amazing."

"You don't know the half of it."

"How long have you been doing this?"

"Eddie, listen. I know how curious you are. And maybe later we can talk about that stuff. How long. When. How much. Those are details we can talk about later."

"But did the accident happen?" Edward felt no sense of worry, or anxiety, or anything. He was empty of everything disruptive.

"Yes. It happened, and when this is over we have to reckon with that, I guess. Hell, maybe we won't leave this place. Maybe it is heaven after all. Maybe we did die. To tell you the truth, Eddie, I don't understand it. I wish I could explain it better. The one thing I know is that if you could put your head back a minute and close your eyes, well, that's a good thing to do here. But I know how it is. You being so young and all. You think there is an answer to everything. That all mysteries have solutions. That's what they teach you. But a mystery is always a problem. And problems disrupt the soul. And *too many* problems destroy the soul. Too many mysteries rob the juice out of life. Not knowing ain't a mystery. You can not know something and let it just be that. You don't have to make it into a mystery. Once it's a mystery you figure you have to solve it. Some things can't be solved, Eddie. That's what kills so many people. They're trying to find answers to questions that don't have answers.

"My mother, Eddie, my mother, probably just like your mother, was an incredible woman. Whatever my failures, I don't think it was her fault. She lived for me. There was this one time when I was a little bit younger than you, I must have been about eight, one of my teachers, a white man—a skinny, pimple-faced guy—smacked me upside the head. He thought I was the one that hit Matilda Jones with a spitball. But it wasn't me. Back then I wasn't thinking about no Matilda nobody. I was just foolish, you know? I mean I saw the boy who did it, Hershal Hewett. But Hershal was smart enough to put his head down and look serious while I was smiling like a fool. So Mr. Miller drags me into the hall and smacks me upside the head. And then when I went home and told my mother she just got up out of her chair, grabbed a sweater—I remember that sweater, too, it was like a lime green with little knots all over it. I remember because whenever she reached for that sweater I knew somebody outside the house was in trouble. And without saying a word, she starts walking the three blocks to the school. And I followed right behind her. And instead of going into the classroom where I knew Mr. Miller still was, she marches into the principal's office and tells him what I had told her, and then we all went to the classroom. I can see it like it happened yesterday. The principal sat in a student's desk and I stood at the door while my mother dressed Mr. Miller up and down. She said that I was like a flower, a little flower that deserved to be loved and nurtured and taken care of. And first, she didn't believe that I had shot no spitball, and second, if I did, he should have sent me home with a note. I was so happy. Happy to be hers. Happy that someone was there for me. Mr. Miller turned red. He tried to tell her that it was better that he disciplined me, that it would make me a better person. And then like glory personified, my mother, her name was Louise, my mother says to him, 'I know you think you know best. And I can tell by the look in your eyes that you think my child is some kind of heathen that you have to show right from wrong. But, Mr. Miller, I don't know you from John the Baptist.' That's what she said. 'And I especially don't know what is right and wrong to you. Or how you go about determining who did what and why. I know we're poor and you're white, but that don't mean that I automatically believe you know what you're doing.' Then she looks at me.

" 'Did you shoot a spitball at anybody. Tell me the truth, Rufus.'

" 'No, Mom, I swear, I didn't do it,' I said.

"Well, she turned around and stared at Mr. Miller like he was the devil. 'Now, are you gonna call my boy a liar?'

"And he sat down on the side of his desk, his suit all marked up with chalk from brushing up against the blackboard, and he says that maybe he'd made a mistake. And she said back to him, 'Your mistake is a welt on my son's head. And ain't nothing gonna happen to you, is it? When I walk out of here, you'll go home to somewhere in Maryland or Virginia and forget that you smacked my son on the head for nothing. And I have to try to make him forget it. You just made my job harder.'

"Mr. Miller apologized again and he never messed with me after that. The principal neither. And it's not the fact that he hit me, that don't mean nothing. Didn't then, don't now. It's the fact that she was there. That she said all of that. I was so happy. So happy."

Edward was lost in Rufus's words. They wafted about him like a dream.

"Anyway, the most important thing is that before she died, and she died really young—I was ten—she used to talk to me. She had TB, so she knew she was dying; lots of folks were dying from it. But she used to tell me how hard she wished that I would not take on the weight of the world. She said don't drink. Don't mess around with bad people and all that stuff. She wanted me to stay pure. Without worry. She told me that life was a series of choices, and for a black boy, making those choices was all wrapped up in a situation that made it so much worse if I made the wrong ones."

"But you've made a lot of bad choices."

"I know, Eddie. But when I'm in this place, all I want to talk about, all I can think about, is the times when I was happy. You ever watch squirrels?"

"Not really."

"Once when I was about six I sat on my front steps and watched these two squirrels, a boy and a girl, running all around our little yard. We was living in Anacostia at the time. I watched those squirrels for an entire afternoon. Up the tree, hopping to each branch. They'd stop awhile and kiss and then they were off again. Two little brown lovers wrestling in the leaves. And he never let her out of his sight. That's love. You know what 'frolic' means, don't you? Well, I don't know many colored men who ever use that word. Frolic. That's what those squirrels were doing. That's what I think love is. A frolic in the sun. Up high in the trees, beyond the dirty air and unpaid bills. How I looked forward to finding me a partner to frolic with. That's what Edna was.

"We spent so much time walking on the boardwalk and eating cotton candy I thought I was gonna break out in pimples. You know that roller coaster they got over there? Well, we rode that thing three, four times a week. Edna screaming and pinching my arm till the blood stopped flowing. I said to her, 'Edna, you ain't no spring chicken now, you gonna have a heart attack.' And soon as the ride was over she'd look at me and say, 'Let's do it again.' That was Edna, threw herself into fun with wild-eyed not caring.

"And boy, she could make me feel special. She wasn't the most tender of women, you know, but she'd do things for me. Fix a nice meal, buy me a shirt or something. She wasn't much with sweet words, but her hands—no, it wasn't just her hands, it was the power that emanated from her skin. Aw, Edward, I know you don't know what I'm talking about, but, boy, when I would walk or sit next to her, I could feel her there. And I'd want to touch her. And back then, she'd want me to."

Rufus ran silent. Looked forward. Edward was finding it difficult to even want to open his eyes. He had done as Rufus suggested. Let his head come to rest on the back of his seat and closed his eyes. And with his eyes shut, everything Rufus said became pictures.

And then he heard Rufus's voice starting up again, like a little motor. "When I was little I used to play tops. I was one of the best on Ferry Street. It was all in what kind of top you had. Most boys had to play with Mason-jar tops, but me, I'd go down by the grocery and get me a pickle-jar top. It was white and smooth, really really smooth. So it would glide right on over cement or tar or whatever we had drawn the game box on. You ever play tops? Yes. All boys should play tops. The trick you know is to knock somebody else's top into the Dead Man without ending up there yourself. I was the best."

Edward suddenly felt a tinge of pain in his stomach. He opened his eyes and turned his head to Rufus. "What does all this mean? Why are you telling me this?"

"I don't know, Edward. I guess I'm just so ashamed of what you know about me. You're the first person in a long time to want to be around me. I tried to scare you off. But you wouldn't listen."

"You never told me not to come back."

"Yeah, I reckon you're right about that. To tell you the truth, I wanted you to keep coming. Since my mother died I feel like there's nobody who's really been interested in me besides Edna, and when she turned her back on me, that was it. Anyway, when you started coming around, even though I didn't want to admit it, I liked it. And at first I couldn't figure it out. What *was* I talking to you for? It confounded me. But I couldn't stop. Every time I saw your little behind coming my way, I couldn't help but get a little excited. What kind of tragedy is that? You tell me. A grown man like me, all jazzed up to have a little half-pint like you asking me a thousand questions when I can barely remember my own name or where I am. Still, that's the way it was. But it dawned on me that something must of been bringing you to me. But when I'm in that world, no matter what my mind is trying to think, it all goes the same way. Backward. All history. All the things I did wrong. All the ass-whuppins. All the disappointments. That's all I can talk about. I always feel guilt-ridden and shameful in that world. Everywhere you go there's somebody looking at you like you don't belong. Like you're some kind of insanity unloosed to frighten them. And that ain't no kind of thing to be talking about with a boy your age. You need to be like your father and mother. You need to avoid what's happened to me. So at first I thought I was telling you these things so you'd know what not to do. But you know, that ain't it either. The real reason is I need you to see me the way I really am. I need that from you, Eddie. You the last one. If you can't see me like I am, like I am here. If you don't believe I can see the flowers, or have fun; if you can't see the fire that once danced in my heart, then I will have lost my last chance. I need you to believe in my innocence."

"Uncle Rufus?" Edward could feel a rising throbbing pain now more clearly on both sides of his body.

"Yes."

"Did you kill that man, T Hall?"

"Yep. Cut him up like a piece of salt pork."

Edward paused and then asked the question which had drawn him to Rufus in the first place. "Why did you eat Mr. Peabody?"

"Eat who?"

"Mr. Peabody. My pet snapping turtle. You took him out of his cage and cooked him."

Rufus's eyes lit up with recognition. "Ah . . . The turtle. Eddie, I didn't take that turtle out of no cage. I was in Edna's garden gettin' me a tomato and I seen him there. I was more shocked than anything. I couldn't figure out how a turtle that size could ever have gotten that far inland. But I didn't wonder about it too long; I love me some snapper soup, you understand. But more important, Edna loved snapper soup. I made it to give to her. I never knew that was your pet."

"But you killed him. And you killed T Hall. Then you can't be innocent. You committed murder. How could you want me to think you were innocent. You just confessed."

"I did that and I'm still innocent. Look, Eddie, I killed a man in an instant. You know what happened. And when I'm back there, I mourn it all the time. But I'm talking about the man who's sitting beside you right now. This man is innocent. Because this man ain't angry about nothing. About not having a job or not getting a raise or watching some frail white boy who is as dense as a two-by-four get treated cordially while you get spit on. *This* man would have no reason whatsoever to hurt a living soul. But this man can't make it over there in that world. Too much stuff being manufactured to sit on this man's shoulders. Can't walk with that much weight on you. Can't stand up proper. Can't do what you supposed to do. You get all tricked up and you start getting frustrated and then angry and then find yourself sleeping with Despair and loving it."

Edward considered what Rufus was saying. Rufus wanted Edward to see that if he had lived in a world where he wasn't angry or hurt, then he would have never killed T Hall. "But my father always tells me that when I do something bad it always comes back to me. And he says, saying you're sorry or making excuses about it doesn't make what you did go away."

"I know, Eddie, but innocence is something no colored man has in that life. You start off guilty. Committing the crime is just the proof of it."

"I'm not guilty of nothing. And I'm not going to be." Edward's face contorted in pain.

"Maybe that's why we're together. I want you to remember you said that."

12

Ragtag and limp, Rufus came back to Rehoboth Beach a full five years after he had fled the police after killing T Hall. He had already disconnected from the normal flow of life. He carried nothing more than a bag containing his few clothes and a five-dollar bill when he pulled into Rehoboth's makeshift bus station.

As he stepped off the bus, he looked back at the driver as if he were a sheriff who was leaving him at the entrance to the county prison.

He wanted to be mad at the driver. But it was him who set Rehoboth as his destination. And he knew it. He came back for Edna.

But Rufus did not know that Edna had expected to never see him again. With her successful business, she had paved over the hole that he had left. Horace had visited her two years after Rufus had gone and told her that they had closed the case. Rufus had disappeared.

"I can't spend my whole life lookin' for one colored man," Horace had told her. "Anyway, the way I see it he did it in self-defense. Besides it was just that crazy T Hall anyway. I got to worry about my record, you know."

"Yes, Horace, I guess you do." Edna hadn't questioned him. She figured that they had killed Rufus and were just trying to cover it over. She didn't believe he could have gotten away.

Edna spent most of her days cooking and doing favors for people, but at almost any time, she was liable to turn tough and nasty. It had become her anchor. A tool to keep things in their place and maintain her control of the situations that might confront her.

To her credit, she had taken over the responsibility of a daughter of one of her cousins in North Carolina. Christine, at seven years of age, had become the object of whatever compassion and concern Edna had left. She needed constant help and supervision and provided Edna with a sense of purpose. Besides, the extra money Edna received from her cousin for keeping Christine had helped to solidify her finances.

At the bus station there were no crowds, not a person there to greet him. Even if Edna had known he was coming, he thought, she would be too busy or too unconcerned to be there.

He looked around. What this was was not a bus station at all, but a hut with a horseshoe driveway around it. The buses in waiting, numbering three, were parked in the back, and nobody was waiting for anything. Only two or three buses traveled in and out of Rehoboth on a given day anyway, and practically no one traveled by bus to get there. The rich drove limousines and the poor hobbled down the highway from Philadelphia, Washington, or Baltimore in scarred and battered cars.

As he walked toward Edna's as if hypnotized by some old spell, he passed the post office, where Edna kept her mailbox, and the five-and-ten, where Edna had bought him a pair of tennis shoes which he had always loved. The shoes had long since worn out.

Another block and he was walking past the Thunderbird Shop, where rich tourists spent their money on artifacts associated with being a tourist in a resort town.

Beyond the normal dehydrated horseshoe crabs and the seashell ashtrays, the Thunderbird Shop displayed a unique number of gifts one could not find in the city, like rawhide whips and swords made to look as if they came from Spain. Rufus kicked sand as he walked by the Thunderbird Shop.

Trudging along, half in fear and half in anticipation of seeing Edna once again, Rufus walked around the fruit-and-vegetable displays creeping onto the sidewalk. He reached the bridge that crossed the canal that divided Rehoboth Beach and looked down and to his left to see who might be on the piers crabbing. There was no one there, which was unusual. No little boys with legs trailing into the water, testing the stupid crabs, no traps and no proud fathers watching their sons and daughters enjoy the sport of taking advantage of the situation.

As he crossed the bridge, the grating that composed the middle of the span provided him with an unusual view from the top. He looked down as he walked, counting the powered boats with white people draping the decks, Coca-Cola frosting in glasses held by dainty and uncallused hands. Each time a car passed him he would tremble as the sound caused by the rubber of the tires squishing over the grating etched its way into his skin and made him shudder.

His thoughts fluctuated between joy and dread. After having lost all of his money on the ship, Rufus was empty of hope and little knew or cared very much what was in his future. He had thought long and hard about the money. About Otis. The captain. He knew he'd never know what happened. He just knew that they all had a part in destroying his life.

Another fifty yards beyond the bridge and he turned right and took a path that would shorten the distance between him and Edna.

As he walked that path, on his way to West Rehoboth, his thoughts grew even dimmer. He began to see people he knew. He tried to make himself into a shadow. A ghost. He averted eyes. No one seemed to recognize him. No one came up to him to speak. He'd almost forgotten the thick beard that he'd grown over the past two years. He'd planned to shave as soon as he got to Edna's. But, he reasoned, that must be why people seemed oblivious to him. Still, he turned down the defunct railroad tracks in an effort to avoid meeting others in the path.

Rufus now walked through the wooded area between downtown Rehoboth Beach and West Rehoboth. As he broke through the wooded area and left the tracks behind him, he turned up the road to his left. He passed houses constructed of shattered, rotting trees and tar paper, as children played in the yards, kicking up sand as they ran. Rufus kept his head tilted downward as he walked.

In the yards of these poor black folk were chickens and chicks pecking in wonder at the ground, searching for their meager portions.

Little children with nappy heads and pigtails of braided hair clothed in simple cheap garments made of scrap cotton or bought for little money downtown played aimlessly in the afternoon sun. Of course, Edna had a hand in their clothing. Nearly everyone had been a recipient, at one time or another, of clothes from Edna, which she received regularly from relatives and friends in Philadelphia and Connecticut.

The road on which he traveled soon intersected with Hebron Avenue, the road that led to Edna's. At the corner of this intersection sat the Do Drop Inn. The place of his demise. The source of his nightmare. The place where T Hall had lived and died.

He remembered the nightly crap games in the back, the blaring music. T Hall turning his angry eyes on him. T Hall in his face. Now the vision of T Hall was often joined by that of Captain Sparks and Otis Jessup. Sometimes they pushed T Hall's face into the shadows.

Standing in the yard in front of the Do Drop Inn, Rufus could not resist the urge to enter. Maybe, he thought, the police were still looking for him. Maybe somebody had already recognized him and called the cops. He had to get a sense of what was going to happen.

It was a Wednesday afternoon, bright and hot, a day in sunny July, the heart of the tourist season. This meant that the Do Drop would not be crowded. As he walked in, he was immediately embraced by the damp, dark interior. Sitting on a stool, he called for a drink, and the bartender, a man whom Rufus did not know, served him without saying a word.

After a couple of sips, amid the rush of alcohol, Rufus began to relax. The thought of T Hall and the Otis Jessup gang gently slipped away and he looked around. A small dark man sat five stools away from him, staring into his beer. Rufus recognized his profile.

"Jack Bonds? Is that you?" he asked tentatively.

The man looked up and squinted his eyes toward Rufus. "That's my name, and it makes me right nervous to have somebody recognize me and know my name when I can't even see who the hell it is."

"Well, don't be too nervous, Jack; it's Rufus." Rufus left his stool and sat down on the one next to his old acquaintance. This would be the big test.

Jack had not yet reacted as if he knew Rufus. He was staring at him, hands on his chin, fingers running through his whiskers, thinking. The time had outrun them both. However long it had been, things had changed for Jack. His eyes had gotten tired and begun to give way to fuzziness and outright darkness. His ability to relate places and people had taken flight. Now he fought to remember.

"Rufus? Rufus? Yeah, I believe I recollect. Yeah, I believe I do. You Hattie's boy, ain't you?" Jack said to Rufus.

"No, you old mangy bastard, you know who I am; Rufus, Edna's old man. Remember?"

"Oh, yeah, Rufus." Jack sprang to life, then he froze. "I thought you was dead. They told us you was dead. Didn't you die up in New York somewhere?"

"Do I look dead, Jack?" Rufus was dumbstruck. They had killed him. They had purged themselves of him. How many times were they going to kill him?

Jack was shaking his head. "Rufus, well, I'll be goddamned. Well, if you ain't dead, where the hell you been, man? Goddamn, I'll be a son of a skunk. Rufus." As he spoke, he pounded on Rufus's back.

Rufus just sat there staring into space.

"Shit, how long you been gone? Where the hell you been?" Jack's grin spread across his wrinkled worn face.

"Out to sea. I been out there on the water for a long time."

"Well, where'd you go? Tell me all about it."

"I will, Jack, I will. But first, why don't you tell me a few things. Does everybody think I'm dead?"

"Yup. Gone." Jack took a drink.

"Edna, too?"

Jack looked Rufus in the eye with a grin. "Who you think told everybody? She said that old shitty cop Horace told her you was gone for good."

Rufus was almost giddy. He had been right at least in figuring he was safe. "So what's been going on around this town while I been gone? Tell me about Edna."

"Edna? What's to tell?"

"Come on, Jack, I been gone for over five years, what's the news?"

"Oh, I don't get around like I used to, Rufus. Naw, I don't rightly know what Edna's doing these days. All I do is stop by there in the evening to get me something to eat. I don't say much and don't many people say much to me."

Rufus was not satisfied. "Don't give me that shit, Jack. I don't know what's wrong with your eyes, but I know you well enough to know that you can tell me what's been going on 'round here."

"The only thing I can tell you, Rufus, is that Edna was goin' out with a fellow named William for a time. But that didn't last but about a month or two. Shit, since you been gone, Edna ain't been doin' much of nothing except makin' money."

"I kinda figured that," he said, thinking about Edna's ambition. "So she ain't hitched up to nobody?"

Jack laughed a cracking, grainy laugh. "Man, you must be crazy. I can't see Edna with no man and I can't see for shit. Edna with a man, that's a good one."

Rufus reached into his pocket and took out his last five-dollar bill. He placed it on the bar and ordered a beer for Jack and another shot of rye for himself. "Make that a double," he said to the bartender as an afterthought.

Rufus gulped down his drink and ordered another. "Well, Jack, if you ain't made me a happy motherfucka. If I'm lyin' I'm flyin."

"Yeah, well, Rufus, I wouldn't get too happy if I was you. Edna ain't the woman she used to be."

"Watch what you sayin', Jack. She still my woman." Rufus turned sour.

"You'll understand what I'm trying to tell you when you see her. She's not the same, Rufus. I reckon time did something to her. I don't know. But I do know she's different now."

"How, Jack?" Rufus asked, not really wanting to know.

"Well, she don't smile and joke a lot like she used to. She's right gruff about everything now. Don't take no shit off nobody. You know how Rehoboth is. We got characters around here mean enough to bite your damn head off. And even the really bad ones don't go down to Edna's 'cause they know she don't take no stuff off of them." Jack paused and took a long swig. "She's different than before, that's all. She ain't no young girl actin' like she got the world on a string no more."

Jack bought a couple of rounds and Rufus spent the rest of his money as well. Five drinks later Rufus stumbled from the bar of the Do Drop Inn and headed down the road to Edna's. It was dark now and the Do Drop was much more crowded, although Rufus had been absorbed in too much thought to take notice. In fact, none of the people there had even recognized him, although many of them had once known him. By the time he left, his mind was reeling and all he wanted was for Edna to come running when he hit the door.

There was always much traffic between the Do Drop and Edna's. People would sidle up to the bar and not arise until they were sufficiently inebriated. Thus numbed, they could stand the hot sauce Edna would wipe on her pork ribs. It was the thought of those ribs which would push them out of the Do Drop into the hot summer air, destined for Edna's.

But since Rufus had been gone during the time Edna had made her fame, he did not know what to expect. In this drunken state, his mind focused on a beautiful woman, brimming with the potential magic that lovers can identify, and waiting with open arms for his return.

Rufus turned into Edna's driveway, staggering, drunk, and dirty. He had left his bag in the Do Drop and carried nothing but a hope that Edna would be there. He knocked on the screen door. He heard music and people talking inside, but he was unsure of himself and thought he should wait until she came to open the door for him.

While he stood there, for it seemed to him a long time, two teenage boys walked up and entered.

As one passed him, he stared at Rufus and finally asked, "You need help in getting in, Pop? I know the food's good, but maybe you ought to go sleep it off first. You can get Edna's barbecue any day of the week except Sunday." The boy laughed to his friend and they slammed the door in Rufus's face before he could respond.

"Edna? Edna? You in there?"

Rufus waited.

"Who is that?" Edna said as she walked to the door.

"It's your Rufus. I just got in this evenin'." Rufus couldn't think of what to say and so he left it at that. He faced her, scraggly, weaving, waiting for her response. He felt T Hall's dead breath on his neck. He heard Otis laughing.

Edna squinted her eyes and grabbed her heart. She looked on a ghost.

Behind Rufus, the lights, which were affixed to the house to illuminate the entrance, gave him a spotlight of sorts. In the haze of the light were swirls of mosquitoes and moths. The man before her was oblivious even as the bugs were trying to suck his every drop of blood.

For the briefest of moments she felt as if someone had snatched the breath right out of her lungs. She almost slumped down in a gasp of pain. She held the freshly painted screen door tightly as she groped for perspective.

She knew this man. She knew the weave and the rubbery legs. She could see through the facial hair. The smell of whiskey was enough to drive off the mosquitoes but didn't.

She immediately lapsed into prayer. She asked the Lord for guidance. She asked him to remove this ghost from her presence. She waited, hoping something special would happen. She wanted the pain to be replaced by joy, surprise, hope—something. Instead, it remained the way it was: a cramped stomach of ageless pain.

Still, she reached her hand out to touch him. "Rufus? Rufus, is that you?" She grabbed his dirty white T-shirt in her hands and pulled him gently toward her. "I thought . . ."

"You thought I was dead. I know. But it's me, baby. I came back home to you."

Edna closed her eyes. "Rufus, the police . . . they . . ."

"Edna, don't you worry. They don't want me no more." Rufus was tired of standing in the door. He wanted to get his arms around her, but she held him away.

"You killed T Hall."

"That was then, baby. Let me come in and we can start all over again." Rufus tried to shake his arms loose, but her grip was like steel. He stood his ground.

"You're drunk. How can you just come back like this? Five years and you walk in here stinking and reeling." The words were out of her mouth before she could catch them. It wasn't that she wanted to begin that way. What else was there to say? But saying those words had triggered something in her. His reappearance had momentarily pulled her out of herself. For an instant she had considered the future with Rufus. Had thought that maybe she shouldn't push him away. But it was the Rufus that stood in front of her that she had to be afraid of. Not the killer. Not the wild, ill-tempered jealous man who had taken T Hall's life. It was the drunken, dreaming ghost that was to be feared.

She drew a deep breath. "Rufus, I'm real happy to know that you ain't dead. It's good to see you, but you can't come in here. You just can't."

"What? But, Edna, I—"

"No, Rufus. I will not let you back in here. This is my life. You can't just move back in."

"But I love you, Edna."

"Don't give me that, Rufus. You come back here, jeopardize my business, my whole life, and you think I'm gonna just let you in because you say you love me. You don't understand love, Rufus. You don't know nothing about it."

Rufus tried to focus his thoughts. "But I don't have no place to stay, Edna." He started to cry. The tears, like the tears he'd given to the dolphins, began to flow in strong streams. "I got nothing. They took everything from me."

"Rufus, I'm sorry for the way things turned out. But I can't do nothing for you. You can't live here. I'm keepin' one of my cousin's little girls and I can't let you stay here with us. If somehow the police do start lookin' for you, this is where they're comin'."

"But, Edna . . ." Rufus convulsed into tears and unintelligible pleas.

Edna stood there silently. She would stand there all night. She would stand there for a week if he needed someone to be there when he cried. But she wasn't going to let him in.

Through his tears Rufus tried to make eye contact with her, but her gaze went through him. He stepped back and looked around. "Ain't you got a room or something. I can see you've added on."

"I told you, Rufus."

"What about that shack 'round back? What about that? Anybody livin' there?" Rufus was desperately trying to identify some way to pronounce his own sentence upon himself.

"No, Rufus. Nobody's livin' back there, but I don't want you back there neither."

"Just for tonight, Edna. Just tonight. I love you, baby. I know you mad at me. But just let me stay tonight, then we can talk tomorrow and maybe we can work something out. I won't be no trouble, I promise, baby. Please. Just tonight."

"Go on, Rufus." In the end, Edna couldn't send him away that night. She considered his proposition. "Just tonight. In the shack. No trouble, Rufus. And I'll come back there tomorrow and we can talk when you're sober. Okay. Now, if you'll wait right here I'll get you a sandwich. If you come across this door I'll kill you myself. You hear me?"

"I hear you, Edna."

"You wait here." She turned to go.

"Edna?"

"Yeah?"

"It's good to be home."

"You ain't home yet, Rufus. You just come back to where you started." Edna turned back toward the kitchen.

Suddenly he felt sober. He stood straight, pulling on his shirt, as if he realized the wrinkles and the dirt for the first time. He wiped his lips with the back of his hands. This was where he would serve his time.

13

Edward's eyes snapped open. He was still in excruciating pain. Rufus's face was still just inches from his, although this time Rufus looked downright insane, his face screwed into a wild contortion. His lips moving, words tumbling out in total randomness. Edward screamed. This scream was everything in him trying to get out. This scream was panic. His insides scurrying around, trying to find a way to vent the cut glass that was rolling in waves throughout his body.

"Hold on, boy. I swear for God, just hold on. You gonna be all right. Somebody be here directly. Just try to stay sane. Just try to steady yourself and understand that it ain't gonna ever be like it was and that you can't control every goddamned thing under the goddamned sun. You just have to go with it. Eddie, just ride with the pitch of the drink and never let one side list too much. You got to stay afloat."

Edward was crying again.

"And don't be so goddamned ready to fold your hand. Fix your face and your voice and your body to do what you set out to do. Right now, you got to live through this. You got to suck it in like air and laugh at it. Tell it to go on and do what the hell it's gonna do to you and then you got to be ready to fight it back without losing your goddamned soul. Stand up to it, boy. You'll make it. 'Cause you're strong. I seen the way you look at me like you some kind of authority. At your age even. Like you know even more than I do. Maybe you do. But right now you just have to breathe."

"It hurts, Uncle Rufus. It hurts."

"I know, boy. I know. But it ain't nothing to give in to. Old folks say God won't give you more than you can handle. But I think that's a bunch of bull. I seen more people collapse under the weight of this rotten life than I can count. Hell, if I had a nickel for everybody that I seen laying in the road after thinking they was strong enough to handle what was standing in front of them, I'd be a rich old man. I couldn't make it, Eddie, but you can. You can do it."

In the distance Edward heard a siren. How long had they been lying there? He smelled the fragrant odor of fresh grass and the dense musky smell of damp leaves. He could still hear cars rolling by on the road above them. When he focused on Rufus again it was as if the man had worked himself into a trance. His eyes were showing only white and Edward started to panic again.

"Uncle Rufus. Uncle Rufus," Edward screamed in terror. "Uncle Rufus." He heard a low-level groan from Rufus's mouth.

Edward tried to shift his weight. Rufus stirred. "Uncle Rufus, are you okay?"

Rufus was lost in an abyss. "Damn. They tried to kill me again. I can't do nothin', go nowhere, without them trying to kill me."

And then Edward heard people around them. And the thin whine of machinery being put into place. And then, like a sun which revealed itself from behind a deck of thick dark clouds, a white man's face appeared in front of him.

"How are you, son? Can you answer?" Edward recognized the policeman as the one who had stopped him and Edna on his second day in Rehoboth. Horace was his name. He swallowed and felt it roll like a marble down his throat and into the pit of pain below. Even though his whole body was yelling at him, he realized immediately this situation was dangerous for Rufus. This was *the* Horace who had let Rufus slip through his hands once before.

"I'm stuck. I can't move. My sides hurt real bad."

"You just hang in there. We're gonna get you out in a jiffy. Are you bleeding anywhere?"

Edward hadn't thought about blood. He hated blood. "I don't think so. I can't move my arms."

"Okay, son, okay; they're working on it right now."

Edward felt people gathering around them and now lots of noise. Rufus had been strangely quiet since the police arrived. Edward whispered to him when he felt Horace's attention diverted.

"Don't worry. I won't tell."

"Won't tell what, Eddie?"

"That you were driving like you were. I'll make something up. Don't worry."

"It don't matter, Eddie. I'm pretty much done for. I just hope you're all right. These peckerwoods been waiting on me a long time and here I go and just lay down in the road for them to run over me."

"No, Uncle Rufus. You just keep quiet. I'll figure something out." And then the weight on his body vanished. And he heard a group of people grunting as they guided the machine that was helping to separate the bread from the meat.

Finally Edward slipped down a couple of inches before a group of white arms snaked under him and lifted him to a stretcher. In a few seconds Rufus was lying next to him. Rufus was staring into space. Whenever someone asked him a question he just looked at them. When they were freed from the wreckage, the pain in Edward's body subsided greatly. Now it was only excruciating if he tried to move. But lying there still, it was bearable. And then above him was Horace and another police officer.

"What's your name, son?"

"Edward Massey."

"And who is this, Edward?"

"Ah, his name is, ah . . . Otis . . . Mr. Otis Jessup."

"I see. He must be hurt pretty bad, huh? He hasn't said a word."

Someone was lifting the stretcher up and suddenly his face was much closer to Horace's. "I don't think he's hurt too much. He just can't talk that's all." Edward thought back to a case of his mentor, Poirot. It was a situation where a woman had participated in the murder of her brutal husband. She was much younger than him and had taken a lover. And then, when the husband's violent nature against her was too much to bear, she and her lover conspired to kill the old man. But of course Poirot caught them. And yet, because he sympathized with the woman and had a tender spot for young love and detested the brutality of her dead husband, he looked the other way. *He* determined justice. His integrity, his arrogance, his sense of right and wrong had already justified her actions. Edward felt the same way about Rufus. He knew everything now. It was up to him. If Horace figured out who Rufus was, he'd surely arrest him.

"What relation are you to him?"

"I'm his nephew."

"You say he can't talk?"

"He's mute and he can't hear neither. Lost his voice in the war, I think." Edward was proud of himself. Horace looked a little confused and Rufus was staring at him with laughing eyes. It was like being silent now was precisely the right thing to be. And then they slid Edward's stretcher into the ambulance. But Edward heard Horace trying to talk to Rufus anyway.

"Hey, boy. Can you hear me? You hear what I'm sayin' to you? You been drinkin'? Otis? That your name?" Horace turned away and said to his partner, "I tell you, Jim, these dumb jungle bunnies gonna drive me crazy one day. I ain't never seen this one before; you?" Jim shook his head no. "Damn damn damn. I swear I think he's drunk."

And then Horace stuck his head into the ambulance. Edward felt him there and spoke first. "Aren't y'all going to take me to the hospital. It don't hurt as much as it did, but every time I try to move it gets pretty bad."

"Yes, son. I know, we're gonna try and squeeze this, ah . . . your uncle in here with you in just a second. You're gonna be fine. I reckon you just broke a rib or two. But we're gonna get you out of here. I just wanna know what happened."

Edward was ready. "We was driving down the road and I was playing like I could drive better than him and I turned the wheel by mistake. It wasn't his fault at all. He was trying to keep it straight. But I steered us off the road. I'm really sorry."

"So you did it?" Horace rubbed the whiskers on his face.

"Yes, sir. One day I want to be a race-car driver."

"I see. Okay, well, I'll be in to see you at the hospital in a bit. I hope you feel better."

"Thank you."

And then Horace stepped back and they rolled Rufus in beside him and someone closed the door. With great effort, Edward looked at Rufus, who was almost smiling, and winked his eye. And then there was a great commotion outside the ambulance and the door flew open.

Edna stood at the door with a waning sun behind her. When Rufus looked in her direction Edward saw panic in his face. Edna was there.

She craned her head in the tight compartment. "You'all all right?"

"Yes, Aunt Edna. We just had a little accident." Edward spoke first and grimaced as he did.

"A little accident? Both of you gettin' carted off to the hospital and you call this a little accident? Rufus, what the hell were you doin' out here with Eddie? You know better than that."

Now Edward was afraid. He couldn't see beyond Edna, so he wasn't sure where Horace was, but he wanted her to lower her voice. "Aunt Edna, I—"

"I wasn't talking to you, Edward."

"I know you wasn't, Aunt Edna, but if you tell them who he is, they gonna get him for that T Hall murder. I told them his name was Otis Jessup."

"Who?"

"Otis Jessup. It's just a name. If they find out he's Rufus they'll arrest him."

Slowly Edna understood what the boy was saying. "I see."

But Rufus could be silent no more. He didn't see Horace and suddenly he didn't care anymore. That's just the way it was. He might give the silence a chance after he said what he had to say to Edna. He wanted to apologize. To erase time. "Edna, listen to me. I'm sorry. I'm sorry it all turned out like this. I wish it was different."

Edna stood straight. The denim-blue wraparound skirt that hung just below her knees fluttered in the soft breeze. "It's too late, Rufus. Too late. You can't ruin somebody's life and then, ten years later, say 'I'm sorry.' It ain't enough."

"But, Edna, I didn't know what else to do." Once the subject was opened, Rufus lost his control and wavered between anger and tears. They were becoming the same.

"You could have just not done what you done. Things probably would have been different." Edna turned her back on him and then thought better of it and leaned in again. "Rufus, maybe if you change yourself. Maybe become Otis whatever or somebody else, I can think about it different. For now, you and Eddie take care and I'll meet you at the hospital." She stepped back and the doors closed.

Edward caught Rufus's eyes and held them tight. "Uncle Otis, you know we never made it to the dump. I really wanted to do that. Do you think maybe we can do that sometime before I have to go back to Philly?"

Rufus raised his arm just an inch and then let it fall limp at his side. "We'll see, boy. We'll see." Edward broke into a smile and closed his eyes. He could feel the truck finally beginning to move and then he heard the sirens. This time they were just above his head. The sound nestled itself between the folds of his experience. There was still a month left to his summer vacation. The great mystery solved. A great adventure complete.

"Uncle Rufus? I mean Uncle Otis?" Rufus looked at him. "How did I know about T Hall? About Otis? Were we really there?"

Rufus smiled, and decided to speak at least once more. "You wanted a mystery, didn't you? Well, Eddie, you got more than you bargained for. You done got inside my world and you'll be trying to figure it out for the rest of your life. You'll have something good to tell when you get back to the city. And you tell them that Rufus taught you what you know. Rufus put the bug in your ear. Rufus set you straight."

"*Oui, mon ami. Exactement.* Edwarrrd 'Hercule Poirot' Masseee now knows all." Edward whispered and forced a smile as he felt his body pulsing with pain every time he tried to talk. He relented and let his body relax. The pain instantly subsided. He felt the ambulance moving on the road, and thought about how much fun he was going to have telling Sonny and whoever would listen about the story of one Rufus C. Brown.